Praise for K.A. Mitchell's
Life, Over Easy

"Emotional and well-balanced, with great sex and a strong combination of plot elements."

~ *Dear Author*

"Life Over Easy is a very emotionally charged romance with sizzling passions and enough generated heat to make any reader sweat."

~ *Sensual Reads*

"K.A. Mitchell has a knack for creating great characters, bringing them to vibrant life, and making readers love them."

~ *Jessewave*

Look for these titles by
K.A. Mitchell

Now Available:

Fragments Series
Life, Over Easy

Custom Ride
Hot Ticket
Diving in Deep
Regularly Scheduled Life
Collision Course
Chasing Smoke
An Improper Holiday
No Souvenirs
Not Knowing Jack
Bad Company

Print Anthologies
Midsummer Night's Steam - Temperature's Rising
To All a (Very Sexy) Good Night
Serving Love

Life, Over Easy

K.A. Mitchell

SAMHAIN
PUBLISHING

Samhain Publishing, Ltd.
577 Mulberry Street, Suite 1520
Macon, GA 31201
www.samhainpublishing.com

Life, Over Easy
Copyright © 2011 by K.A. Mitchell
Print ISBN: 978-1-60928-176-2
Digital ISBN: 978-1-60928-146-5

Editing by Sasha Knight
Cover by Mandy M. Roth

First Samhain Publishing, Ltd. electronic publication: August 2010
First Samhain Publishing, Ltd. print publication: July 2011

Dedication

For someone who makes life—and love—very easy
Kathy.

Chapter One

John Andrews' first experience with public education was as a twenty-one-year-old freshman at the University of Albany. In his first class of five hundred, one girl passed out, two other girls made out and a drug deal went down two rows in front of him. By the end of the week, John had learned that college wasn't all that different from training camp. Less weight training, still lots of bad food.

In that week, seventeen different flyers for parties, clubs and political rallies came flying under his dorm room door. Each of them went up on the otherwise empty bulletin board in his room, except the one from the Disabled Students' Association, which had been hand delivered. The guy with the hearing aid had been the only one who'd even noticed, or at least said anything about, John's cane. That flyer in eye-hemorrhage-inducing orange went immediately into the trash.

John didn't need it, or the Disabled Students' Association, or the handicapped room the university had given him—though having no roommate and a private bathroom was a plus. John wasn't exactly disabled. He didn't always need the cane—unless he made a quick move and lost his balance, but it didn't happen all the time anymore. He just couldn't drive. Or watch a tennis match. Or look out of a second-story window.

Or ever get on a dive platform again.

One of the flyers he'd saved was for a get-to-know-you

meeting for some environmental club. Everyone wanted to save the planet. Maybe that was something he could do. Life: Plan B had to start somewhere.

Four fifty-six Madison Place was somewhere downtown, and it took him two buses and a walk down a couple of dark blocks to get there. John had discovered walking was easier in the dark. No contending with the blurs from bright light, less noise. And even if he did stagger, fewer people were around to see him trip over apparently thick air.

Now that he was on the right street, it wasn't hard to tell which house it was. Lights on, music blaring bright enough on its own, and the added confirmation in the form of a young man puking off the front porch. Getting to know the members of the environmental club seemed to require large amounts of alcohol.

John propped his cane up behind some definitely non-recycled trash on the porch and went inside, remembering just in time not to shake his head in disgust. He didn't have a problem if people wanted to play beer pong and call it a club meeting. He just thought that if they were going to call themselves Students for a Greener Tomorrow, they might use non-plastic cups and recycle their empties.

He hadn't needed any pills today. No headaches. No heaving. He could probably have a beer. It wasn't as if he was driving. And hey, at least the cups were green.

John negotiated his way to the keg. He'd been to his fair share of parties all over the world. The Germans usually had something going on in their dorm at any event, and if they didn't the Brits did. The Brazilians threw a two-week-long celebration during the Pan American Games, though John's memory of it was a little fuzzy because he'd gotten knocked down to silver by two freaking tenths of a point and had decided that it was a good time to experience being spectacularly drunk. The resulting hangover had been the benchmark worst experience of his life—until he found out how bad things could really suck.

He found a wall to lean on and watched the beer pong game.

John was aware of the look for a full minute before he began the slow process of turning to see who was aiming it at the side of his head. He hoped it wasn't someone trying to remember where they knew him from. It usually turned out to be from the cereal box. He'd already suffered through five tearful—on their part—encounters with girls who thought it was so very tragic and how could he bear it and what was he going to do with himself now.

John wished he knew the answer to that last one.

He turned, and sometimes it didn't matter how slowly he did it. Something clicked over in his brain and the world burst into glittering confetti and kaleidoscopes—two things he'd never enjoy again. Nausea set his stomach on the spin cycle and pain sparkled silver and white through his head. The flashes of color slowed, settled into refracted light. Almost like a bad 3D effect, bending the edges of whatever he tried to focus on.

And in this case it was a guy's face. The pain faded and took the nausea with it, which John thought was only fair since they always came as each other's date. But the weird scattered crystal effect kept going on for a full minute, white with red and black streaks, as John tried to focus on the guy's face.

Red lips, dark for a guy, but the color didn't look artificial, more like he bit them a lot. Hair a warm brown, close-shave on the sides and spiky on top. Now that the broken-glass effect had faded, John finally got a good look at the guy's eyes. Maybe this was a new perceptual distortion from the fall, but those dark eyes looked back at him like John had every answer in the world. Like John was Jesus and a gold medal and the guy holding a check for a million-dollar endorsement all at once.

John's hands got cold. And then the dark gaze dropped

before making a long, slow trip back up John's body, pausing for a hard stare at John's crotch where even the loose fit of his Dockers couldn't hide what that attention was doing to John's dick.

The guy noticed all right. His tongue swept over his full bottom lip. Sauna heat rushed over John's body, prickling his skin even as it melted his bones. Jeez. Was it really this easy? After all that sneaking around and crap with Roald on tour, here you could just have a guy check you out at a party and that was it?

John might not have a lot of experience, but he knew what this was. Cruising. He'd even seen the 1980s movie with Al Pacino. It hadn't worked out too well for the characters in that movie, but it wasn't the 1980s anymore.

So. In the middle of this party with straight couples slobbering on each other and people half-passed out on the beer pong cups, the one gay guy had found him. And it hadn't even taken a flyer from whatever gay student organization they had here.

No, John didn't have much experience, but he had seen a lot of movies, though not as many of the kind that would help him out in this situation as he'd like. He hooked his thumbs in his pockets so that his fingers framed his dick and met the look in the other guy's dark eyes. He smiled and walked up to John, steps nowhere near as steady as his gaze.

"Wanna get out of here?"

John would have nodded, but that would have gotten the whole kaleidoscope going again, so he blinked. Apparently that was good enough because the guy knocked back whatever was left in his cup—which didn't smell like beer—and tossed the cup away.

No way was John getting into a car with this guy. Sexy lips, eyes and seriously ripped arms or not. His life might suck right now, but he wasn't ready to become a drunk-driving statistic.

"I don't have a car."

"Me either."

John thought of the long bus ride back to his dorm. "I live on campus, uptown."

The other guy hooked his finger through the belt loop on John's khakis and pulled him close enough that their hips touched. The guy's breath hit John's cheek, warm, almost enough to burn with the fumes from whatever had been in that cup. "I'm right around the block. Okay with you?"

A hot guy's hand was a few inches from John's very happy dick, and his lips were even closer to John's ear. Like any second he'd be kissing him and yes, it was okay with him. This guy wasn't Roald and evidently didn't give a shit if anyone else knew he was gay. And since no one was handing out endorsements for brain-damaged former gold medalists, neither did John.

Belatedly, John realized the guy was waiting for an answer. "Umm, yeah."

"So let's go."

They threaded their way through the front room of the party, which was now made up of people jumping up and down to some song, pounding out muddy reds and oranges as the thump of their feet hit the floor just a split-second off from the beat of the music. Between the color wheel and the moving bodies, John wondered if his brain was going to provide him with another one of those fly-eye faceted views where he had to decide which of the dozen images was the right one so that he would not trip over what had moved in his path, but the other guy reached back and slid his hand just under John's shirt and pulled him along.

When they got to the door, the guy stretched out one of those hard-muscled arms and yanked John close. Roald didn't kiss. And kissing one of the girls on the synchronized diving team had only confirmed what John had already suspected about him and girls.

This was what he'd wanted, right? A chance to get in all the stuff he'd missed during twelve-hour practices and plane rides and tutors.

John opened his mouth for his first kiss.

A dizzy lurch in his stomach that finally had nothing to do with the new way his brain saw the world. This was like flying, like springing into air and daring gravity to catch you. The closest thing he'd had to his old life since he'd woken up in the hospital. His body buzzed, alive like it had only ever been when he walked out on the platform.

He brought his hands up, palms sliding across the crisp fuzz on the sides of the other man's head, and sucked that spicy tongue in deeper. A contact high was what they called it, right? Getting drunk or stoned off someone else's buzz? That had to be it. Because if kissing felt this good, why didn't people do it all the time? Why didn't Roald want to do it?

A shift, a pause and John knew he was supposed to kiss the other man back. He gave it what he had, stroking his tongue over those full red lips, following into his mouth where everything tasted even spicier. And it definitely wasn't beer.

The other man pushed him away. "Fuck. Umm…?"

"John."

"Mason." The other guy offered his own name. "You're eighteen, right? Please tell me you're eighteen."

"I'm old enough to buy my own beer. Legally."

"Okay then."

He pulled open the front door. It wasn't that cool outside, but after the heat from all those bodies, the shift in air pressure made John wish he had his cane. Hanging onto the siding for balance, he stepped toward the pile of trash where he'd left it.

"You'd think if they were concerned about the environment, they'd be more into recycling," he commented to Mason.

"Huh?"

"Students for a Greener Tomorrow. The meeting?" He pointed at the house.

"That's not a meeting. That's Friday night at Billy's."

"But it's four fifty-six Madison Place."

"No, that's four fifty-six Madison Ave."

"Crap."

"Did you really need to be there?" Mason had come up behind him, heat against John's back, a particularly warm and heavy press sliding along his ass that felt good and terrifying at the same time. Like trying a reverse off the three meter for the first time.

"No." What John needed was to finally find out if sex was everything people said it was. Especially if you had it with someone who wasn't just using your mouth because he had no one better to do.

"Then let's go."

If Mason had a problem with John's cane, he didn't say anything, which was nice because a breeze sent the few fallen leaves spinning across the sidewalk in front of them. Without the cane, John would have ended up tripping over one of the eight curbs he saw in fragments after the leaves had passed.

At the corner, they turned down a much darker street. No cars moved past, and the maple hung heavy and dark over the narrow pavement. The breeze stirred the leaves, a higher pitch to the rustle now, bringing a touch of gray to it. During the summer the sound had been dark as molasses.

Maybe John could become a weatherman. This thing, this whatever in his head that gave colors to sounds, maybe it would help him predict the weather. *There will be a bright orange cold front tomorrow, with a fifty percent chance of light blue freezing rain.* Yeah. That was why he'd kept this color-hearing thing to himself. The rest of it, the dizziness and the headaches and the shattered-glass confetti were bad enough. They'd probably lock him up if he told them he heard colors.

Mason's hand had been resting on the small of John's back and now it slid down to cup his ass through his Dockers. His dick liked that a lot. He hoped it wasn't far to Mason's house.

"So, John, what do you like?"

His voice. Screw the wind, Mason's voice curled around John's ears like dark purple velvet. John's favorite color, a purple so dark it was almost black. The same color as the collared shirt he'd worn to the party. It was bad enough for the sound to have color, but to feel it? That purple voice slid against his skin.

"You up for fucking?"

"I—uh—"

"Oh, man." Mason moved closer, and that just made the color more intense as he whispered into John's ear. "First time? That's kinda hot."

Mason's hand landed on John's dick. Maybe he was just being nice, trying to make sure John was really interested, but John thought the fact that he was here answered that already. And they might be in Albany, New York and not Waco, Texas, but John didn't want to stand out here as a target for anyone who decided that tonight was the night to get rid of some queers.

"C'mon." Mason tugged him down a driveway made up of two uneven strips of sidewalk that ran parallel to one of the houses on the street. They climbed up the back porch steps, and Mason let them into a dark kitchen. As he opened the fridge, the light showed a sink full of dishes and a table full of books and papers and a laptop.

"Want another beer?" Mason asked over his shoulder.

John's throat was dry, but beer had too much vitamin pee in it, and he didn't want to screw this up by having to work on getting his dick to switch functions halfway through.

"No thanks."

Mason uncapped a bottle for himself and drained half of it. Moving more swiftly than he should have been able to, he rolled the icy lip of the bottle across John's lower lip.

"You're fucking hot, but you look scared. You okay with this?"

John wasn't scared, just startled. And he was more than okay with it. It wasn't as if he were saving his virginity for a special occasion. When he found someone, he'd kind of like to know what he was doing. At the rate Mason was drinking, if John did something stupid, Mason either wouldn't know or wouldn't remember. Good enough for tryouts.

"I'm fine."

Mason tipped the bottle, and John let some of the beer slide down his throat. With a small smile, Mason moved the bottle down over John's lips to his chin to his throat, until it rested in the notch of his collarbone. John shuddered.

"This is gonna be fun." Mason finished the bottle and added it to the dishes on the counter, and then tugged John close for another kiss. Definitely beery this time, but still good, setting his heart pounding, blood reheating all the spots that Mason had chilled with the bottle.

"C'mon," Mason said again, though John had hardly been the one to hold anything up. He left his cane at the foot of the stairs and followed Mason to a room with piles of clothes on the floor and a tangle of sheets on the bed—which was just a mattress on the floor.

Mason flopped on the mattress and unbuttoned his jeans. "Get naked. I can't wait to see what you've got."

Mason had his jeans around his ankles and was kicking them away as John peeled off his shirt.

"Oh shit. Never mind. Slow down." Mason reached up and pulled John onto the bed, running first his hand and then his mouth over John's chest. He jumped when Mason's tongue flicked hard over a nipple.

"All right. Let's get your pants off before anything else happens." Mason's fingers had trouble with the rivet, so John arched his hips and shimmied out of the pants himself.

Mason did much better lifting the elastic of John's jockstrap. "Mmmm. This is why your ass felt so good even through those pants." Mason dragged the elastic down over John's knees and tossed it away.

John was wondering if he was supposed to say something too. Mason was still in his T-shirt and shorts, so John couldn't see much besides his legs. He was glad Mason had left the lights off. It was easier, and John's head exploded less when it wasn't too bright. He was thinking he'd need to wear sunglasses to class, even if everyone called him Stevie Wonder.

Apparently, Mason didn't need any conversational skills from his bed partners since he pushed John onto his back and started flicking at his nipples with tongue and fingers.

"God, what I'm going to do to your ass."

It was fine. Because John could just let that voice float all around him, wrap him in that warm purple velvet while every stroke of Mason's tongue made John's dick pulse and twitch.

"Gonna eat you. Loosen you up with my tongue until you beg for my dick." Mason's mouth moved below John's navel and not talking was good because he was pretty sure that the only thing that would come out of his mouth was "Finally." Roald didn't kiss, and reciprocating a blow job was out of the

18

question.

"You're gonna scream a little when I get it in you, but then it's gonna feel so good." Mason's thumbs started under John's balls and stroked up in the crease of John's thighs, coming to rest on his hips like he was going to hold him down.

Not necessary. John wasn't going anywhere.

"Sweet cock." Mason licked the head. "Anybody ever do this to you before?"

"No. No one." Maybe holding John down wouldn't be a bad idea because he wanted to arch up, slam his dick to the back of Mason's throat, and as he knew from personal experience, that took a minute or so to work up to.

Mason's lips wrapped tight around the head, tongue flicking the slit. Hot. Wet. Oh God. This was so worth...

The tongue stopped moving, the pressure eased. John brought his hands to that soft prickle of hair just above Mason's ears.

"Mason?"

Silence. John lifted his head and then propped himself up on his elbows.

If John didn't have a sense of proportion, he might have thought it was the shittiest thing that had ever happened to him. But shitty or not, Mason had passed out, head heavy on John's thigh, lips slack, stuttering breath teasing the wet skin on John's dick.

John let his head flop back against the mattress. This was so not his year.

A million laser light beams forced their way under Mason's eyelids, and he squeezed them shut. The skin might as well have been rice paper for all the good that did. He thought of the bottle of Jim Beam tucked between the head of the mattress and the wall and scrubbed at his face with his hand.

Not today. One day he would. One day it would just be easier to drink away his hangover and never come back. And it would finally be over. But today, he still liked living enough to put up with the pain. All of it.

Christ, he reeked. The bourbon bled out of him and into the sheets, soaking them both with the stench of sour sweat. He curled his nose. One thing he didn't smell was sex and that was weird because he could have sworn he'd brought someone home last night.

He used his fingers to pry his eyes open, looking for signs. No uncapped lube on the nightstand. No condom wrappers. Actually the new box wasn't even open. Maybe he'd imagined the whole thing. He swung himself out of bed and his toes tangled in a piece of elastic. He squinted down and kicked the jockstrap away. Okay. So there had been another guy here last night, because Mason sure as hell had never been high enough to wear a man-thong.

So. If there was no come on the sheets and no condom debris, what the fuck had happened?

His stomach soured more than what he could blame on sour mash alone. Shit. Had he done someone raw? Or...he tightened his own ass. No. He hadn't been fucked, unless the guy had a No. 2 pencil for a dick, in which case things would never have gotten that far.

Shit, shit, shit. He buried his head in his hands and tried to remember. Billy's Friday party. A guy. Thinnish, until he took off his shirt and then damn. Muscles like carved marble. Okay. That much he remembered. Tall too, tall as Mason. He'd remembered the random thought that had made him need that last beer when they got to the house. Eye level, he'd thought as he leaned in to kiss the guy. No chance of a crick in his neck or that strain in his knees like when he'd hunched down to kiss Alex.

20

So there'd been that extra beer. And maybe an extra round with Jim when they hit the room. And then...Mason shut his eyes. An ass that clenched every time Mason touched it. A virgin. He'd fucked a virgin bareback? A guy too innocent to know you couldn't trust any asshole who just wanted to get his dick in your ass? He wouldn't. No fucking way.

Mason tumbled out of bed and across the hall. With the shower on arctic, he stuck his head under the blast and then staggered downstairs.

"There he is." Lizzy's voice was a blare, carefully calculated to send off more sirens in Mason's bourbon-soaked brain. But that wasn't the worst, because sitting at the kitchen table, dumping sugar into what looked like the last fucking cup of coffee from the sixteen-cup coffee maker Mason had bought for the house, was the guy whose jockstrap had practically killed Mason when he tried to get out of bed this morning.

Maybe the last was an exaggeration, but it was hard to think between the hangover and who's-making-more-coffee and the holy-shit-what-did-I-do?

A waffle popped out of the toaster, and Lizzy dropped it on a plate which she handed off to jockstrap guy. Mason would have glared at her, but it hurt too much to focus his eyes. Carrie was unrepentantly belting out Britney Spears as she and her headphones danced at the sink and occasionally washed a dish. Even the fourth member of their household, Kai, who never seemed to come out of his room now that he was studying for the LSATs, looked up from the papers he was highlighting to watch the entertainment.

It wasn't like Mason never brought guys home. He'd just done it last...a while ago.

"Don't worry." Lizzy put the syrup bottle in front of jockstrap guy. "He's always like this on Saturday mornings."

"And Sunday and Monday. And Wednesday and Thursday."

Carrie sang the days to the beat in her head.

"Tuesday is his designated sober day, right, man?" Kai added.

What the hell? Why was this so fucking entertaining for everyone? Mason and Kai had been roommates since freshman year. He barely had to lift a finger to flip him off.

He ignored his tormentors and watched the quiet guy pouring syrup on his waffle. The one missing his jockstrap, the one with the soft, innocent-looking eyes and the far-from-innocent sweet curve of ass Mason hadn't been able to keep his hands off as they walked from the party.

Which brought him back to his question.

"Need to talk to you."

The guy put the syrup bottle down. Kai capped his highlighter. Lizzy stopped fussing over the guy like he was her long-lost son, and even Carrie took out one of her headphones.

"Alone," Mason mumbled.

The gray eyes blinked, kind of like a subliminal nod.

"Don't forget, I'm going to drive you back uptown," Lizzy said as jockstrap guy pushed away from the table.

"Thank you."

The guy went out onto the back porch. Mason stared after him and then remembered they'd come in to the house that way. At least part of his memory was clear. You *could* bounce a quarter off that ass.

It was warm and bright, and the birds were really chirpy. Mason decided to get this over with. "What happened?"

The guy blinked again, like he had to translate the words into another language before piecing together an answer.

"It was too late to catch a bus home so I slept here. I was on my way out and your housemate Lizzy offered me breakfast and a ride."

More bits came back. Dorm. No car. And that whispered, "No, no one," as Mason wrapped his lips around a slick red cock.

"I mean, what happened before? Did we have sex?"

"Define sex." That blink again, slow, steady and fucking infuriating.

This guy could not possibly be as innocent as those eyes and that creamy skin made him look.

"Did anyone come? More specifically, did I put my dick in your ass?" The without-a-condom part he kept to himself for now. One freakout at a time.

"I sure didn't come."

Shit again. He'd fucked a virgin, done a crappy job and probably scared the kid off sex for life. The guy looked about seventeen. But he'd been at the party. He'd had a beer. *And how many times did you get smashed before you hit legal age, Mason Jackson Kincaid?* He'd fucked an underage virgin without a condom. Not one of his finer moments.

"I don't know if you came," the guy went on. And now he looked amused instead of blinking like a fucking owl. Only an owl wouldn't have eyes like that. Not that shade of gray. Not with the tilt at the corners that looked out of place in such an all-American face. "Since I slept on the couch," the guy finished.

"The couch."

No nod. Just a blink.

"So—"

"You passed out with your mouth on my dick."

"Um—" Maybe there were worse things than fucking a virgin without a condom and screwing him up for life.

"C'mon, John. The food's getting cold."

Mason had told Lizzy to take her codependent mothering shit somewhere else. She had. She mothered Kai and Carrie,

23

K.A. Mitchell

and him she just watched. And now she was mothering—
"John."

As Mason called him, he turned slowly, and Mason noticed
the cane in the guy's right hand. Mason hadn't seen it before
and it surprised him because he had been watching the guy's
ass and he knew damned well he didn't have a limp.

Why was John looking at him like that? *Because you called
him back, idiot.*

"So could we maybe do this again sometime? I promise..."
not to pass out on your dick? "...it'll be better."

John blinked and then smiled. "I don't think so."

Chapter Two

John gripped the door handle for a quick exit as Lizzy stopped her car directly over the words labeling the area "Fire Lane No Stopping or Standing", putting John as close as possible to his dorm on State Quad. She didn't offer to help him out of the car or anything crazy like that, but she did wait until he was on the decorative cement that delineated the campus from the road.

"You all right from here?" She leaned out of her window, crystal-pierced lip and eyebrow flashing in the sun, like the warm honey-colored pieces of glass John's screwed-up vision showed him radiating from her black hair.

John waited for the images to settle, then waved. "I'm fine. Thanks a lot."

"You know, Mase really is a good guy. He's just—going through a phase."

"What kind?" Did people really call alcoholism for someone in his twenties a phase?

"The kind where he's an asshole to everyone. See you around, John."

According to the university website, there were 13,432 undergraduates enrolled. He doubted he'd see anyone from that household again. Which, given how badly his balls had ached until horniness had trumped embarrassment and sent him to jerk off in their bathroom, was fine with him. He gave her another wave and his best press-friendly smile and watched her drive away, the buzz of her small engine leaving behind a stream of soft baby blue.

Of course, Mason dreamed about Alex. He dreamed about him almost every night. There was the dream where Mason could feel him and see him but every time he reached out, Alex disappeared. And there was the one where Alex was trying to tell Mason something, but he couldn't understand Alex because he was mumbling or speaking another language. Mason was used to those dreams. He was just glad he never dreamed about that night. If he had to relive the accident every time he closed his eyes, he would have killed himself a long time ago.

This dream was the one that freaked him out. He could understand Alex. Could hear his voice all around. But every time Mason turned toward the sound, Alex wasn't there. Even knowing it was a dream while it happened didn't make it any less frustrating, because Mason couldn't shake the feeling that if he could find him, he would somehow be able to bring Alex back with him. That he'd wake up, and Alex would be next to him. Then Mason could explain that he'd just had a really freaky dream, and Alex would wrap his arms around Mason and hold on tight.

But Mason's empty bed and empty life were the reality. And the only way he got to be with Alex was in those dreams.

So he was more pissed than usual when Lizzy yanked him out of it with a tug that hauled him half off his bed.

"What?" Mason struggled back toward his pillow.

"Is this it? Are we there yet?"

Mason focused on the rest of the room and then back at Lizzy. The sooner she got to her point, the sooner he could get back to sleep. Maybe this time it wouldn't be one of those scary dreams, it would be a sex dream, bodies inside each other, everything wet and hot and so good he woke up coming.

"Are we where?" he asked. Maybe Lizzy was stoned. It would be just like her to bogart the good stuff when Mason could have used the help right about now.

"Rock bottom."

Ah. Got it. The intervention speech. Which would get her out of his hair faster, pulling Jim Beam out of his hiding place or making fun of her? "Yes. We have. Despite my consumption of endless empty calories, my bottom remains rock hard."

"How's your dick?"

"Now, Lizzy, you know I don't swing that way. You're going to have to take your heterosexual perversions somewhere else."

She smiled.

Shit. He was missing something.

"I just thought that since you were now too drunk to fuck, you might reconsider your decisions."

"I wasn't too drunk to fuck." He'd gotten hard last night, hadn't he? He'd wanted to. Wanted that firm ass under him, wanted a taste of something new. Something to chase away the bitterness for an hour or two.

"If you weren't, why was piece of ass number twenty-seven on the couch instead of in bed with you, begging for more?"

"Shut up." Twenty-seven? There had been a lot of guys when he first got out of the hospital. Mostly because he wanted to prove to himself he still could. When he'd been trying to get back to the guy he'd been before Alex, when a hot ass and a nice cock was all Mason needed out of life. Of course, Lizzy had known him then, their first year in the dorms when he never came home before five in the morning. But there hadn't been as many the past spring and summer because he'd been working.

27

And tired. It had nothing to do with the bourbon he'd been pouring down his throat these past weeks as he tried to figure out how to fit back into his old life without Alex.

"Maybe I wasn't that interested. You know, sometimes when you get your new toy out of the package, it's disappointing."

"Right. It's not you, it's him."

"Is the lecture over?"

Apparently it wasn't, because Lizzy dropped down next to him, her head flopping against his thighs. "We gave you a month of wallowing."

"That's nice considering I've only been in town for three weeks." Was his grief on some kind of fucking schedule? New school year. Time to move on. Ten months was plenty of time to get over losing the better part of yourself.

"You know, we miss him too. Me, Kai, even Carrie."

His muscles went tight and his teeth sank hard into his lip to bite back something even more vicious than what came out of him. "Don't. Shut the fuck up right now." He didn't care how much he loved her, if she tried that I-understand shit for a second, he was going to shove her right onto the floor and walk over her on his way out to...wherever.

"Fine." But she didn't move.

How was he supposed to go back to sleeping off his hangover if she wouldn't get off the bed?

"Why are you still here?"

"I'm not going anywhere until you get up and take a shower."

"We're doing tough love now, is that it?"

"Who said I loved you?" She started humming, some musical theater thing that Alex would know, the hum growing louder until she squawked the words to the song.

"Christ, I'm up." He rolled her onto her side and pushed away from the bed. "I wish you'd leave me alone."

She was lucky he was already slamming the door when she said, "Yeah well, I'm not doing it for you. I'm doing it for Alex."

Art History was boring and lame, but it was still John's favorite class because it took place in the dark. As the professor droned on, describing the image he had on the board, John's digital recorder took notes. All he had to do was avoid the moment when the professor pushed the button to change the slide so that the computer-generated spinning transition didn't require five minutes of concentration before John could see the new slide.

Today they were finishing up Raphael, and John tried to absorb the professor's monotonal information about the artist's portraits and commissions and study with da Vinci. When the professor's hand came up, John looked down to avoid the transition.

As he looked back up, he was really glad he had the digital recorder because the last thing John heard from the professor was something about an uncharacteristically heavy use of shadow and light. Then his brain supplied a single word as the sharp beautiful face on the board came into focus: Mason.

Well, not that Mason had long hair, or wore a funny velvet hat, but he had that sharp nose, the intense promise in his eyes and lips. Especially those lips. Dark red, full curvy lips that had for one blissful second looked—felt—so good around John's dick.

Did this guy screw you over too, Rafe?

John would have to wait until playback to hear what the professor had to say about the pose, but to John, it was clearly a tease. That over-the-shoulder look? Maybe this guy had passed out on Raphael's dick after too much—what did they drink then? Mead? Wine? John had heard some of the girls in class whisper that all of the important Renaissance painters were bi. Which probably explained why so much of class time was spent looking at hot, naked or almost-naked guys. And why most of the class was girls. As the class went through the Greeks and the Romans and the Renaissance painters, (who were easy enough to remember if you'd ever seen *Teenage Mutant Ninja Turtles*) there was more dick on display than in a locker room.

This was different than all those other nudes—for one, it wasn't a nude. No skin but the guy's face. Still, John couldn't help thinking that there was no way an artist would paint a guy that way unless he'd had those eyes and lips promising him something that made his belly execute a back two and a half with a twist.

John needed to get laid.

The professor had moved on to a portrait of some pope— and the only thing *his* eyes promised was eternal damnation. John didn't believe in hell, but he did know he was twenty-one years old and he'd almost died a virgin. It was time to reorder his priorities now that winning Olympic gold no longer dominated every aspect of his existence.

John looked back down at his notebook and started making a list. He didn't actually label it "How to Get Laid" but he figured he'd remember something that important. It wasn't as if he was still having those little brownouts of memory like he'd had right after the fall.

So. Finding a guy to have sex with. Random parties? Definitely out. Clubs? Like with the Keith who kept sticking Disabled Student Association stuff under his door? Nope. He crossed that one out too. How did people meet? Work? He'd have to find something he could do that didn't involve moving his head quickly. Or walking a straight line. Or being up high.

Or—he crossed that one out. Friends? He'd have to make some first. He'd never had that problem before, but here, everyone already had friends and they seemed to travel in a pack. As soon as John made eye contact with one of them, they shifted and closed ranks.

The professor moved to the light switch, and John shielded his eyes.

"On Thursday, we'll begin the later Renaissance. Be sure to read the articles on the Baroque influences."

John blinked, wondering if his eyes had adjusted enough to prevent him from falling as soon as he stood up. When he uncovered his eyes, there was a girl with a pierced lip and eyebrow and a familiar smile standing in front of his desk.

"John, right? I thought that was you."

"Hi." Then his brain came up with a name to match the familiar face. "Lizzy."

"Are you getting some lunch?"

He didn't want this to be like that awkward thing with the girl on the synchronized dive team. Lizzy had to know he was gay, right? He'd spent the night on their couch, but she must have known why he was there. She'd apologized for Mason.

He pushed to his feet, slung his backpack on and grabbed his cane.

"You're a freshman, aren't you? Let me show you a shortcut to the food court."

John followed her out of the lecture hall. "How do you know I'm a freshman?"

"Art history. Standard freshman fare."

"Then why—I thought you were—" *Older* sounded rude.

"I needed the humanities credit. Core courses. That's mostly what I'm doing this year. I did all my heavy lifting last year."

Instead of heading out into the sunlight and up one of the innumerable flights of stairs that made John wonder why the campus had such a "disability friendly" reputation, she turned and pulled open an unmarked door in the wall.

They walked into a narrow dark corridor that opened into something like an underground street.

"These tunnels run under the whole campus, like Disneyworld. Only without the people in costumes," she explained.

The space smelled like exhaust and tar. Deep blue hums rolled from machinery.

"Everyone with a brain ends up using these by November. The campus was designed for some place in Arizona, not New York." Lizzy stopped and they waited as a miniature truck buzzed by. John shut his eyes just before the spinning amber light on top could send him into his own dizzy spiral.

Lizzy pointed up. "We're under the Podium." She said it with that emphasis, the capital *P* people used when they were talking about the great big rectangle of cement at the center of campus where people hung out, instead of just the little stand where professors lectured. They crossed the main strip of asphalt, heading for another set of doors. "This leads right into the campus center and the food court."

John measured this quick path against the trip he would have taken. Out into the sunlight, up the stairs to the Podium crowded with people, dodging guys on skateboards. Then up more stairs and into a building and down more stairs into the basement food court.

"Thanks."

"If you go exploring, just watch out for the maintenance guys and their carts. They act like it's NASCAR down there."

They joined a line of students with trays. Lizzy put a single yogurt on her tray, and John looked down at his sandwich, chips and pudding cup. He wasn't working out ten hours a day anymore. Maybe it was time to start thinking about that. He put the pudding thing back and gave his prepaid meal card to the cashier. Lizzy handed over some cash, and they found a table near the windows that looked out on the lower half of the campus.

All of the windows on campus were narrow slats of glass, no more than four inches wide, more like an archery slit in a medieval castle than a real window. The pattern they made reminded John of prison bars. And he'd thought he was finally free.

"Is this okay?" Lizzy pointed at the windows.

"Yeah, it's fine."

And it was. At least with the windows so narrow, he didn't have to worry about a lot of movement in what was left of his peripheral vision.

"The tunnels are great in the winter." Lizzy opened her yogurt. "But there was another reason I wanted to show you." She paused.

John was getting used to the way people came at mentioning his injury sideways, as if the fact that he had permanent brain damage was something he didn't know. Like he could ever forget it.

"I thought you looked familiar the other day. And it wasn't because of art history class."

And the next part was the sorrys. They made John feel like he was attending his own funeral. *Please accept my condolences on the loss of your life. Good luck with the rest of your nonexistence.*

Lizzy went on. "And then I figured it out. I—um, know who you are. Were. Whatever." She pointed at John's head with her yogurt spoon. "That really sucks."

As condolences went, it wasn't bad. "It does. Thanks." A

cold flush spread across his skin, the sickening chill he got when he knew he'd been a few inches off when he left the platform. Did Mason know? Had he pursed those lips and sighed out something about poor John? The last thing John needed was pity from a guy like Mason. "Did you tell him? Mason, I mean?"

He thought she might smile, but she just scooped up more yogurt. "Why would I? Did you want me to? I didn't think you guys really hit it off."

"We didn't." Didn't get off either. John considered his list of opportunities. Friends. Maybe Lizzy knew other gay guys. Guys who weren't assholes like her housemate.

"So what else are you taking?" Lizzy changed the subject, and John had another reason to thank her.

After listening to John's random course list—he still had no idea what he planned to do with his life—and offering suggestions based on what she'd heard about various professors, Lizzy picked up her tray. "I've got a class in ten. But I'll see you Thursday. Hopefully, the later Renaissance has more hot naked guys, right?" She offered him a big smile.

She might be a connection to one of the most humiliating experiences of John's life, but it wasn't as if he had friends to spare. He smiled back.

After she was gone, John crumpled up his trash and decided to get his laptop from his backpack so that he wouldn't look quite so lonely and pathetic sitting by himself. Off in the distance, he saw Lizzy stop to talk to someone. Despite the weird confetti and fractured way his sight worked these days, he still had perfect distance vision. It was Mason.

John bent over farther than was necessary to retrieve his laptop. He didn't expect that Mason would want to talk to him. He ought to be just as embarrassed—more embarrassed than John was.

John pulled his laptop out of his bag and put it on the table. When the world stopped spinning, Mason sat across from him.

"Hey." That voice again, the dark purple rub like velvet against John's ears.

He looked better than he had that night. Eyes clear, no stubble on his sharp chin, skin warm and tan. The weird little crystals of light around his head looked different too. No smoky black, or veined white, mostly red. John really wished he had someone to talk to about those. The sparkles around people's heads shouldn't have colors too, should they? But talking meant more tests, and more meds, and possibly more hospital, and John wasn't living through another two months in a rehabilitation facility which—no matter what amenities it claimed to have—was worse than living in the training dorms. If another person ever said, "How are we feeling today?" to him, John was going to see how effective a cane was as a weapon.

"Umm. Are you going to say anything? I was kind of hoping to apologize, but it's kind of freaky to have you just stare at me," Mason said.

John blinked. "I guess I'm just surprised to see you upright." He gently smacked his head. "But I forgot. It's Tuesday. Your designated sober day."

"Yeah, well, my housemates might have been kind of exaggerating."

"You mean you're only drunk four days a week instead of six?"

"Okay. I guess you're entitled to that one. I'd wanted to tell you I was sorry for being an asshole the other night. And the next morning." Mason took a deep breath through those dark, full lips. "It's just been a little weird being back. I took some time off from school to...uh, work, and I guess I got carried away when I came back."

"Okay."

"So that's it? Okay?"

"Pretty much." John had no idea why this guy gave a crap what he thought. It had just been a learning experience in John's new life, and he wouldn't be making the same mistake again.

Mason smiled, slow and easy. His face changed, his eyes glittering in a way that sent a hard pulse of blood to John's dick.

John reminded himself he was supposed to learn from his mistakes. "Look. I'm sure you're a really nice guy. And you can tell your friend Lizzy that you apologized."

"What the fuck does that mean?"

"It means I saw you talking to Lizzy before you came over here. And I get the impression that she tries to keep you in line. But—"

"But what?"

"I'm not interested."

That smile and glitter came back. "In what?" Like Mason knew it was a lie. That John's dick was pretty interested in Mason. But really, he couldn't be the only guy in Albany who could make John's dick hard, right? And it was the other stuff, the getting-carried-away stuff that John didn't want any part of.

"In dating you," John said.

"Define date."

John realized Mason was mocking that morning-after awkwardness and had to smile. Then he realized he had no idea what a date was, other than what he'd seen in movies. And they didn't feature a lot of guys dating. Or for that matter, any.

"A date. Two people getting to know each other by going out to eat and going to the movies. And having a conversation." He remembered Mason's words acting like a hand on John's dick.

Remembered promises filthy enough to be sweet threats. But mentioning them would derail this conversation. Even thinking about them was going to make it difficult to get up from the table unless John wanted everyone to get a good look at what Mason's voice did to him.

"I'm pretty sure it's rude to talk during a movie. And talking with your mouth full? Isn't that rude too?" Mason said.

"Not as rude as passing out on someone's dick."

Mason sucked in his breath, a thin silver sound. "Yeah. Can I have a pass on that?"

"Why?"

"Let me take you out and I'll show you why."

Mason certainly hadn't been as much of a jerk as Roald—at least not deliberately—and there was John's whole how-to-get-laid list. It wasn't as if lots of guys were jumping up to offer themselves to a guy with a cane.

"So, what are you doing this Friday?" Mason asked.

"I think I'm—"

"Saturday?"

"Uh—"

"How about Sunday?"

John smiled.

"Okay. It's a date then." Mason grinned.

"Which?"

"All three."

That voice sent another spike of blood to John's dick. "Three?"

"I said I'd make it up to you."

Chapter Three

Mason decided he'd head straight out the door and wait for John on the porch. That way he could avoid any smart remarks from the rest of the 10 North Pine household. Three steps from the front door, Lizzy's wolf whistle brought him up short.

He faced his three housemates. "Friday night, guys. Don't you have anything better to do?"

Kai looked up from his laptop. "Than see you sober? On a weekend? I think we need pictures."

"Fuck. Off."

Lizzy swung off the couch and stepped close enough to sniff audibly. "Smells like you think you're going to get some. Anyone we know?"

Mason met her arched brow with his best poker face. She knew. He knew she knew. And no one else needed to know anything.

"Spiffy," Carrie called out from where she and her iPod were tucked in the butterfly chair. "Did you get him a corsage?"

Mason looked down and smoothed his dark green button-down shirt over his jeans. So he hadn't given much thought to what he'd thrown on in awhile, or to whether what he was throwing on had recently been thrown off and had skipped the visit to the washing machine—two or three times.

"Better yet, do you have condoms?" Lizzy asked.

"When you get smashed, try not to puke on his shoes," Kai suggested.

"I hate you all."

Mason went out onto the porch. At first he ignored the battered wicker couch Alex had rescued on a trash day, then sat on it anyway. It wasn't as if the couch was the only reminder. Much as Mason would like to blame his housemates for rubbing his face in his change of habit, he wasn't likely to forget that this was the first time he had made plans to go anywhere with someone since Alex.

One of the reasons he was hiding out here was that he didn't want to answer Lizzy's questions. Because if she wanted to know why Mason had been so intent on making a date with Mr. Innocent, his only answer would have been "Beats the fuck out of me."

The guy was hot, but Mason had never been anyone's first time, and he was thinking that showing a virgin the ropes would take more effort than he managed to put into anything these days. But when he'd seen John again, sitting alone in the cafeteria, embarrassment over what Mason had done suddenly couldn't compare to the forever humiliation of never making it right.

He twisted the silver ring on his left hand, remembering what Alex had said. *It's not about what you owe anyone else, you owe it to yourself to fix your mistakes.*

Right, babe. And as long as your boyfriend's mistakes didn't include wrapping the car around a tree, you'd get a chance to.

Alex could still make Mason wish he was half the man Alex had been.

Okay. Mason would make this right. Work off a fraction of his karmic debt. He'd send the guy off to the Magical World of Dick with a hell of a lot better intro than Mason had had. Then maybe Alex would smile at Mason in his dreams.

Of course, there were other selfish reasons. His buddy Jim Beam might have softened the edges of last Friday, but Mason could still feel the tight curve of Mr. Innocent's ass as it filled Mason's palm, still taste the sweet hunger from those not-so-innocent kisses. He hated to give Lizzy too much credit, but actually finding himself too drunk to get off had been a bitch of a wakeup call. Since he wasn't dead and still liked to fuck, he'd decided he wasn't ready to crawl permanently inside a bottle of bourbon. Now he was looking forward to some other distractions.

John came around the corner on Western, steps even despite his cane. Cane. Shit. How had Mason forgotten that? Thinking with his dick for one. He'd planned to walk down to Duffy's Tavern. For a second, he actually thought about going back inside to ask Lizzy if he could borrow her car before he remembered he wasn't ever driving anyone anywhere in a car again.

Lizzy could really get off playing mommy and drive them. Yeah. Not happening.

John didn't limp at all, though. Only kept his head down, a slight hesitation every now and then. He was almost at the porch before he looked up, the porch light beaming off creamy skin, turning his hair almost blond. John blinked three times, like the old forty watt was making his eyes water, and then smiled.

"Hey." Mason pushed to his feet.

John's answer sounded more like a question. "Hey."

Mason stepped off the porch to meet him.

John offered a smile, slow as his sexy blink, bright as his hair. "Hey," he said again, with more assurance. "You look great."

The surprise in his voice made Mason laugh. "Thanks." He stepped closer. "You look hot."

Color hit the top of John's cheeks, building on the sweet-wholesome vibe that had Mason wanting to put the guy on his knees and see how pure he looked with a cock in his mouth. His imagination transmitted the image in high-def, sending a rush of heat south so fast it left him lightheaded. Damn, that felt good. How long had it been since he'd felt anything close? He hadn't so much as jerked off since he'd come back to school, the flood of memories of Alex in their house, on campus, even standing next to him in the grocery store had sent Mason straight for the bourbon.

From the quick intake of John's breath, Mason didn't think he'd have much trouble convincing John to just head back into the house and upstairs with him. But there was the living-room gauntlet to run, and Mason was doing this right. If he'd made it without sex for the past three weeks, he could make it another few hours.

He pulled his lips in between his teeth and shifted a bit, making room for his thickening dick and moving out of the range of immediate temptation at the same time.

"You good with walking?"

John tucked the cane in closer to his leg. "I'll be fine."

Mason folded in his lips again, sucking back his own story of the royal pain in the ass—and in the armpits—his life on crutches had been for the three months after the accident. Because once he opened that up, there was no guaranteeing he wouldn't say the hell with making it up to his dick or to John and just go spend the night with Jim.

"It's only a couple of blocks."

"To where?" John fell into step beside Mason as he headed for Western.

"Duffy's."

"What's Duffy's?"

"They have live bands on Fridays. A guy I know is playing

bass in the band that's there tonight."

"So it's a bar."

"Yeah. You got ID?" Mason didn't particularly care if it was fake.

"Yes."

"Not just student ID?"

John's voice was crisp and precise. "I have a state-issued non-driver's license."

Some kind of story was buried under that non-driver's license business, but again, Mason wasn't interested in anything that might get back around to his own reasons for walking everywhere.

"So we're going to a bar?" John repeated.

"And you think I'll end up passed out again, right? Let me see your phone for a second."

John took it off his hip and handed it over. Mason typed quickly and passed it back.

"There. Now you have Lizzy's number. If I drink anything but soda, call her and she'll pick you up. Feel better now?"

"No."

Mason turned to look at him. "Why's that?"

John shifted his cane from hand to hand. "I'd feel better if—if I knew whether we were going to have sex tonight."

Blunt fucker. Mason liked it. And the heat curling through his balls made him like it even more. "Do you want to?"

"Yes."

"Then, yeah. We are." Mason stopped walking and put his hand on John's chest, right over the heavy thump of his heart and felt it jump to meet his palm. "You want to just skip right to it?"

John gave him that slow blink, and the streetlights turned

his long lashes almost white. Mason's brain flashed another image of John on his knees, his mouth sinking down, eyes closed, lashes brushing hollowed cheeks as he sucked. The gauntlet of nosy, staring housemates could come listen at the door for all Mason cared. They'd be back at the house in two minutes.

"No. Let's go hear your friend and his band." John smiled and covered Mason's hand with his own.

Mason shook his head. Mr. Innocent had some damn fine moves. As they started walking again, he tried to find a topic of conversation that would help him keep from dragging John back around the corner. "Where'd you go to high school?"

"I didn't."

"Huh?"

"I...moved around a lot. Had tutors mostly."

Rich, religious or crazy were the only things Mason could think of to explain that. As a conversation went, it was a dead end. He shot a glance over at the guy next to him. Maybe conversation other than *there, harder,* and *oh fuck yeah* was overrated in this case.

"Are we going to a gay bar?" John asked.

"No. But Duffy's is pretty laid back. No one'll freak if you can't keep your hands off me. Why?"

John didn't acknowledge his joke. "I've never been to one."

"Never?"

"No."

Mason had considered taking John someplace where it was dark, loud and full of guys grinding and sweating, until his more selfish sense reminded him that John had every reason to find a better offer and slip away. Right about then, Mason knew it wasn't so much about fixing a mistake, but getting to do this, do *him*, right.

"Disappointed?"

"Not yet."

Mason wanted to answer the challenge in John's voice with a tongue in his mouth and a hand in his pants. Duffy's might be run by an aging hippy couple and the crowd might be mellow, but here on the street between the Price Chopper plaza and the police substation was a whole different thing.

"C'mon then."

John tried to pay his own cover at the door, but Mason had already handed off two twenties before John got his wallet out.

"Wow. That seems like a lot for a place like this."

Mason looked around. Duffy's wasn't a dive, but it didn't draw a business-suit crowd.

"Tonight's a benefit. For the animal shelter." Mason bit his lip, and he turned toward the bar. "I thought since you were planning on joining that environmental club that you would like that."

John started that slow smile again, and it teased something in Mason's memory. "That was nice."

Nice? Mason tried on the label. It didn't fit. His motivations were far from nice.

Owen gave him a half-wave from where he and his band were setting up on the stage near the front door. Mason steered them toward the back, where conversation and an easy escape would be possible.

"Want something to drink?"

"No thanks."

"Not even for the sake of all those homeless puppies and kitties?"

"Fine. Um...rum and coke?"

Owen's band, Four Guys Named Dave, was doing a sound check when Mason got back with their drinks. His own unbourbonned, unrummed, untequiled coke was disgustingly sweet and flat, even with a generous squeeze of lime. He grimaced and put it on the thin rail that ran along the wall. John reached for the other sweating glass, propping his cane against the wall.

Mason wanted to kick himself for not grabbing a table or a stool for John while there were still some available. "You all right with standing? Want me to—?"

"It's fine. I—" Gold lashes dipped over John's eyes. Was there a lie coming? "I don't need it all the time. It's just for balance."

Balance? Part of the reason Mason hadn't asked about the cane was that John didn't seem to want to talk about it, but even more, Mason didn't want to hear about someone else's shitty case of luck, especially if that luck had anything to do with mass times velocity equaling newtons of impact that turned cars into crumpled paper balls.

No he hadn't wanted to ask, but John's mention of balance stirred all kinds of curiosity in Mason's brain. Owen started a bass line, the guitar and drums crashed in, the singer moved to the mike and conversation got difficult as Four Guys Named Dave launched into their weird punk-grunge-folk rock. As soon as the music started, John's attention seemed focused on a spot on the wall over the speakers, reminding Mason of a cat fascinated by thin air, staring at something only it could see.

John leaned toward him. "Thanks. I haven't heard live music since—in a long time. It's really good."

Owen was a good guy and the band was pretty popular, but Mason thought their riffs were whiney and that the singer was inventing a brand-new key that should have been reserved for dog hearing. Still, John's thank-you felt good.

When the band finished their set, John moved close, lips to Mason's ear, as if the music were still blaring. His hair tickled

45

Mason's cheek and then his breath heated Mason's ear.

"Bathroom?"

For a dizzy moment, heat and electricity rocked Mason's crotch until he realized John's question wasn't an invitation. And even if it was, this wasn't Steel or Sammies. A quickie behind the stall doors was out of the question.

"Uh...down there." Mason pointed to the back hall. "I'm going to get another drink. Want something?"

"No thanks."

When John came back, Mason had already sucked down half his club soda. John looked at the glass.

"Nothing but soda, honest. Taste it."

"Okay." John bent his head but instead of sucking on the straw, he licked at Mason's lips, tongue flicking to the corners.

Mason pulled away.

"I thought you said this place was laid back."

"Not enough for what that makes me want to do." Mason put his glass on the drink rail and gently tugged John and his cane-assisted balance to the back hall. The band was starting again, but the bathrooms were still crowded. Mason led John past the kitchen door and stopped, pressing him into the wall.

John put a hand behind Mason's head, tugging him close, and Mason kissed him. In spite of the grip on his neck, John let Mason take the lead. John didn't push his tongue into Mason's mouth, but the flick and suck and glide of John's kiss pulled heat from Mason's gut to the tip of his cock. Mason lifted his head, keeping John's head tilted toward him with a hold on his chin.

"Fuck, John. You kiss like you wished it was a cock in your mouth."

"Maybe I do."

"Jesus Christ." Mason's dick wasn't going to make it long

enough to hit phase two in his date plans. "Let's go."

"Where?"

The bathroom was out, but they were still doing this now. Big Mason was no longer acting captain. The back door was propped open with a box of empties, and Mason dragged John through it. A dumpster to the left was occupied by some guy in white kitchen clothes leaning against it while he smoked. A beat-up blue van was wedged in tight between the dumpster and a fence.

Please, please, please, yes. Owen hadn't locked the back of his van. Mason yanked it open and flopped inside against God-knew-what piled in the back. John followed him in. Mr. Innocent sure as shit wasn't living up to his name because he dove for the fly on Mason's jeans as soon as the door swung shut behind him. No licking around, no preliminary kisses or rubs. And that was fucking fine because Mason didn't need them. The second his dick cleared his fly it was in John's mouth, cradled in wet sucking heat. Mason levered himself up on his elbows to watch John's cheeks hollow. He paid perfect attention to the head, a hand stroking the shaft even as the other slipped through the slit in Mason's boxers to play with his balls.

Oh yeah. That sweet innocent look was a sweet fucking lie, because no way was this John's first taste of dick. Hell no, not when his lips slid down to meet his hand and Mason's cock slipped deep into a tight throat.

"Shit." Mason sucked in as much oxygen as he could get.

John's throat worked on him, once, twice, and his hand twisted hard, fingers lifting, teasing, stroking until it was right there, rolling through his balls, barely enough warning to—

"Fuck. Off. John, off. Now."

John knew that drill well enough too, because he lifted his head and his hand kept the rhythm, sliding on spit, thumb flicking over the head.

Mason came so hard he saw sparks behind his squeezed-shut lids.

It might have been over fast, but damn it was good, dick and balls flooded with heat, the spasms wringing out thick jets. It went on and on, beating out of him faster than his racing pulse until he was dry, empty and sated at the same time.

Mason finally pried his eyes open to see John lean back and wipe his hand on the floor, then use his shirt to clean the come off his chin and neck.

Fuck. If he hadn't come so hard, Mason would have licked that off. He flopped back again to catch his breath.

"Damn. Where'd I get the idea you hadn't done this before?" Mason tucked his cock back into his pants.

"Because I told you no one had ever done it for me." John's rough voice was accompanied by the familiar slap and slide of a fist on a dick.

Mason dumped John off his legs and rolled him underneath, covering his hand to slow his strokes. "Hey. Hey. Wait a second."

John froze, body shaking under Mason's.

"So you're telling me you suck cock like a porn star and no one's ever bothered to return the favor?"

"He said he didn't do that."

"He? One he?" Mason pressed a kiss along John's neck, ran a finger up his cock to feel him shudder again.

"Yeah. He said—he told me he couldn't. That it would get him in trouble."

Christ. So much for fixing Mason's karma. Dragging John into the van and onto Mason's cock wasn't much better than Mason's own introduction in that truck-stop bathroom with piss-soaked tiles digging at his knees.

"What an asshole."

"Him?" John's voice was still rough, but there was a little bit of a laugh in it.

"Yeah, well, maybe me too. But you are seriously fucking hot." A thick vein in John's dick pulsed against Mason's thumb. He licked the matching thump of blood in John's throat and traced the path to his jaw and ear. "You deserve something better than this for your first time."

John swallowed and rocked his hips, sending his dick sliding against Mason's palm. "I wasn't looking for candles. I just wanted you to finish what you started."

"And what was that?" Mason smiled into John's throat before looking up. The guy might suck like a pro, but his face was so innocent Mason wanted to see that mouth form a filthy request.

John didn't say anything, so Mason held John's head and licked the bitter salt taste from between his swollen lips. The groan in his throat sparked new life in Mason's cock.

Mason asked again, "So what did you want?"

"You made a lot of promises the other night."

"Like what?"

John's eyes got darker, a thin silver rim all that was left of the color. He tried to shove Mason's head lower. Grinning, Mason pushed up John's shirt and licked his belly, nose filling with the smell of his skin. That first taste had him wanting more. His tongue dipped below John's bellybutton, getting a stronger taste now, sweat and soap and the hint of his cock in that silky hair.

He raised his head just enough to let the words vibrate on John's skin, so that he would feel the heat of Mason's breath. "Don't you want this somewhere else? A soft bed where you can spread out, where I can get my mouth on every inch of you?"

John's hips moved so that his cock jutted into Mason's jaw. "If you don't do it before someone comes back for the van, I'll…"

"What? What are you gonna do?" Mason rubbed his jaw across the damp skin, sliding on fresh drops of precome.

"I'll tell everyone you suck in bed."

"Yeah, well that would only help me get dates."

Chapter Four

John was going to die. He'd never been this hard and not come. His balls were so tight, the skin on his dick so tight, it was like suffocating. Need drowned him, and he couldn't break the surface no matter how hard or fast he swam for it.

Since he'd figured out what his dick was for, it had always been about getting off fast before he got caught. Even later, it had been about doing Roald quick enough that no one noticed the two of them disappearing at the same time. This was killing him.

Mason kept rubbing his face across John's dick. Nice. A different touch than anything he'd ever known, but still nothing that would make him come, and God, how he needed to come. Mason moved, settling himself between John's legs, hands gripping tight on John's hips like there was any chance of him trying to get away. Nope. Not until he finally got this, even if he had to drag Mason's head down and—

Mason licked him. Licked the head of John's cock. They were both awake and no one was going to pass out. John forgot how to breathe.

Mason lifted his head, and where his tongue had been was cold.

"C'mon." John was pretty sure making it up to him would mean that he got his dick sucked before he died from lack of oxygen. "Do it."

"I like a guy who talks." Mason's voice was a physical touch now. Not just that weird sensation of deep-purple velvet, but a real vibration against John's dick. It felt good, but not as good as his tongue had.

"Tell me what you want." Mason rubbed his chin against John's balls.

"Your mouth. Suck me." It wasn't as much of a whine as John feared it would be, too full of desperation and anger. When Mason finally closed his lips around the head, that desperation wanted to drive John straight to the back of Mason's throat. Grab his head and push inside, like Roald would do to John. Stretch his jaw until his eyes watered and he couldn't breathe. It had been scary the first time, but good too, good enough that John always came in his hand before Roald pumped that bitter taste into his mouth.

John didn't need to grab or push now. Mason let spit leak from his mouth and slicked it down John's cock with a warm hand before sucking him all the way in, over the smooth hard roof of his mouth to the soft, hot space in the back of his throat. Heat coiled tight in John's gut and then Mason started to suck. That pressure all around while the back of his tongue rubbed and wiggled under the head, and at that moment John could have killed Roald for all his bullshit lies about why he could never let John have this. For making him think...God. Better than perfect. He wanted this to last forever. Wanted to do whatever he could to make Mason want to keep sucking him.

John's hips jerked, and Mason's grip tightened, a harsh sound vibrating against John's cock, like Mason growled a warning. John didn't know how much Mason could see, but John tried to nod and relax, at least relax enough that he didn't choke the guy with his teeth right next to John's dick. Mason made a different sound then, and it buzzed against John's cock as Mason's hand pushed inside John's pants, lifted his balls and pressed underneath them.

John forced his hips down, grinding into the hard plastic poking into his butt, and hoped Mason's finger would slide down farther and then prayed it didn't, because as soon as Mason's finger pushed on John's asshole, John was going to come and this would be over. And he didn't want his first blow job to be over.

Just the rub of Mason's finger, like John did himself when he jerked off, and his balls were sparking a warning. "I'm— I'm—"

The sucking went on, deep and hard.

John shoved at Mason's head, but coordination was already sliding away. Like Mason's finger was sliding into John's ass, like a wet wave was lifting him into an orgasm that burst in Mason's throat, shock waves echoing back and forth to make the confetti bright and shimmery behind John's eyes. In front of them too, when he managed to pry them open. Mason stroked his dick gently, breath falling on it as he met John's gaze, sparks framing Mason's face, spinning out from the ends of his hair.

John took a deep, shaking breath. "Wow."

Mason grinned. "Yeah. So what else haven't you tried yet?"

John shifted his feet under the table to let a girl carrying five coffees squeeze by. Friday night was pretty busy at the coffee shop Mason had led them to following his quick apology about hurrying John out of the van. Understanding that the band would probably finish their set in a few minutes and come outside to do whatever band people did in between sets didn't make John any less resentful of the need to fasten up his pants and jump out of the van on legs still shaking from that orgasm. The sharp corner of some case had been digging into his left kidney and something vaguely cylindrical in shape had connected with his spine at exactly the wrong angle, but after having his dick sucked for the first time, John was willing to ignore the discomfort in favor of just lying there and floating on how freaking awesome he felt.

He still felt good, squeezed at this tiny table, legs between Mason's, muscles pressed inside his thighs a memory of Mason's weight on him, pinning John as he sucked him, teased him. He took another long gulp of the shake-like drink Mason had bought him. It tasted as good as this place smelled, a bittersweet richness of chocolate and coffee. Mason had a smaller cup of something strong enough to make even more of the thick warm scent hang over their table.

Right now, John could run four miles uphill while writing an art history essay and solving quadratic equations. Was this a caffeine rush? If it was, he wanted more. It was much more fun than his limited experience with alcohol, even if caffeine did make everyone's head turn into a Spin Art. John could keep his eyes on his non-spinning shake and the already familiar clear and red crystal bits around Mason's head.

"So tell me about that asshole."

John blinked.

Mason's full dark lips quirked in a half smile. "Okay. The other asshole. I know I got a little carried away, dragging you into the van like that. Sorry. I'm supposed to be making it up to you."

"You're making it up, all right."

"You mean you don't believe me?" Mason moved his leg, more pressure on the inside of John's thigh, a slow rub along the inseam of his jeans.

"No. I don't think you're sorry that you got off. And neither am I. Did you hear me complaining?"

"So am I still an asshole?"

"I'll get back to you on that."

Mason sipped his coffee. "So then, tell me about this other asshole, the one who was all about his own cock and ignored that pretty dick you've got tucked in here." Mason shifted again, knee brushing lightly across John's crotch.

John tried a cautious glance around, but between the crowded space and the colors sparkling around everyone's heads, he couldn't tell if anyone was paying attention to them. He didn't want to talk about Roald. How John had been stupid enough to keep believing him when his lie of "Maybe next time, we've got to hurry" turned into "They're testing our team a lot and semen will show up on the test." John had to be the most naive human being in the world to have fallen for that crap. No. He didn't want Mason knowing what a moron John had been.

"Why?" John sucked more of that sweet, rich drink through the straw.

"Might want to slow down. Those things are like liquid speed."

"What is it?" John didn't have to worry about drug tests, or whether every single one of his abs was visible for some promotional shot. All he had to worry about now was whether he'd pick the right one of the three shakes in front of him since someone had just accidentally kicked his chair and turned the room into a carnival ride again.

"It's a Brewed Awakening shake. Lots of espresso and sugar. I didn't want you to fall asleep too early tonight."

There wasn't much chance of John falling asleep. Not if there was a possibility of having his dick sucked again, or even better, of getting to have some even more interesting experiences.

"I'm not the one with that problem."

"Strictly coffee." Mason raised his cup. "So that was the only guy you ever did anything with?"

"What difference does it make? And I already told you he

55

was."

Mason leaned forward. "The difference is, I want you to have a good time." He pulled the straw out of John's shake and sucked it clean. "No. I want you to have a great time. A holy-shit-I-think-I-saw-God time."

Blood thickened John's dick, lightning quick with the added jolt from the caffeine. Mason must have felt the pressure against his knee because he smiled again, a full-lipped smile around John's straw as Mason licked and sucked. John wanted to believe the promise in that smile. He couldn't remember the last time anyone had shown that kind of interest in a John Andrews who wasn't a tragically injured former Olympic double gold medalist. It wasn't just because of what a jerk Roald turned out to be. After the accident he'd figured out damned fast that everyone who had seemed so fascinated by John the diver wasn't very interested in John the college student who had a tendency to stare and blink a lot.

So far, it seemed like he could count on Mason for straight answers. "Why do you want that?"

"Because you have a beautiful cock. Good enough?"

John had seen a lot of naked men in locker rooms, but hadn't particularly seen anything that he'd call beautiful. Interesting, maybe.

When John didn't answer, Mason kept going. "Really. Such a thick ridge, soft slick head, felt damned good in my mouth. Pretty dark pink."

John swallowed. "And you've seen so many they all look different?"

"I've seen a few."

John picked up a sugar packet from the table. "Fingers-and-toes few or the-sugar-crystals-in-here few?"

"Someplace in between," Mason said, though the twist to his lips made John think it was closer to the number of crystals in the packet than the number of human digits.

John couldn't control a widening of his eyes. "Is that because you drink a lot?"

"No." Mason shoved the straw back into John's drink and cupped his hands around his coffee. He didn't look angry, just frustrated. "Like I said before, my housemates tend to exaggerate."

"You don't drink?"

Mason had been meeting John's gaze, a steady look under the warm light above their table that let John see the gold flecks in Mason's brown eyes. Now he dropped his lids, staring down at the black surface of his coffee. The crystalline pattern around Mason's head shifted, the white and red looking scorched with black smoke, like it had been the night they'd met. Was it because the caffeine now and the alcohol then made things look different? John wished there was someone to ask, someone who wouldn't think he was insane. Everyone in the coffee shop seemed to be under their own kaleidoscope of crystal, but Mason's was the only one that had two—now three different colors. What if it was a sex thing? A gay thing? He sucked out some more of the shake. If he drank enough caffeine, maybe he could get it to overload, short out the colors in one blinding explosion, and it would be gone. Forever.

Mason was back to studying John and probably thought he was crazy for the way he'd been staring at the colors above Mason's head.

"It's all kind of hard to explain." Mason's words were so close to what John was thinking that they startled him. "Especially if you haven't—" Mason broke off and looked down at his coffee. "Sometimes something happens and your whole life changes in an instant."

"I know."

Mason looked back up, meeting John's eyes. With a nod,

Mason said, "I guess you do. So yeah. Something like that happened to me last December. It's been hard trying to figure out how to be who I was before it all happened."

If Mason could understand all that, maybe sometime John could tell him about the fall. About waking up to realize nothing would ever be the same. And maybe Mason would have something to say besides *sorry.*

"And drinking helps you figure that out?" John really wanted to know.

"No. It just makes it easier for me not to give a shit."

John wanted to nod, but with the caffeine rush from the shake, he knew a nod would get the world spinning for hours. He tried to nod with his eyes and his lips, to tell Mason that he understood. Mason gave him that half-smile again, the one that suggested he was up to no good and didn't care who knew it.

"So, you up for another round?"

When Mason closed his bedroom door behind them, John wished he could blame his jitters on the shake still settling in his stomach. Mason's question had made him nervous enough to gulp the rest down, and it wasn't that long a walk back to Mason's house. He wasn't sure if he wished Lizzy had been around when they came through the front door or glad he didn't have to face anyone.

Again, Mason seemed to read John's mind. "The housemates are conspicuous in their absence."

"Why?" John glanced over at the digital display on the clock radio. The numbers danced a bit, but he was pretty sure it wasn't quite eleven o'clock yet. That wasn't too late for people to be out on a Friday, was it?

"I don't know. I suspect Lizzy's managing hand. Kai hasn't left the house on a Friday night since he started prepping for the LSATs." Mason pressed John back against the door and licked over his Adam's apple before scraping their jaws together and whispering in John's ear. "Good. Now we can be as loud as we want."

Loud. John wasn't sure anything could make him want to yell more than how good it had felt to have his dick in Mason's mouth. And then he was half afraid there would be when Mason's hands slid around to cup John's ass through his jeans. Mason licked and sucked under John's ear, hands kneading his ass. John didn't know how a guy's hands there could make him so conscious of the space between, of how much he wanted to find out how that space felt when it got filled with another guy's dick.

"No jock tonight."

"No." John wasn't going to explain his naive belief that a jockstrap was what all gay guys wore based on his limited forays into internet porn. The sight of Mason's boxer briefs last week had shown him how stupid that was. And how nice a guy's body could look in them.

"But your ass still feels hot under these tighty-whities. Wanna see it. Want to see all of you." Mason released John's ass and reached for the button on his jeans.

John covered Mason's hands with his own. "Can we turn off the light?"

Mason leaned back. "The guy who fell on my dick like he was starving for it is shy?"

"No." And John wasn't. Not about his body. "It's right in my eyes."

Mason picked up a shirt from the floor and tossed it over the lampshade. "All right?"

The room dimmed to warm light and shadows. Much better.

"Thanks."

Mason pulled his shirt over his head. John took a moment to look before following the request for reciprocation in Mason's arched brows. The muscles in his arms were as hard and defined as John remembered from that night. Now he could see that Mason's chest was tight and smooth, the skin tan all the way down to a tiny stripe of white above his jeans, a trail of hair on his belly leading to what John really wanted to look at.

With a shrug, Mason dropped his pants and briefs. His cock angled up toward his left hip, dark as the skin on his tanned chest, a contrast to the pale skin of his hips and thighs. Not a lot of hair, just the thick tangle around the base of his dick, dark on the tops of his thighs. Mason reached down to stroke his cock until it stretched up toward his navel, full and heavy, veins swelling under the skin.

John licked his lips.

"Uhn-uh. Get naked and get in my bed."

Mason's voice registering with color was one thing, but it was a whole new level of crazy that John could feel it. Feel a warm towel rub across his chest, feel the weight of it against his thighs, his ass, his cock. John's dick was fighting a losing battle with his zipper, and he pulled open his fly. Mason sat on his bed, leaning up against the wall, still stroking his cock. Thumbs hooked in jeans and briefs, John shoved them down.

"Yeah." Mason's voice washed him in rich color again.

John kicked away his pants and started for the bed, dick slapping against his belly. Neither of them had touched it, but it still pulsed hard and thick from the sight of Mason stroking his cock, the memory of those same hands on John's ass.

As soon as John stepped close to the bed, Mason reached up and pulled John down, rolling him onto his back on the tangle of sheets, running a warm, wet tongue over John's pecs, first flicking over, then sucking on his nipples.

"We got this far last time," John said, and then wanted to

smack himself for being more stupid than usual.

"Well, now we're going to get a lot farther." Mason knelt between John's legs and tossed a bottle and a condom on the sheet next to him, like it was some kind of dare.

John wasn't backing down, he didn't even want to slow down. He wanted to move this along before he had time to think too much, because looking at Mason's dick, he was starting to have some doubts.

Mason dropped down and kissed him, weight pressing John into the mattress, hips, chests, cocks lining up for all-over friction as Mason's tongue slid slow and silky over John's lips. John reached up and grabbed Mason's head, the short feathery hair above his ears tickling John's palms as he kissed back, answering every tug and thrust of Mason's tongue.

Mason lifted his head. "Like the way you kiss, John. I'm going to make you feel so good."

John didn't need someone to take care of him, he just wanted Mason to show him how to do this, but maybe it was the voice, because Mason's words melted like caramel in John's stomach, sticky and too sweet to resist. Then Mason groaned as he licked his way down John's chest, as if making John feel good was something Mason needed.

Mason raised his head. "Show me how you jerk yourself off. Want to see what you like."

That made sense. John slipped his hand down his chest, palm flat against his sternum like he was sliding it into loose pants. He grabbed his cock by the shaft and started a steady pull.

"Straight for the good stuff, okay." Mason smiled down at him. "Don't come."

"No." But the word got caught in a stammer. John's own hand felt ten times better with Mason's eyes on him than it ever did when John was alone.

He moved his other hand to thumb across his nipples, squeezing one in the vee of his fingers.

"I can handle that." Mason lowered his head and sucked, his teeth grazing the nipple John had squeezed until John jumped.

"Good jump or bad?"

"Good, but—" John ground his teeth and clenched hard with his muscles to slow down the way his body was sliding into that rhythm of have-to-come-now.

"Okay." Mason blew on the wet skin, provoking a shiver. "Then what? When you're getting close, how do you do it?"

John rubbed his fingers over the head of his dick, collecting enough precome to get them a little slippery.

"I like where this is going." Mason rolled onto his side. "Here. I think I've got this now." He put his hand over John's where it still kept up a steady stroke and followed his movements. "Then what?" He leaned in until his lips were brushing John's ear.

John slid his fingers over his balls, pressing between, lifting them before going back to the head for another slick drop. When he moved his middle finger lower, down far enough to press on his hole, Mason sat up.

"How much, John? How deep do you go?"

"Just a little, just when I'm really close."

"God, you look tight. Oh Christ, that's gonna feel good." He yanked John's hand away and took his cock between those full dark lips, sucking him halfway in before retreating to lick at the head.

His hand covered John's on his ass, finger on top of John's, not forcing, just an extra weight, someone else there, but it sent him bucking up into Mason's mouth.

"Easy." Mason pulled off and tapped his finger on John's.

"You gonna come?"

John figured he could last a minute or two, unless Mason did something completely unexpected. "Not yet."

"Good." Mason left soaking wet kisses up and down the shaft of John's dick, finger nudging John's until it slipped in, spiking the pressure in his balls so that the next time Mason wrapped his lips around the head, John had to grab what hair he could and pull him away.

"Stop."

Mason sat up, straddling one of John's legs. John squeezed his eyes shut, fighting for breath, for control, for a way to stop the pleasure from burning through him.

"Okay, sugar?"

Squeezing his eyes shut wasn't going to be able to help him calm down if Mason was going to talk to him like that. "Sugar?" He opened his eyes.

Mason put a thumb on John's lips. "You do taste kind of sweet. I can taste that shake right on your tongue."

"Are you from the South?"

Mason laughed. "Southwest of Buffalo."

John could breathe again without feeling like he was going to tear a hole in his chest. He reached for Mason's hips, let his hands slide to feel the curve of his ass, and it did curve, soft and sexy, but tight muscles shifting under his palms.

"My turn."

"Hmmm? For what?"

"A taste." John licked his lips, and Mason walked up his body until he straddled John's head.

"You want it like this? Can get kind of rough."

John reached for Mason's dick and brought the tip close enough to lick.

"Okay, sugar."

It was different, Mason pushing his cock down into John's mouth, into his throat, only his hand on the shaft keeping Mason from plunging all the way in until John couldn't breathe.

Mason knew it too. He rocked over John, dick sliding heavy and slick on John's tongue, pressing against the back of his throat before easing back to let John get a breath, get a chance to work his tongue around the head.

"What if I grab your hands and pin you down? Fuck my cock into your throat until you gag on it?"

John licked and sucked, a groan rising from deep in his chest at the thought of Mason holding John down, keeping him from moving. Mason could do it too. He had the weight and the upper arm strength, and John wouldn't be able to use his legs.

"Yeah. You would like it, wouldn't you?" Mason grabbed his wrist, but he didn't pull it away. "But I've got other places I want to stick my dick right now." He backed off to the side. "Roll over."

Gravity suddenly tripled and John couldn't lift himself anywhere. He'd been riding that feeling of Mason using his mouth, using it but aware of him, talking to him, so different from Roald's *hurry-uhn-there.*

"Huh?" He'd heard him fine, but he wanted a minute to process it. And he'd kind of been hoping they would do it face to face. He'd liked Mason looking down at him just now and didn't want to lose that.

"Roll over so I can fuck you. That is why you came back with me, right? If you wanted another blow job, we could have managed it in the bathroom at the coffee shop."

John rolled. He suspected Mason could have rolled him anyway if he'd wanted to. As John settled face-down with a pillow near his head, the sheet rubbed roughly against his dick.

"Oh, that is a sweet ass."

John wondered if all those sugar-crystal guys, the more than a few, heard that. Mason's hands stroked up and down over his ass, hard and firm on the muscles, more like a masseur than a lover.

Then he grabbed on tight, fingers pulling the cheeks apart, and ran his tongue along the crack.

John's chest seized with a shock of pleasure, and he sucked in air. Mason went back for another swipe, tongue flicking hard on the hole. John knew that touching his ass during sex felt good, but nothing could have gotten him ready for what a wet tongue would feel like on—oh God—in his ass.

The touch turned into a kiss, more obscene and intimate than anything John could imagine. That Mason would do this to him—for him—filled John with a sense of power, even as Mason's hands held him open and vulnerable. And it just flat out felt amazing.

Mason slapped an ass cheek, palm raising a sting that tingled even as the caress of his tongue had John squirming back for more. Breath fell hot then cold on John's skin as Mason whispered, "You like that, John?"

Between the sensations of another slap and a wet wiggle of tongue, the best John could manage was "Uhn." He hoped Mason knew that meant *God, please, yes.*

A groan vibrated along the sensitive, stretched skin. "All of it?"

"Yeah."

Mason slapped John again, hand leaving a burning imprint that it quickly soothed away before taking a bruising grip on John's ass. John rubbed his dick against the sheet, found a fold that tugged on the crown in the perfect way as Mason's tongue dipped back in. Flat first, and then pointed. A swirl and a jab. John could come from nothing more than this. From a little humping on the sheet and Mason's tongue in his ass. Could feel

K.A. Mitchell

it start to burn and sparkle in his balls.

When Mason lifted his head this time, his thumb took over for his tongue, rubbing and pushing while his hands kept John pinned open.

"Your ass is all soft and open for me. You ready for my cock, sugar?"

Yes. No. Can't I just come like this? But John only rubbed his face against the pillow and waited.

Mason sucked a hard, biting kiss below John's hip, the pressure fading to licks the instant it started to hurt. A good distraction, because while John was dealing with that, Mason's thumb slid deeper, moving, twisting and prodding, even as John heard a bright snap of plastic followed by the pinkish gurgle as Mason squeezed a bottle. John had never heard the sound before, but he knew what it was, and his stomach and ass tightened as he felt the cool touch of Mason's lubed fingers.

"Relax for me, sugar. I'll make it feel good."

John tried, but Mason was pulling him open, stretching John's ass with two thumbs inside and it burned. A lot. He rubbed his face against a pillow and held himself still, but when Mason's thumbs went in deeper, John dove forward, away from the pain and pressure.

Everything stopped.

"It's okay." Mason smoothed John's back with slick hands. "Okay. You just stay soft and sweet for me, all right?"

The condom wrapper parted on a silver hiss, a dull brown slither followed, the colors flashing against John's closed eyelids as Mason poured out more lube and slicked his cock.

As the slippery head of Mason's dick rubbed the crease of John's ass, muscular thighs pressed John's into the mattress.

John swallowed around a rock in his throat. "I can't move."

"I know, sugar. But if you jerk around, it's gonna hurt

more."

John wanted to trust, to fall into that soft cloud of dark purple that Mason had wrapped all around them and let it carry him wherever Mason wanted to go.

"I know what I'm doing, okay? I promise I won't do anything you can't take. Just breathe and it's going to be good."

A little pressure and it was good. Good enough that John wanted to arch into it, suck it down into his body, but Mason didn't move, wouldn't let him. The pressure was gone, but before John could think about that it was back, more, thicker, but still okay.

Mason dropped a kiss on John's shoulder before he pushed in deeper, and now it did hurt. Why the hell had John wanted this? Why couldn't they have just stuck to fingers and tongues and—

"Umph." John huffed the sound into the pillow as the pressure from Mason's cock seemed to force it up through his body.

Mason backed out again, hand rubbing along John's spine, but the weight was still there, Mason sitting on John's thighs and God, pushing his cock inside. Mason didn't stop this time, and John's body gave in to the pressure, but not without a sting that made his eyes water. He wanted to move. Wanted to get fucked, take it deeper, get it out, forget he'd ever thought losing his virginity was a good plan and just go hide in his dorm room for the next four years.

Mason didn't move, didn't even whisper, which would have been something nice right about now. There was nothing but this stretch as Mason tried to fit inside him and John tried to let him.

John didn't feel any different, but Mason must have felt something because he said, "That's it," and pressed in deeper.

He moved with shallow thrusts then, weight spread over

John's back, holding John's arms down like he held his thighs. John was covered with Mason, full of his cock and even his breath as he kissed John's ear, his neck, his cheek. But now when Mason moved it felt different. He shoved in farther and surprised a gasp from John's lips.

A good gasp. Not that it didn't still hurt, because it did, it just hurt good. Like the sweet pain of coming, hard spasms from gut to thighs wringing his dick dry. But John didn't come, only groaned every time Mason pushed more of his cock inside John's ass. Mason pressed down on John's hands, chest lifting from John's back, and went all the way in, so deep Mason's balls slapped against John's.

Just breathe, Mason had said. John didn't know what good breathing was supposed to do when every breath, every beat of his pulse, made him even more aware of the thick cock in his ass. Mason's weight flattened John against the mattress, only Mason's hips moving so that he stabbed quick and deep. John tipped his head back against Mason's shoulder.

"Better now? Is it good?" Mason licked the words into John's ear.

It was. Especially when Mason went fast. It made heat spill from John's ass to his belly and balls, hot waves prickling over his skin.

"Yeah. It's good."

Mason raised his chest, but his thighs still held John down. He moved in and out, cock dragging along nerves and muscles that couldn't seem to make up their mind about whether in or out was better. He pulled all the way out and rubbed the head up and down the crease.

Out was definitely not what John wanted anymore. He reached back for Mason's hip.

"Oh fuck, John. Such a sweet tight ass. Makes me want to pound it."

John's stomach leapt at the thought of it, of slick friction and burning pressure, of Mason holding him down and fucking away until John shuddered and came. "So do it."

Mason shoved in again, gliding deep inside on one stroke. "Not yet. Give it just a little more time, sugar."

Still dark purple sound, but the rasp in Mason's breathing made ripples of something else in the color, the way the live music from the band had rippled and splashed against the walls of the bar. John grabbed Mason's hip, Mason drove them forward, weight settling on John's back, lips licking the sweat on his neck, his cheek, his forehead.

A little faster, good deep strokes that made John want to ride this forever. Mason supported himself on his arms and drove straight down into John's ass, into his gut, farther inside than should have been possible, but still too slow, no faster than their hoarse exchange of breaths.

Then Mason stopped, pulled out and panted against John's back.

"What's wrong?"

"Nothing, just—" Mason moved off John's legs and scooped an arm under John's hips to pull him to his knees before pressing back inside. "This good too?"

It wasn't right away, because it hurt again, almost too much, but then Mason grabbed John's dick and started jerking him off.

"Yeah."

Mason's other hand reached up to John's chest, pulling him down and back and that was better. Eyes-rolling-back-in-his-head, dick-leaking-precome-like-a-faucet, whole-body-wanting-to-shake-from-it better.

"C'mere, sugar." Mason lifted John farther back onto his lap so that they were both kneeling, Mason's cock pushing John up, arm pulling him down, dick wrapped in perfect friction.

"Harder." John wasn't sure if he meant the hand on his cock or the dick in his ass, but he needed something.

Mason gave it to him, nudging John's legs farther apart so that all his weight forced Mason deeper into John's body and moved them faster, shocks of pleasure burning back and forth from his ass to his cock.

"Gonna come for me, John? Want to feel your sweet ass go crazy on my dick when you do." Mason kissed his neck and his cheek before John turned to offer his mouth.

It was there, that perfect moment of tension before he left the dive platform, muscles coiled, everything clear and sharp and ready to explode into flight. He squeezed Mason's arms, mouth opening to try to take more of Mason's kiss.

Mason groaned into John's mouth and slammed up in lightning-quick strokes, palm shifting on John's dick to rub the head, and the orgasm crashed into him, no color, no sound, just pleasure radiating out from his ass and cock until it poured out hot and aching from his dick.

And through it all, Mason was there, body, hands, mouth, cock, closer than skin in a way John had never felt. No, not even when he shot in Mason's throat was it like this, sharing feelings with another body.

John dropped his head on his chest and caught his breath, opening his eyes to see Mason's fingers laced with strings of come, a blob of it up on the pillow. He shuddered and Mason's hand gentled, thumb light on the head. Mason's other hand slid down John's chest to push just above his cock, as if Mason wanted to press out every last bit of pleasure in John's body.

Mason caught John's weight as he fell toward the mattress, turning him away from the come on the sheet and the pillow. His body was incredibly relaxed, but not so much that he didn't know there was still a hard dick in his ass.

"How do you feel?"

John went looking for an answer and came out with the truth. "Crazy." He did. Just not in a way that had anything to do with his skull fracture for a change. He felt energized and exhausted. Good but sore. And most of all, he felt a resentment that he'd had to wait all these years to find out what sex was, coupled with the relief that he'd been able to find out from someone like Mason instead of an asshole like Roald.

"Seems right." Mason shifted, a little movement magnified by the fact that he was still buried inside John. "So. Are you sore? Do you think you could take me in here until I get off?"

John wasn't sure, but he could try. "Okay."

"Not gonna take long." Mason put an arm behind him and came up with a towel from somewhere, wiping off his hand and John's stomach and some of the sheet before rolling John face-down again.

Mason moved in steady thrusts, hard rough breaths stuttering over John in flashes of color. The motion ached inside, the way muscles burned after a hard workout, but every once in a while there was a little shudder of good friction. Mason reached up and clutched at John's hands, and again, John couldn't help comparing him to Roald. Like Roald ever cared if John was more than a hole for his dick. Mason wanted John with him, and that made him want to put up with a lot more than a sore ass to make the other man feel good. He tightened his muscles, and Mason groaned.

"Oh yeah, sugar. Damn you feel good on me." Mason lowered his head, kissing and biting on a spot just off John's spine, strokes getting faster, shorter.

John squeezed his ass again.

Mason lifted his head. "Christ." He drove in hard and deep and stayed there, shaking and jerking before collapsing on John's back.

Mason's breath tingled across the back of John's neck

where Mason's lips and teeth had left a spot John could feel swelling and pulsing with blood. He was pretty sure he had his first hickey.

"Damn," Mason said, and rolled to the side, hand resting on John's hip. "You, John, are an awesome fuck."

John didn't have any basis for comparison to return the compliment so he just said, "Thanks." He didn't think he'd done much. Mason had done all the work but still... "I'm hungry."

Mason laughed. "Well, my dick's out of commission for a few. I'll see what's in the fridge."

Chapter Five

John was as sticky as he'd been when he worked a cotton candy machine for a Special Olympics fundraiser. He slipped into his shirt and jeans and then into the bathroom to clean up as much as he could without taking a shower. Mason still hadn't come back upstairs, so John stripped the bedsheets but couldn't find anything else to put on the bare mattress.

Mason came in, dressed in a pair of paint-splattered sweatpants, balancing a glass of orange juice and pizza slices on a paper towel on top of a brown margarine tub. "Going somewhere? Got another date?" He looked at the bed. "And what happened to the bed?"

The crystal shards around Mason's head shimmered and shifted colors, red and clear bright white almost fighting for space like a rope of chasing Christmas lights. After a second, John realized Mason was pissed.

"I thought the sheets were—I came all over them so I took them off."

Now John realized the bed was the only furniture apart from a table with books and a laptop and a wooden chair that had been painted so many times John could see three different colors showing through the chips. And real colors too. World colors were not as bright as the colors that came from his head.

Mason put the food on the table, shoving some papers onto the floor to make room. "Trust me. The sheets have seen worse."

"Oh. Right. Sugar packet."

"Yeah. Whatever." Mason bent down and picked up John's briefs and tossed them at him. "You always leave your underwear behind? Must save on laundry."

"I went to wash up and I didn't know if—I figured we were, you know, done."

"Christ." Mason dug through some of the piles of clothes, but didn't appear to find what he needed. "That guy, the asshole you were blowing, he go to school here?"

"No. Why?"

"Because someone really needs to kick him in the balls. I was going to offer to do it."

"Huh?"

Mason turned around. "That guy really treated you like shit."

"It was just getting off." John had no idea why he tried to defend Roald, especially when it had been much more about Roald getting off than John, but he couldn't understand why Mason was angry.

"Just because it's just sex doesn't mean people have to be assholes about it." Mason found the balled-up sheets and tried to shake them out. "Fuck." He threw them down to join the other dirty laundry piles on the floor. "Don't you remember when I said I'd make it up to you, I asked you what you were doing all weekend?"

"Yes."

"So why are you so ready to hit the door? Did it suck that much?"

"No." John couldn't believe Mason didn't know that. He was too sure of himself, too sure of what he'd done to John not to know that John had loved every minute of it.

"Well, all right then. I'm going to go steal a sheet from Lizzy.

You'll have to explain it to her, though."

"So you want me to stay?"

"Unless you've got other plans." Mason turned back to lean on the doorframe. "But hey, part of the fun of being gay is getting to have sex both ways."

John swallowed. From the grin on Mason's face, John would be willing to bet his eyes almost popped out of his head. Mason was going to let him...

"You got a roommate back in the dorms that'll call the police if you're not back by three or something?"

"No."

"So grab some pizza. And take off your pants." Mason disappeared through the door.

The pizza was plain, with thin sauce and covered with congealed cheese, but as soon as John brought it to his mouth he realized that he was starving. When Mason came back with a set of sheets, he stuffed half his slice into his mouth and wiped his fingers on the paper towel before starting on making the bed. The action tipped his ass up and the pizza got hard to chew. If it felt that good to have a dick in John's ass, how good would it feel to put his dick in one? And if it did feel good, how was he supposed to remember to do it like Mason had, going slow enough that it didn't hurt? John forced down the pizza with some of the orange juice.

"Mmm. You're licking your lips again." Mason came back and covered John's hand on the glass, pulling it and the juice toward Mason's smiling mouth. He gulped twice, and John would have sworn Mason did it to deliberately draw John's attention to the way his Adam's apple bobbed as he swallowed.

Mason released John's hand. "Does that mean you're going to blow me before you fuck me?"

"Should I?"

Mason smiled but didn't answer. He took the brown tub and carried it over to the bed, waving a spoon. "Still hungry?"

John was, he just didn't think he could eat, stomach aching with the good kind of nervous he got before competition—the hyper focus that kicked in the second he heard the murmur of all those voices echoing off the still water and tiled walls. He shook his head. But unlike when he breathed in chlorine and came into that echoing space from the locker room, this kind of focus made his dick swell instead of shrink.

Mason dipped the spoon in and scooped some noodles into his mouth. "So, you moved around a lot, huh? Where was your favorite?"

John's brain, damaged though it was, had settled on a pretty nice loop of mouth-dick-ass, for once the images having nothing to do with weird color-sounds and everything to do with how it would feel to have Mason hard and hot around him. To have the strength that had held John down yield as he pressed in. And Mason wanted to have a get-to-know-you chat like it was some team-building thing at training camp? Maybe he wasn't ready yet. John tried to steal a glimpse of Mason's dick, but the way he had his leg up on the bed made it hard to do without being obvious.

"Um, a lot was boring." What could John say that wouldn't give it away? He didn't want to lose this anonymity, this chance to have someone just want him, John, and not the John who came bundled with everything else. "Arizona was nice. Pretty but hot."

"Funny. Everyone said the way the Albany campus was designed was meant for Arizona. To maximize the wind. Sure as hell does."

Mason couldn't seriously be interested in talking about

school. Not now. But John couldn't figure out a way to say "I thought you were going to let me put my dick in you" that didn't sound weird, given the direction of the conversation.

John tried to think of something to say and Mason laughed. "So not what you had in mind?"

"Huh?"

"You told me a date was conversation and eating."

John felt the laugh hit his own stomach. "You are such a dick. And the movies. We didn't go to the movies."

"Oh, right." Mason moved his head to the side. "I think there's a couple midnight shows at the Madison. Want me to get the listings?"

John took the plastic container out of Mason's hands and put it on the floor next to the mattress before grabbing him and pulling him underneath. Warm skin, hard bones and muscles, and a cock hardening as John brushed it with his thigh. John held Mason's head between his hands and pressed his thumbs against his laughing mouth.

"So I'm a dick now," Mason mumbled under John's hold. "Is that a step up from asshole?"

"You're—" Amazing. And hot. And John wanted to stretch this night out for a month or maybe forever, because this was how it was supposed to be, right? It's what everyone else seemed to have. You met someone who got you hot and bothered and could make you come and make you laugh and was a nice person and then you fell in love. Until you told him about the fact that you could see colors and people's heads looked like the center of a Spin Art and then you were screwed.

So for now, "—going to get fucked." John whispered it, but he knew it was the right thing to say, because Mason groaned and hiked his legs up so that his heels rested on John's lower back.

John bucked his hips hard, grinding their dicks together.

"That's it, John. You want it, you gotta take it."

"You're going to take it." John had meant it to be a tease, but it came out deep and raspy from the back of his throat.

There was something about Mason's body under John's that made him want to mark it, own it. He grabbed Mason's hip, fitting them together even tighter, fingers creeping down to pull on Mason's ass. Then the memory of how carefully Mason had eased John through the sensations of letting someone into his ass blasted him with guilt. John froze in place.

"It's okay." Mason reached up and grabbed John's neck. "I've done it before. Just make it a good ride."

John understood. He'd have to try not to come the second he got inside, like he had in Mason's mouth.

Mason was angling for a kiss, but John wasn't sure how much his self-control could stand. Already the friction of their cocks rubbing together was enough to make a whine fill the back of John's throat the way he begged silently for something when he jerked himself off, for that last bit of something that would send him flying off the edge. He kissed Mason, and it felt like all their other kisses, Mason licking and teasing open John's mouth until they were groaning into each other's throats. John shuddered and ground his hips down, need hitting hard and fast.

He crawled backward and bent down to lick the head of Mason's dick. He tasted like come and a little like plastic and a lot like the skin everywhere on his body, kind of spicy and sweet. John moved his head lower, licking at Mason's balls, lifting them to suck one side into his mouth.

Mason's hand landed heavily on John's head.. "Hold on, sugar. I'm pretty primed already."

John sat up on his heels between Mason's legs.

"Let's get you ready." Mason's voice was rough again, rippling and shifting color. He tore through the condom wrapper and rolled it down John's cock.

John could have cried in gratitude. He'd never tried that, not once, and he'd probably have made a total ass of himself figuring it out. Mason slipped the latex down to the base and stroked his fingers back up, circling the shaft.

"Can't wait to feel this ridge in me. Want you to fuck it in and out." He demonstrated with his fingers around the head until John had to wrench himself away, diving for the plastic bottle of lube.

Mason grabbed it from him. "I'll do me, you do you." He squirted some of the runny gel into John's hand.

John coated his dick. It was an odd sensation, his hand slick but his cock couldn't feel it, making it almost like he wasn't quite touching himself. Maybe it wouldn't be as hard as he thought not to come too soon. Then he saw Mason sliding his finger down under his balls and everything roared back like a power surge. Mason's finger slipped inside his body and he puffed out a grunt.

"Can I?" John blurted. "I want to."

"Sure. Do it with me."

John put one of his slippery fingers on Mason's hole, next to the knuckle just above the rim. As Mason nodded, John pushed in, right next to Mason's finger, a strange sensation of hardness against the wet heat and squeezing soft muscles.

"Uh." John couldn't help making the sound even if Mason smiled at him. Then made it again when Mason's muscles tightened on John's finger.

John had never gotten this far in his jerk-off fantasies, always imagined a guy's cock taking the place of his own tentative finger. But now he was going to do it. Put his dick into that tight hole and make Mason feel what John had felt. Make every nerve in Mason's ass pulse pleasure into his dick. Mason trusted John to give him that.

Mason pushed his finger in and out, and John copied the movement, moving faster until Mason gasped and pulled his finger out, grabbing John's wrist to stop him.

"Want me to roll over?" Mason asked.

"No."

"All right. Wait a sec." Mason grabbed the pillow from over his head and shoved it under his hips, putting his ass level with John's dick. "Okay, sugar."

John rubbed his dick against the warmth of Mason's ass, the sensation slippery even though John couldn't feel the lube on his skin. Mason's pulse beat hard against the tip of John's cock. Holding his breath, John looked down at Mason's face. The crystals around his head shone all red now, pulsing like the thump of blood in Mason's ass, the throb of it along John's dick. The color was almost opaque now, full and thick and hard.

"C'mon. Do it." Mason pulled his lips in between his teeth and closed his eyes. A bit of white flashed in the red.

Keeping a careful watch on Mason's face, John pushed in.

He didn't go anywhere except down the crease of Mason's ass, and they both groaned in frustration.

"It's okay, John." Mason's eyes opened, and the crystals went solid red again. "Just hold your dick in your hand to keep it from sliding."

"All right." John aimed his dick and held onto Mason's hip with the other hand. This time he had the right spot, but as soon as he felt the pressure around him, Mason gasped and John pulled back.

"Keep going. I'm fine." Mason didn't look fine, but John didn't know how he could tell. Mason's smile was there, but his eyes were closed. The crystals were pulsing slower, like whatever made them glow was fading.

John lined up again and pushed. The head went in.

"Fuck." Mason's curse wasn't quite a yell, but it was the loudest sound either of them had made. "Don't pull out."

"But—"

"Tell you. A secret." Mason grunted the words out between short, quick breaths. "God. Don't move."

John tried to make even his breathing move a minimum amount of muscles. "What?"

"Always hurts. A little. At first. Go."

John pushed in farther and kept going, sinking into that incredible heat and pressure, feeling the muscles shift against his cock as he went as deep as he could. He tried to hold still again, like Mason had done for him. But when Mason let out a long breath, John couldn't help it. A tug in his belly jolted his hips forward. When he looked down and saw his dick inside Mason's body, the pull got stronger until John's muscles cramped with the urge to move hard and fast until the heat spilled out of him.

Mason shifted and a tighter pressure rippled up John's dick.

"God, Mason. You feel good."

Mason blinked then opened his eyes to look at John, eyes dark, gaze steady. "Fuck me."

John moved his hips like he was fucking his own fist, but it wasn't the same. Then he tried a long deep stroke that felt really good on his cock, those muscles inside pulsing, gripping him, trying to keep him in, then friction fighting him on the downstroke. He didn't care about the condom anymore, this was way better than his fist had ever felt on bare skin. Mason's ass worked him everywhere at once and John moved faster.

"Yeah." Mason nodded and tipped his hips up.

The movement made John slide all the way out as he

rocked back, the tight ring squeezing the head of his cock as he left Mason's body.

"Yeah. Like that. Please, John."

Mason was begging him. This guy, the one who'd given John something better than anything else he had felt since he realized he could never get back up on a dive platform, was begging him. Wanted him. And not because John was convenient or naive enough to screw with or famous, but because John could give Mason what he needed.

John held Mason's hips and made fast little dips into the sudden give as Mason's body opened for the head of John's cock again and again. It wasn't as tight as it had been the first time, when Mason's hole had been tight enough to hurt. Now it just felt good, every quick stroke tugging hard on the ridge on the head of his dick, pressing over the sensitive spot under the head.

"Christ." Mason's fingers dug into John's forearms. "Good, so good, b—sugar." Mason raised his legs higher, hooking them over John's shoulders, and grabbed for John's hips. "Faster. More."

Heavy legs, voice, hands, all dragging John down, Mason was trying to pull all of John inside, dick first, and John sank into the need, into the strength all around him, using just his stomach muscles to shift his cock as Mason held John too tight to let his hips move.

"Fuck." Mason let go of John's hips, arms flopping out to the sides, fingers twisting in the bright blue sheets. "Harder."

John's legs and hips could power him cleanly through the air in time to make three perfect flips. Shoving Mason's legs over his head, John let all that force drive his cock into Mason as hard and fast as he could.

He lowered his head and kissed him, startling Mason's eyes open. John saw no pain there, just the hunger that John could feel building at the base of his own spine. The hunger for every last bit of pleasure their bodies could wring out of this, for that moment when everything would go tight and loose at the same time, for what they were climbing to together.

Mason turned his head away and closed his eyes again. His hand worked its way in between them, his knuckles scraping John's belly as Mason jacked his cock.

John didn't know why, but without Mason's eyes or smile to go by, John found himself staring hard at the color around Mason's head, trying to hold on until Mason came. Something like smoke touched the far edges, and the red throbbed like it was trying to squeeze out that gray color, like a video John had seen of blood cells rushing through an artery. Mason's other hand came up to grab at his necklace, a silver ring he wore on a black cord, and white sparked over the red.

It was distracting enough that John didn't lose the last of his control when Mason's ass tightened on him in quick hard pulses and come splashed warm and thick between them. John kept pumping his hips, though his throat ached like something was stuck in it as he watched Mason's face.

Mason's legs slipped off John's shoulders. "You gonna finish in me, sugar?"

John planted his hands on the mattress and pushed up. He didn't know if it would take ten seconds or ten minutes. He'd been close before, but now he— Mason's ass squeezed John's dick.

"Yes." John started moving. He wasn't even sure it would take ten seconds now. Not with Mason's hand dragging a sticky bit of come up toward John's nipple. A rub, a flick, and then Mason's fingers pinched. The sensation echoed all the way to John's dick, burst of pressure and pain, and then nothing but pleasure pouring from him until he emptied his balls into Mason, eyes squeezed tight to block out the distractions of colors framing that face with its knowing grin.

He eased back, one hand holding the condom on his softening dick, and Mason rolled to his side. It seemed right to snug in tight against him from behind after stripping off the latex, but then he didn't know what to do with it.

"Just toss it on the floor. I'll get it in a minute when I get up." Mason's voice sounded farther away than it should have since it was only coming from right under John's chin.

John hesitated and then put his arm around Mason's waist. After a minute, Mason covered John's hand with his own. Something heavy and cool rested against the heat of John's skin. A ring. John tipped his head to look down, but he already knew he'd see a thick silver band to match the one on a cord around Mason's neck. The ring he'd held on to just before he came.

John might not have spent a lot of time around people who weren't sports freaks, but he had seen a lot of movies. Mason had loved someone, someone who had left him—or was probably dead. So despite what John had tried to convince himself, he was only another substitute. For Roald's girlfriend back in Copenhagen. For his father's failed career in pro ball.

It sucked. Probably not as much as having someone you were in love with die. But it still sucked. John wasn't sure when or why he'd started to think that it mattered that Mason thought more of John than just a way to get off, but the news wouldn't have bothered him as much if he hadn't.

Mason linked his fingers with John's and rubbed the sides, sending warmth down John's arm. He shared it in a kiss on the damp skin behind Mason's ear which made Mason roll off the mattress onto his feet.

Mason grabbed a towel from the floor. "I'm going to go wash up a little." He stopped at the door. "You don't have to get dressed. And you don't have to change the sheets, all right?"

Relieved that he wouldn't need to call a cab to take him

back uptown at two a.m., John stretched out on the bed. "Why? Is there more?"

"You up for more?" Towel around his waist, Mason leaned against the door.

John wanted more. More of the pleasure, the friction of skin, more of Mason. He'd just have to remember that however nice Mason was, he wasn't the answer to finding someplace to matter again.

"Maybe." John rolled onto his back.

"Don't write a check your sore ass won't want to cash. We'll see."

After Mason left, John found the condom on the floor and tossed it into the wastebasket. His thighs and ass and even his dick ached, but thanks to the Brewed Awakening shake, his brain was still far too awake for sleep. He stretched out on the mattress, arms and feet hanging off the ends. His fingers brushed something hard and heavy wedged between the mattress and the wall. Grabbing it and pulling it free, he found a small flat bottle of Jim Beam bourbon.

Wow. John knew some guys on the tours, guys who couldn't compete without their hit of speed or poppers, guys who took their chances and prayed they wouldn't get selected for testing. At least Mason must have really wanted to have sex with John if Mason had been willing to give up his bourbon for a night. As John slipped the bottle back into place, he decided to consider it a compliment. He knew why Mason did it now. It wasn't like the guys on tour who needed the edge in a competition where every contraction of muscles had to be precise and perfect. This was because of the ring around Mason's neck. John knew what it was like to have that kind of hole inside, to lose something that you'd give anything to get back, but he'd rather fill it with something that tasted—and felt—better than liquor.

Mason came back in and pulled off the towel, holding it up in one hand and a washcloth in the other. "Thought you might want to get despunked too."

"Okay." But when John reached for the washcloth, Mason dropped it on John's belly and started a tickling scrub.

The colors around Mason's head were back to their usual pattern of white and red, solid, not flashing or pulsing. If John could go back and see those guys from the tour now, would they have two colors as they carried their addiction around with them?

"I can wash my own dick, thanks," John said as Mason dragged the cloth lower.

"Yeah, but so what? It's not like I haven't seen it. Tasted it. Had it up my ass." But Mason didn't fight when John took the cloth away.

"I think I'm going to crash for awhile." Mason's lashes cut off John's view of his eyes.

"Yeah. Me too." John looked down at the mattress. It hadn't been too small when they were on top of each other, but it wasn't that big. "Um. I'll go down to the couch."

"Nah. Room here. And when we wake up horny, we can do something about it." Mason plucked the washcloth from John's hand and tossed it on the floor before scooting onto the mattress.

John rolled next to the wall to make room, but Mason put an arm over John's chest and pulled him back. As Mason wrapped himself around John's back, breath tickling the back of John's neck, John stared at the wall and thought about colors.

Chapter Six

Mason knew it was a dream all along, just like he knew what he was looking for in this house with too many damned rooms wasn't Alex. Because Alex wasn't there, not even in his dreams anymore. Mason had to find the shower because fuck if he would cry in front of—but when he yanked open the door, it was a kitchen. A shining chrome kitchen he'd never seen before and John was there with his bright innocent smile, holding out a mug of coffee so hot that heat licked at Mason's balls. Then he was awake and John's mouth was *there*, hot and wet, gentle suction, nose bumping the base of Mason's dick, the sensations dragging it from half-ready to let's-go in a few good sucks.

From virgin to cockslut in just a few hours. No, that wasn't exactly true. Someone had already trained that mouth. Someone who'd used him and left the poor kid hanging. Mason knew his anger at the asshole was disproportional, but he couldn't help it. At least the anger was better than the sick guilt his dream had left him with. No Alex, just John serving up something sweet and hot. It didn't take Carrie's major in psychology to figure that dream—or his guilt—out.

He wished he had respect enough for the both of them to say he pushed John away and went to either cry or jerk off in the shower—either action ending with him whispering Alex's name—but John's tongue was pressing under Mason's balls now, and besides, John wouldn't understand why Mason was being a prick. That obvious a rationalization wasn't something you needed a psych degree to label either, but at least Mason could share the goods.

"Hey, sugar. Shift your sweet self up here so I can get a little dick too."

Maybe John had started the blow job half asleep because he seemed out of it as he swung around to straddle Mason's head. Mason barely avoided a knee to the nose and caught it with his ear instead, the blow making his head ring.

"Sorry." John followed up his apology with a firm lick between Mason's balls, so Mason was inclined to forgive him.

Who would think sixty-nine had such a high degree of difficulty? Every move John had made from dropping down on Mason's dick in the van to letting Mason pop his cherry to fucking Mason stupid had been beautiful to watch, grace in the way John's muscles held unbroken lines of strength, never a wasted motion. This awkward tangle made a startling contrast, John's actions full of sloppy desperation. Well, Mason wouldn't take any prizes for morning mental or physical coordination without a dose of caffeine, but he figured he could still manage to suck cock. John didn't make it easy—he dove down on Mason's dick while his own hung just out of reach. Mason had to do an abdominal crunch just to get the tip between his lips.

"Easy, sugar. I'm not going to take it away. Get down here."

John took Mason to the back of a throat full of vibrating moans and swallowed, but the hitch in his breath and the twitch in those muscles made Mason think John was starting to gag. A mouth on John's cock ought to slow him down, so Mason wrapped his arms around John's hips and dragged him down until his balls rested on Mason's chin. Giving them a rub with his jaw, Mason licked his way back toward John's hole over the hot, salty skin. John jumped in Mason's hold but didn't pull away. The pressure eased up on Mason's dick though, and he set a slower pace. Blowing on John's wet skin, Mason stretched his neck to flick his tongue over John's hole. This time when John jumped, Mason was ready and held on tight, pulling his cheeks farther apart.

John didn't stop sucking, but he was distracted enough to get sloppy, which was what Mason was after. With John's devastating skill, Mason was afraid another blow job from John would be a repeat of the blink-and-you'll-miss-it one in the van. Insane as the idea was, Mason hated how good John was at getting Mason to empty his balls in ten seconds or less because it felt like the practice to get there had been something John had been made to do. If Mason ever found the guy who'd done it, he'd kick the asshole's teeth down his throat.

Forcing back the irrational anger, Mason flattened his tongue for long wet strokes as John's muscles twitched everywhere. "Yeah." The word hummed against John's spit-slick, stretched-tight skin, pulling a deep grunt from the mouth around Mason's cock.

He'd forgotten how sweet this could be, the taste of a man on his tongue while his own dick slid into sucking heat. He moved his head so he could reach John's balls, pulling a nut into his mouth and letting it roll on his tongue.

John pulled off, gasping. "I don't think I—"

"I don't want you thinking. I want you to fuck my mouth."

"I can't. Please. Just let me do this."

Maybe mastering sixty-nine was too much this early in John's career. Mason dropped his head onto the mattress. "Okay." Besides, turning down a blow job wasn't something Mason had managed to get the hang of yet.

He fisted John's dick and tugged just enough to keep him veiny hard, while John groaned and dove back onto Mason's cock. Tension shivered out of John's hips with a sigh Mason felt on his balls. Hands tight on Mason's ass, John lifted Mason so that the wet slide went all the way to the root of his cock. Under the rush of pleasure, a dark swell of anger tugged in Mason's gut. So good, such damned good pressure squeezed out all Mason's plans to be making things better for John, until all Mason wanted to do was grab John's head and force him to stay down, lips locked tight on the base while the muscles of his throat closed around the head again and again.

It wasn't supposed to be this easy, he shouldn't have been able to feel this good, shouldn't let the best ever bl—a gold-medal blow job—wash out all of his guilt in a flood of heat. He made one last try for John's cock, straining to kiss the tip, but John started bobbing then, hard and fast and wet. Mason couldn't think about anything at all.

It hit him fast and he tried to hold onto it, wanting to stay safe from the guilt forever while the pleasure burned him clean. But there wasn't any choice. Never had been. His balls drew up tight, everything locked tight until it broke free, pumping hot and loose into John's throat.

As soon as the last pulse left Mason's dick, he pulled John down to him, dick finally slipping past Mason's lips.

"C'mon," he grunted.

John didn't give him much but Mason worked with it, sucking, using his tongue on the thick ridge, the knot of nerves underneath, lapping salty drops from the slit. Anger shook off the rest of the buzz from coming. Anger at John for holding back. At the asshole who made John think he had to. At himself for thinking he had any business trying to be the good guy. Anger at the stupid deer for not staying on its own side of the road. And anger at Alex for saying he needed Mason to drive. He wanted his jaw to ache and his throat to burn. Wanted the excuse of gagging for the tears burning behind his eyes.

He yanked John down harder, trying to pull him all the way in. What the hell was his problem with getting his dick sucked? John sure as fuck liked it. Dick iron hard, blood thick in the vein on Mason's tongue. Why couldn't John let Mason show him how good it felt to fuck into a willing throat?

John might be able to hold himself up while he was on top, but Mason wrapped his arms around John's hips and rolled, weight pinning John to the mattress. Now that thick cock would go as deep as Mason wanted it, John would lose control and start dragging Mason's head down, and everything would be the way it was supposed to be.

John wiggled like he might try to get out from under him, gasped and smacked at Mason's arms, but John was still a guy and Mason knew what he was doing, and the struggles turned into little quick jerks of the tense muscles under Mason's arms as John pushed deeper into Mason's throat. Mason rocked them, eyes watering, head light from lack of breath until John's muscles locked down and he pumped his load down the back of Mason's tongue. Too far down to taste it really, nothing but a hint of bitter and the choking pulse of it pouring in.

Mason pulled back in time to catch a little on his lips and cheek and then rubbed it into the patch of hair at the base of John's dick, sucking in full breaths of the smell of their sweat and come together. Mason had moved enough to the side that John could get a hand on Mason's damp cheek.

"Mason, what—"

Mason rolled free. "I'm going to shower, find some breakfast. You hungry?"

"Yes, but—"

Mason shut the door on whatever John wanted to know and crossed the hall. Fuck if Mason had the answer for him when he wasn't exactly sure what that was all about himself. All he knew was he had to get in the shower before someone found him crying in the hall.

He wasn't in there longer than it took to blast away some of what was eating him with hot water and one of the girls' lime-scented body wash. He sucked his lips in between his teeth and chewed on them, which had been working for as long as he could remember to keep a lid on whatever felt like it might sneak out. Except around Alex. He'd always taken one look at Mason with his lips turned in like that and said, "Spill it. You're going to sooner or later."

Mason scrubbed at his hair and chewed harder, half afraid John would come in here looking for him.

John didn't. He was dressed again when Mason came back into his bedroom, and this time there weren't any tighty-whities left behind on the floor. Mason lifted his towel to his hair and rubbed before digging through a maybe-clean pile for shorts of his own. With boxer briefs and sweats on, it felt easier to breathe. Mason took a big lungful.

John looked down at himself and sniffed. "Should I have showered? I mean, I'm just going back uptown."

Mason couldn't help it. That creamy skin looked good with a blush. He stepped closer and sniffed. Nothing like stale fuck, still something a little innocent underneath the musk and sweat.

"If you want to smell like come that's up to you. Might be a help on the bus." Mason stepped back and took another deep breath. "But what I really smell is EBC rolls from Brewed Awakening and I'm going to grab one before they're all gone."

John followed him downstairs, and Mason braced himself for some more whistles and catcalls, but the housemates were suspiciously well-behaved.

The box from Brewed Awakening was open on the table, slick spots showing on the paper that Lizzy had gotten a dozen, bless her. Mason scooped one up on his way to the coffee. Egg, bacon and cheese deep fried to heaven, and still warm. The tips of his ears burned as he considered for a second if Lizzy had timed her run to Brewed Awakening to the sound of their orgasms this morning.

"God, Lizzy, I love you," Mason mumbled through the mouthful of cheese as he fished a mug out of the dish rack.

"I bought them," Carrie said.

A thin stream of pop issued from her earbuds as Mason dropped a greasy kiss on her hair. "God, Carrie, I love you."

"I paid," Kai added.

"Thanks, man. Love you."

"Wow. That was almost heterosexual of you, bro. Keep practicing and you could make the team." Kai lifted his mug in a toast.

Mason flipped him off since his mouth was full again.

"What are those?" John stood in the doorway, fists in his pockets.

"Here, sit down." Kai moved some papers off a chair.

"Coffee?" Lizzy got up and grabbed the last clean mug out of Mason's hands and then beat him to the carafe.

"No thanks. I had enough last night."

With an opening like that, any one of the housemates could have slipped an aircraft carrier full of smart remarks through, but there was a long moment of silence, only broken when Carrie coughed into her fist, cheeks red.

After a beat, Lizzy said, "Orange juice?"

"Yes, please." John smiled at her.

"Gonna give him a bib and wipe his mouth too, Liz?" What was it with these guys and John? How did he get the VIP treatment?

John's hand tightened on the back of the chair he'd been about to sit in. "I should probably head out to the bus stop."

Lizzy opened her mouth as if she'd argue, closed it and turned to glare at Mason.

K.A. Mitchell

Fine. John didn't really deserve Mason's bad mood. Lizzy and Kai on the other hand were up to some kind of shit, and Mason was going to figure out what. Was it any wonder he'd spent the summer back in Dunkirk?

"Nah. Sit down. You've got to try one of these." Mason handed one of the EBC rolls to John.

"What is it?" John looked at it like it might suddenly start crawling up his arm.

"If there's fried food in heaven, that's it," Lizzy said.

"I always vote for fried food in heaven. That's cheese, egg, bacon and bread, deep fried. But the guy who makes them won't tell anyone what's in the batter," Carrie explained.

"It's a lawsuit waiting to happen." But Kai's litigious opinion didn't stop him from grabbing another one.

Mason washed down the rest of his roll with his coffee. He'd barely even tasted it, but Lizzy would probably smack his hand if he dared go for a second before John ate his. There were three left. Mason did some quick math. Assuming three for Kai and two each for the girls, he should be able to get one more. While Lizzy poured John some orange juice in what looked like it had been a jam jar, Mason snuck out a second roll, savoring the full greasy taste.

John bit his and smiled. "You guys remind me of some people I used to know. How long have you known each other?"

"Kai and Mason met as roommates freshman year." Carrie poured a pink packet of sweetener into her coffee. "And Mason and Lizzy met—"

"At orientation." Mason choked down a mouthful in time to interrupt. "When she made a drunken pass at me and was sadly mistaken about her odds for success. We moved in here June after our freshman year to get out of those shithole dorms."

"Jeez, that time of the month, Mason?" Kai took another
94

roll, the bastard.

"Fuck you." The girls rounded on Kai before Mason could defend himself.

Mason grinned. "Bad play, man. Misogyny rears its ugly head at 10 North Pine. I can see it on Facebook now."

"You might think you're as slick as your freshly shaved balls, Kincaid, but you're still the bitch in the doghouse around here."

John laughed, a good big long laugh, and Mason realized that aside from when he'd teased John about their date last night, he hadn't heard him laugh at all. He had a nice one. Teeth white and even, sweet cock-sucking mouth wide open, eyes sparkling slits as his cheeks hid them. The sound invited everyone to join in, and the girls did. A cozy Saturday in the kitchen like they used to have. Like John really belonged there.

Hell, he belonged there more than Mason did now. He couldn't remember the last time he'd made a Saturday breakfast, that tradition Alex had started in the house. Definitely not since Mason had been back. Without Alex, Mason was a stranger in his own fucking life.

He pushed away from the counter and headed for the hall. "I've gotta take a dump. Might want to stay out of the bathroom till it airs out, girls."

But he didn't fool Lizzy. She found him in the alcove off the living room, the one the girls had turned into some kind of combination jungle-library. Wall-to-wall plants and books.

"You should tell him," she said to his back when he didn't turn at the sound of her footsteps.

"What for? He's just a fuck."

"Even if I believed that, he's still entitled to an explanation for you being a belligerent asshole."

"He's leaving, anyway."

"And I'll see him in class on Tuesday. And I intend to be his friend. Sooner or later someone's going to tell him."

Mason pushed past her on his way into the living room, heading for the hall, though whether he'd go back upstairs and dig out Jim or head outside and walk till he didn't feel like punching things he didn't know. "You know, Lizzy, my mother might be a raving homophobic bitch, but at least she isn't up my ass like you are all the time."

But when he came around the arch into the hall, Kai and John were there, Kai's dark eyes wide with shock. But it was the look of pity and disgust on John's face that really tore a fresh hole in Mason's gut.

"Way out of line, Mason," Kai said. "I'm driving him uptown because I'm going to the library. You can ride with us and explain your drama-queen shit, or I'll tell him. And then maybe we can talk about you finding someplace else to live."

Mason was way out of line. And he'd apologize to Lizzy. But he wasn't riding uptown with Kai as an audience. Like Alex had told Mason, it was never either/or. There were always lots of stops in between.

"If the Gestapo will give me a second, I'll handle it. John?"

The guy flinched at the sound of his name, but he looked straight at Mason.

"Can I talk to you for a minute?" Mason couldn't stand being in the house anymore, so he led them out into the postage-stamp-sized yard. Yeah. Perfect place to relive the humiliating conversation from last week. But unlike last time, Mason knew exactly what sins he'd committed.

"Look. Last December I was in a car accident." Mason took a deep breath. He hadn't needed to do this much—or at all. No one back in Dunkirk knew Alex and everyone here already knew everything. Mason waited for that sharp shock of pain, the one that seemed to cut the tendons in his knees, make him want to fall to the ground and pound on it until it gave him Alex back, but despite what a shit he was to his friends, he wasn't that much of a drama queen. He didn't have to fight the impulse. Just this once, the pain didn't come. He let the breath back out. "And—"

John watched Mason steadily. "And you don't really have to tell me the rest. I've got it. Someone you love was killed, right? And that's his ring?"

Mason's hand went to Alex's ring on the cord around his neck. "Yeah. Alex." It actually felt good to say his name, warm rather than piercing loss as it echoed in his head.

John blinked hard. What did he have to cry about? But at least Mason wasn't sucking his lips in between his teeth to chew the tears out of existence. Wasn't hearing the snap of Alex's neck as they hit that tree, wasn't looking over to see that there was nothing left of Alex in that broken shell. No chance to say *good-bye*, or *I love you*, or *don't you fucking leave me*.

"So, aren't you going to say something?" Mason asked.

"Like *sorry*? Would that help?"

"No. Mostly it pisses me off."

John shrugged. "I get that. So the drinking and being an asshole to your friends, does that help?"

"Fuck you. You don't know me."

But John didn't back off, even from Mason's anger. "No. I don't. And I don't really think I want to. But, even with that, I'm glad it was you. Last night, I mean. Thanks."

Shouldn't this guy be a little upset, pissed at least? Where the fuck did he get off being so condescending and understanding?

"So what about you, what's your story?" Mason said.

"Me?"

"Yeah, Mr. All-Seeing-Mystic. That cane is new. And what

97

about that whole *I understand what it's like to have your life change in an instant*?"

John looked away, first at his cane, then at the ground. "I fell. From about two stories up. And now I lose my balance sometimes. Things get blurry and I can't drive." He met Mason's eyes again.

It explained a lot. The blinking. The deliberate grace and slow movements.

Sorry was on the tip of Mason's tongue, but like John had said, *sorry* was good for shit.

"That sucks."

"It does."

Mason was angry again. "So what, I'm supposed to see from your great example how to move on, suck it up and deal?"

"I don't know why I should care what you do just because we had sex." John started for the porch steps, and then slowly turned back. "But your friends here, they're kind of amazing. You might want to do something about that."

Chapter Seven

John's dorm walls started to feel closer than an airplane bathroom's, and he escaped to the lounge with his economics text and a blue transparency to keep the text from turning into swirling rivers of color. The lounge was full of torn, stained furniture, the wooden arms bearing graffiti, predominantly penises. Since John didn't think there were that many gay guys in this dorm, that meant lots of straight guys were dick-obsessed. He couldn't see girls drawing veiny shafts and hairy ball sacs on the arms of furniture, but then he didn't know lots of girls who weren't divers. The lounge did have a TV bolted to the corner, with a college football pregame show full of talking heads blathering to the empty room.

He was still alone, but at least he didn't feel like it was a coffin. He hadn't minded all the time alone until now. At first it was nice not to have to share living, breathing and bathroom space with lots of other people like in training camp. But being with Mason's housemates this morning had felt nice and familiar, like the good times on tour, when you'd been squeezed together so often you knew all the same people, all the same jokes. John had missed that. But his only way into that familiarity had been on Mason's ticket. As usual, he didn't belong anywhere on his own.

And even without the fact that Mason didn't want John there, John couldn't be there. Could he tell Carrie that the pale

K.A. Mitchell

green around her head blurred with the beat of the music in her ears? How would a guy like Kai take hearing that there were pink crystals around his head? Dark pink vibrating with anger when Mason had yelled at Lizzy, pink that turned clear and soft as a dawn sky when Kai watched Lizzy at the breakfast table.

So the lounge was fine. No other people, no freak colors, just the muddy recorded stuff he could ignore from the TV.

"Hey."

The whisper was so unexpected John almost jumped.

"Hi." John turned in his chair.

A guy in a purple T-shirt with the university's gold UA on it dropped into a chair across from John. "I'm Keith." His voice was still a raspy whisper.

"John." He shook the offered hand.

"John Andrews. I've wanted to meet you." Keith pointed at his throat. "Damage to my vocal cords from intubation after a car accident. Hey, at least I'm alive."

John was alive too, and his brain took a bit longer but it could still process things. Speech-disability Keith. From the Disabled Students' Association. Great. No easy escape.

"But you, man," Keith went on. "I can't believe you didn't crack your skull wide open. I must have seen it a million times on ESPN and CNN."

John hadn't. Never wanted to see it. "I don't remember it."

"That's got to be a relief. But a month from your second Olympics? I heard you clipped your head on the platform the dive before you fell, right?"

John would have been happier if Keith just wanted an autograph, or to see the medals—even if they were in a safe in his parents' house down in Westchester. "That's what they tell me." And they'd told him that he'd said he was fine, and it wasn't even bleeding, that he had insisted on going back up.

100

But as he'd walked out on the platform he'd slid off the side, only a freak instinct in his muscles curling him into a ball so he landed half on the deck and half in the pool, the brain that had been sent rattling in his skull from striking the pool gutter changed forever. The biggest moment of his life, and he only knew it as a story that happened to someone else.

"Sorry, John. I forget some people don't like to remember that stuff."

"I can't."

"Oh right. But I've been wanting to ask you. Do you think you could have done it? Hit that 6243D in competition?"

His handstand back double with one and a half twists. So Keith knew his diving. But that hadn't been the dive that had finished John. He knew he could nail that one anytime. Had the upper arm strength to get enough push for it. He'd hit his head on the reverse three and a half.

Keith didn't wait for John's answer. "The guys from China were trying it. When you couldn't go they pulled it from their rotations."

And still took gold and silver, platform and springboard. Not that John had watched.

"What do you think of that kid from Ireland? The one people are all talking about?" Even with his whisper Keith sounded excited. There probably weren't many people who followed FINA diving. Keith couldn't know that John would rather talk about theories of macroeconomics than what had been his whole life for ten years.

"I don't really follow the sport much anymore."

"God, I'm so sorry. It must—I'm such an ass. I'm really sorry." Keith looked so embarrassed John felt sorry for him.

"It's not a big deal."

"Please. Let me make it up to you. Maybe with coffee or

lunch at the food court?"

It took a second, but the hopeful look on Keith's face finally made a connection in John's brain. Had he looked like that when Roald was around? Eager, almost pathetic? Keith was cute and nice, if overly friendly, and John felt bad for the guy, but not so bad that he wanted to take an uncomfortable morning deep into an awkward afternoon.

"I really should catch up on this. Been putting it off for weeks. And my..." he waved at his head, "...makes it hard to read. Maybe some other time, okay?" He should have felt guilty for using his brain injury as an excuse, but it was true.

"Oh, right. That would be great." Keith stood up.

He had a really nice smile. If he came on a little less strong, John could get to like him. Out of nowhere, heat flashed in his cheeks, along his dick. Along with the blood rush was the memory of Mason slapping his ass. *You like that, John?*

So maybe he did like guys who came on strong, but only if they were emotional basket cases.

Keith stopped at the door. "I still think you would have nailed that dive, John."

He was gone. John looked up at the muddy stream of sound from the TV and wondered why he couldn't remember what color had shimmered around Keith's head.

By the time Mason went back into the house, 10 North Pine was echoingly empty. He did some penance in the form of a week's worth of dishes, swept the floor, wiped the counters, then even mopped and cleaned the bathroom.

When no one came home to appreciate his efforts, Mason caught a bus uptown to Stuyvesant Plaza and picked up everyone's favorite chocolates from the specialty store and left them at their bedroom doors. Kai and Carrie would forgive him. Kai had seen worse, but Lizzy. Yeah. Lizzy knew how much Mason hated his mom and throwing that comparison at her was a new low, especially when he couldn't hide behind the bourbon as a cover. He thought about adding his hidden bottle of Jim Beam to her offering, but he wasn't ready to hit belly in the groveling declination. He was sticking to his knees for a bit. He'd save the next step for if they were going to throw him out of the house.

He tinkered with a few programs on the computer they were trying out, one more brownie point with Lizzy if he could get the software to talk to the driver for the hardware she'd designed. He was asleep before nine, face pressed into a pillow that smelled like John and fucking, and ended up arguing with Alex on the back porch.

And he knew it was a dream, because he wasn't drunk or crazy, because Alex was dead, so he couldn't be standing there with one arm bent behind his back like he did when he was pissed, waiting for Mason to climb the back steps onto the porch.

Alex started bitching him out. "When did I ever give you the impression that I was into a three-way, especially if I wasn't the one getting fucked?"

His voice so clear, Alex right there, solid and real from the dark curls on his head to the fraying hems of his jeans over bare feet on the wooden porch boards. Mason reached for him, but Alex stepped back.

"Answer the question, Mase."

Question. About a three-way? What the hell? Mason had never wanted another guy once he'd hooked up with Alex. Never even thought about it. "I didn't. I wouldn't."

"So what was last night about? Do you really think I wanted to get dragged into that?"

"Dragged into what? Baby, I don't understand. You know I'm nothing but trailer trash. You gotta use little words with me."

It worked. Alex's arm came out from behind his back, fist opening, palm coming toward Mason's face, and Alex stepped into his arms, stood on tiptoe and buried his face in Mason's neck.

"You're not stupid and we both know it. I love you, Mason Jackson Kincaid. And I always will. But, baby, you've got to let me go."

"I can't. How the fuck am I supposed to do that, Alex?"

"You've got to figure that out."

"No. Please, baby. Stay."

"I can't do that either. So stop dragging me around."

"I don't understand. Alex. C'mon. Please." His chest burned with the anxious need to fix this, to make Alex stay and not be mad anymore. "What do you want me to do?"

"Mason, wake up."

First it was Alex's exasperated snap, and then it wasn't. It was happening outside him. Like the hand on his shoulder.

"Mason."

That was Lizzy.

He blinked and snapped back into reality...on the back porch, curled up next to the recyclables which reeked of mold and rotting sugar.

Lizzy crouched next to him, eyes wide in her pale face. The naked light bulb on the porch was right over her left shoulder, the brightness stabbing his eyes and making them water.

"Jesus, Mason."

He grabbed at her hand. "Lizzy."

"I thought you had alcohol poisoning. I fucking thought you

were dead. How much?"

Somehow his fifth of Jim Beam from behind his mattress was in his hands, the seal still unbroken. He shoved it at her. "Nothing. Look at it. Honest." He huffed a cloud of breath in her face.

She pulled back but looked less angry.

"What the hell's going on? I went to your room because the light was still on and I saw you through the window. Walking around in the yard in the middle of the night. God. I thought—" She shook off his grip. "I thought you were going to kill yourself."

"A selfish asshole like me? Never gonna happen."

She smacked his arm.

"He was here."

"John?"

"No. Alex. He was here. On the porch. I was talking to him. He's mad at me."

"Oh, Mase." She slid onto the boards next to him, but he pulled out of her hug.

"I know he's dead. But it wasn't like a dream. More like—"

She waited. Lizzy wasn't like the rest of the girls Mason knew, the kind who couldn't let a space go by without filling it with a question.

Mason got his thoughts in order. "Like a ghost. But not really that either. Not like in a movie. It was just him. And I think he was mad about John."

"Why would he be?" Lizzy's hand moved like she'd try to touch him again, but she was too smart to go through with it. "You don't think he never wants you to be with anyone again, do you?"

"I wasn't *with* John. We fucked."

"And you've fucked other guys since, right? Did you dream

about him being mad then?"

Mason bit off the response that it wasn't a dream, because of course it was, no matter how it felt. "No. I dreamed about him, but it wasn't like this." But Mason hadn't slept with any of those other guys in his and Alex's room. Hadn't taken them out to an animal shelter benefit. Hadn't felt good just being around them.

"And he wasn't mad."

"Stop trying to be so fucking logical."

"Sorry. I'll put my bimbo hat on now. Oh wait. You had it last."

Thank God for Lizzy. He could breathe again now. Breathe without that panic, that crush of worry from Alex standing there, hurt and angry, accusing him of...cheating?

"So. What was different this time?" Lizzy said.

He took it back. She could just get lost. "Nothing."

"Right." Lizzy picked at the floorboards with her nail. "You know I felt it too."

"You felt John's dick?"

She ignored that. "It's like he's got a force field of mellow. It just feels nice to be around him."

Mason remembered standing there, telling John about the accident, waiting for the big wave of grief that didn't come. "I was too busy feeling his dick to notice."

"Yeah. I thought I might have to borrow some headphones from Carrie." Her eyes gleamed and she tipped her head at him, like a bird about to stab at something with its beak. "That it? You let him top?"

"Jesus Christ. How much time do you spend thinking about my sex life?" That she was right and he hadn't bottomed for anyone since Alex only made him more frustrated.

"It consumes my every waking moment. Especially when it

106

goes on next door."

"I'll buy you a fucking iPod."

"You know Alex would want you to be happy, right?"

She had him trapped between the trash and the recyclables. But he was too tired to shove any of the three of them away.

"I know." And that was why the *dream* had hurt so much. Why should Alex be angry? And what the hell did he mean, dragged into a three-way?

"I miss him." She blinked hard, but tears still leaked out of her eyes.

Mason moved his legs to let her sit between them.

She wrapped her arms around his waist and pressed her head against his chest. "Sometimes it's like you're the only one who's allowed to."

"Selfish asshole, remember." He turned his lips in and chewed on them, but he held her while she cried.

John let Lizzy steer him to another lunch on Tuesday, where she treated him to an impression of the art history professor's monotone and then they Googled some Baroque painters, trying to decide on a painter with the hottest male models to use for a paper that was due next week. She never mentioned Mason, which was as okay as it was a little awkward. John wondered if they'd made up. He hoped they had. As nice as Mason had been in seduction mode, out of it he was an emotional time bomb. Maybe his friends would defuse him before someone got hurt.

John wanted to cut Mason some slack because he must have cured John of all the desperate-virgin vibes he'd been giving off. First Keith on Saturday and now after economics class on Thursday a gorgeous guy with a jock build veered into his path and said, "Hi. I'm Tyler."

"John."

Tyler fell into step next to him, and John tried to figure out what his sport was. He wasn't big enough for football, too short for basketball, not lanky enough for swimming. John felt a blush hit his cheeks when he realized he was staring at the pale yellow sparks that drifted around Tyler's brush-cut blond hair as if they'd give him an answer.

"Do you live on campus?" John asked.

"No. You?"

John didn't know where they were walking to, but the focus of Tyler's blue gaze was doing interesting things south of John's belt. "Yeah. But I don't have a roommate." It suddenly seemed important to add that.

"Cool." Tyler stopped walking. He was shorter than John, a gold glint of stubble on his chin as he tipped his head up. "I've seen you coming down the stairs after class a couple times."

As sure as John was that Tyler was coming on to him, he had no idea what the next thing was he was supposed to do. Invite him for coffee? Ask him what his major was? Grab him and kiss him?

"So, John, you want to fuck?"

Tyler pressed John against his bedroom door as soon as he got it closed. Tyler didn't ask about the cane. He didn't ask if John had any experience, Tyler just kissed him, one hand diving down to rub John's dick through his jeans. "Damn. I was going to do you, but I think I'd rather see what you've got."

Was there something that different about John's dick?

He gave Tyler's a good look as he stripped. It looked kind of like Mason's, thick and dark pink with a shiny head. Then Tyler dropped to his knees and yanked down John's jeans, and John was too busy concentrating on not coming right away to make many more comparisons.

Tyler pulled off him with a wink and after looking at John's bed, just bent over it with his ass in the air. John had to stammer out a confession that he didn't have any of the supplies Mason had produced so easily.

"No problem." Tyler was as cheerful and polite as if John had asked for something as commonplace as a repetition of an economics reading assignment. "Pocket of my jeans. There's a pack of lube in there too."

John found the little pillow-shaped container and the plastic-wrapped rubber. At least Tyler wasn't watching John while he figured it out. Fortunately, the makers of condoms and lube must have had a guy's lack of patience in mind when they designed the things, since John worked it out pretty fast. When he looked back up from putting the lube on his dick, he saw Tyler stick a couple fingers into his own ass.

Tyler glanced over his shoulder. "Did you leave some for me?"

"Huh?"

"Lube. It's okay. I'm pretty—oh."

John took over, and Tyler didn't have any more suggestions for a few minutes.

But only for a few minutes.

"Can you jack me while you fuck me? I like that."

Again, Tyler's voice sounded as if the request was on the level of "Pass the salt when you get a chance."

As John complied, he took a look at the lemonade-colored bits around Tyler's head. They weren't as bright or distinct from the back, only there when John really thought about it. The whole thing should have been a relief, none of the overwhelming assault on his senses, on what was left of his equilibrium like it had been with Mason, but still good. Feeling good with someone else.

It was tricky to make the rhythm work like this, with a hand on Tyler's dick, but Tyler reached back and grabbed John's hip and that seemed to steady them. Tyler made the kind of sounds that had John thinking he was doing something right, proof in a pulsing ripple on his cock and warm jet falling on his fingers. He slowed, waiting, but Tyler squeezed John's thigh and urged him to motion again, and John drove himself faster, eyes shut as he raced for the edge.

He collapsed on the bed after he came, holding the condom around his cock as he slipped free.

Tyler looked down and grinned at him. "Nice. Do you have a come rag? I've got class in an hour. Hey, you have your own bathroom. Do you mind?"

Mind what? John's muscles were still vibrating with aftershocks. "Go ahead" was the easiest answer.

A few minutes later, Tyler came out of the bathroom shaking the water from his close-cropped hair and toweling himself off. He picked up his jeans and briefs from the floor and started dressing. "So, what are you doing tomorrow night?"

Panic froze his throat. Tyler didn't think that John had—

Tyler laughed. "No. Not like that. Sorry. I'm not big into second dates. I'm going out with some friends. You should come with us."

"Out?" Dick still in a come-filled condom and brain still fighting for some blood, John felt like he'd done a belly flop from the springboard.

"Yeah. To the bars. Downtown. If you need a fake ID—"

"I'm twenty-one."

"Okay. Simon lives in Indian Quad. The guys on campus

are meeting there about nine. In front of the tower."

Tyler didn't live on campus, which meant if John showed up, no one would know him.

When John didn't answer, Tyler said, "If you think you're going to go, I'll hang around, catch a ride with you guys."

John thought about trying to deal with a bunch of new people with their Spin-Art heads and his cane and the shifting kaleidoscope world, and then he looked at the narrow walls of the room, the slotted windows. *What are you going to do with the rest of your life, John?*

"Yeah. That would be great. Thanks."

Tyler gave him another wink. "See you then."

Chapter Eight

Mason ignored Lizzy the first two times she beat on his bedroom door, but when she started kicking it, not even the Mudvayne on his speakers could drown her out. He unhooked the lock and found her there with a knife held over her head.

"Jesus Christ. Don't kill me."

She held it up to show him. "Butter knife. I was going to unlock the door." She waved a hand in front of her face. "God, you haven't left this room in two weeks. And it smells like it."

"I have."

"When? Because the last time I checked they were still having classes two miles away."

"I've been to class. I'm working on the goddamned computer that is six fucking credits of our independent study. If you'd put in the kind of motherboard I told you we needed—"

"It would have fried as soon as you touched the power button. But that's why I was going to break in. Midterms are next week, so Dr. Martin wants to see what it is we're doing for our six credits of independent study. We've got to get it up to her office by two thirty."

Mason checked his phone. Eleven eighteen and almost that many missed texts and voice mails. "Yeah, well then you'd better help me get the operating system to recognize the driver for the fucking mouse you built."

The computer had been their design, all three of them. Him, Lizzy and Alex. Alex was the artist, his sketches were what had sold his collector uncle on fronting the money for a one-of-a-kind clockwork, glass and brass laptop. Lizzy built the hardware, all Mason had to do was make the fucking thing work.

Alex had imagined something amazing, poking at Mason in the middle of the night to ask if certain things were possible. As Mason worked on it, he heard those questions again, caught a buzz off Alex's excitement, tasted the bitter dregs of the coffee as the three of them sat in the kitchen until dawn creating the reality of the computer on paper.

Lizzy tipped her chin up at him, and Mason turned away from the sympathy in her eyes. It had been more than two weeks since she found him on the porch. More than two weeks without a sip of bourbon or a trip out to find something else to occupy his body if not his brain. Two weeks spent on nothing but the computer. She could believe he was just doing it for Alex, and she wouldn't be completely wrong, but Mason liked the work. Writing code was better than bourbon because it didn't leave room for anything else in his head. Not Alex. And not former virgins with hot asses, hotter mouths and an infuriatingly frigid serenity.

"Have you dreamed about him again?" Lizzy asked, leaning against the doorframe.

He walked back to his desk. "Don't start, Lizzy. I've got two hours to get these two stupid pieces of shit to talk to each other."

"Dr. Martin didn't say it had to be done, she just wants to see our progress."

"Well, I don't exactly feel like losing everything I've done so far this morning so if you're not going to help, give me some space."

"But have you dreamed like that again?"

"Not exactly." Most of them had been the usual crap, but once it had been that odd shift from the usual random stuff into a very real experience of sitting in the kitchen talking to a glaring Alex with his arms folded across his chest. Alex said *What makes you think you get a choice about it?* and then a siren screamed out on Western and Mason was suddenly sitting alone at the kitchen table at three in the morning.

"What?" she said.

"Once I woke up in the kitchen."

She was going to say something which would probably end in "maybe you should talk to someone" so he cut her off.

"It's fine."

She huffed but dropped the subject. "Okay. Let's see if we can get these two stupid pieces of shit to talk to each other and then get this puppy in a box."

If they'd brought Dr. Martin an entire box of puppies she wouldn't have cooed more than she did over what they'd done on the computer. But the shine of pride wore off the second she insisted on keeping it overnight. Mason hadn't even let it out of the room since Lizzy had handed it over for him to work on. He stared at Dr. Martin's office door long after she had shooed them out.

Lizzy tugged on his arm. "The day comes when we have to learn how to let our babies go."

But, baby, you've got to let me go. Mason jerked away.

"I felt close to him when I was working on it too."

Mason chewed hard on his lips and forced back the heat in his throat. "And I thought you were getting your degree in real science. Not that psychobabble shit like Carrie."

"Someday when they have real AI, the computers will need psychotherapy. And I'll be glad of a few psych courses."

Mason heard the well-modulated voices from computers gone rogue in the movies and then imagined Yul Brynner's robot in *Westworld* reporting for counseling on a stereotypical analyst's couch. And she'd made him laugh, damn her.

"C'mon." She tugged at his arm again. "I'll buy you a consoling drink."

"On a dry campus?"

But he followed her to the campus center food court and let her get them coffees.

A loud laugh dragged his attention to a table of guys twenty feet away. Most of them Mason knew by sight. One of them even better. John. Formerly innocent, newly Zen-master John laughed as Tyler Granger mimed sucking someone off. Something Tyler had a hell of a lot of practice with.

Lizzy came to stand beside Mason, making a whistling sound that at first he thought was directed at the table he was watching until he realized she was blowing through the plastic lid to try to cool her coffee.

"Yeah." She nodded at the table. "John's made some friends. Good for him."

"Friends. That bunch of sluts?"

Lizzy studied the guys at the table. "Tyler Granger. Didn't you two have a fuck-off freshman year? With tally sheets on your dorm doors?"

"I was seventeen."

"The race was close, but then he pulled off that group thing and beat you."

"Shut up."

She looked over his shoulder at the table, which Mason had deliberately turned his back on. "And Simon's president of

GLBTQ Pride."

Mason rolled his eyes. "God bless you." Fucking alphabet soup. Soon there would be so many initials in the movement that it wouldn't fit on a protest sign.

"Wow. Bitter again. Did he out-fuck you too?"

"I'm not bitter. I just have moved on from that crap."

"The fucking or the caring about civil rights? Or John?"

"I told you he was just a fuck." He started walking away.

"The car's parked this way." Lizzy nodded at the doors that would take them past the table where John sat. Mason clomped on ahead of her, trying not to look at the table while looking like he wasn't not-looking, but Tyler waved a hello. Mason had to return it and ended up trapped by John's startled expression.

He forced a smile to his lips, and John returned it, a tight one at first, but when Mason didn't do anything crazy, the smile got bigger. Mason nodded and held the door for Lizzy.

Once they were outside she said, "Explain this to me. So you haven't moved on from fucking whatever looks good."

"Christ, Lizzy, it's not some true/false logic problem to solve. I just meant—" But he didn't know what he'd meant, or why the sight of John at that table had felt like such a kick in the gut. Maybe because John had been kind of a project, and Mason had failed epically. Hanging around those guys who spent four nights a week getting lit and laid probably meant John was spending more time with people who'd treat him like that guy who'd taught him to drop to his knees if you waved a cock in his face. "I just hope he's being careful."

"Why?"

"He deserves better."

"Than what? All the fun you had freshman year? He's a freshman, Mase. He might not be seventeen like you were, but it's his first time away from home."

"Did he tell you anything about that? About his home?" If John had been raised by crazy bigots who made him think he'd go to hell for being queer—something Mason knew too much about—that would be a good reason to cut loose once he got away. But the John he'd met didn't seem anything like the kind of guy who needed that, who'd been desperate to wash off that shame in an endless parade of guys.

"Wow. That's a lot of interest in someone you claim to be uninterested in." Lizzy had learned to arch one eyebrow after she got it pierced. She loved doing it. Mason hated it.

"He seemed nice. We had fun. But sex doesn't have to mean anything."

"True. But it doesn't have to mean nothing, either. Something I'd think you'd know."

Yeah. It had just taken once with Alex.

Living with Lizzy was like having stitches yanked out of a fresh wound every day. She'd introduced Mason to Alex, knew them both too damned well. The only thing worse was the idea of being cut off from the only other person who'd really known Alex.

The space between the buildings lived up to its reputation as a wind tunnel, even in mid October, turning the breeze into a cold blast, and he wiped his eye as they walked back to the car.

John watched Mason hold the door open for Lizzy. Good. They weren't fighting and Mason had seemed sober. But as glad as John was that Mason didn't seem quite as close to a messy explosion, John still intended to ignore what that single look had done to his dick, the way it had blasted across his skin hot-sauna air. He controlled a shiver.

"You know him?" Tyler leaned in to ask. "Mason Kincaid?"

John had gotten better at nodding. And if he stayed away from caffeine, the sparkles around people's heads and the light bending around objects were dimmer, less distracting.

Tyler laughed. "In every sense of the word, I bet. Mason never did waste time."

John shrugged.

"So how was he?"

John hid a shock of surprise. He'd have bet Tyler would know that himself. In the past few weeks, John had learned that a fuck for Tyler was like a handshake for most people, just his way of saying hi. Even if Tyler had sex on the brain all of the time, he was honest, funny and direct. He didn't ask John any questions he didn't want to answer. With his habit of saying whatever he thought and living in the moment, Tyler made John the most comfortable of any of the people he'd met since he got out of physical therapy. The crystals around his head were small, solid and unmoving, and close to the color of Tyler's hair. John could almost forget about the whole freaky business when he was with Tyler.

John owed his friend an honest answer. "He was intense."

"And manipulative," Simon added from the other side of the table. The color around his head reminded John of the orange Jell-O they'd served so often at rehab, and like Jell-O it always seemed to want to ooze out, expand like some science-fiction monster, like it would suck in everyone else's crystals into a gelatinous mess.

"What do you mean?" John asked.

As usual, Simon was quick to offer an opinion. He'd tried to have John signed up for his gay-rights organization five minutes after they'd met. John held him off with vague promises of "next meeting."

"He knows he's good and uses it to get his way."

"That was before," Drew added. At least someone seemed to

118

be on Mason's side.

"Yeah," Tyler agreed. "Before Alex Mendez."

John knew about Alex and he didn't. Suddenly he wanted to. Wanted to know everything about the Alex whose ring Mason wore everywhere.

"Who's Alex?" John asked.

"Alex was like SuperGay. Majoring in theater, minor in fine arts. Sexy as hell but not stuck up about it. You'd hate him for being perfect if he wasn't so damned nice to everybody." Drew was nice to everybody too, but with Tyler and Simon around, it was hard to get a word in.

"Great voice too. Probably headed to New York for theater. He sure had the looks," Tyler added.

Whoa. No wonder Mason had gone off the deep end. He'd been with Mr. Perfect.

"They were together for what, two years?" Drew said.

"Probably headed for the aisle—if the legislators ever get off their fat asses and do something about marriage equality in New York," Simon said.

"But they were in a car wreck last year. Alex was killed and Mason just disappeared. I didn't even know he was back." Tyler slurped on his straw.

"Who was driving?"

John thought he already knew the answer, but he wanted confirmation of the guilt Mason carried around like the ring on his neck. Maybe that's what that second color was. Guilt. Not an addiction to alcohol. He still hadn't seen anyone else with two colors around their head.

"I don't remember much, except that I know it wasn't a drunk-driving thing. Just their car. Ice or something I think. Shitty luck," Drew said.

"I'd be wrecked," Gavin said, or maybe it was Garrett.

119

They'd been introduced as a pair and John still couldn't tell them apart. They were both tall and thin with bleached and bed-headed blond hair. They looked more like twins than lovers, even the colors around their heads were only slightly different shades of blue. They spent as much time in jealous bitching as they did making out. Today was a cuddle day. Gavin/Garrett's arm across the back of Garrett/Gavin's chair. The one who'd spoken gripped the other's hand and squeezed.

"Who wouldn't be?" Drew asked, but he sounded less affected by the story than anyone at the table.

Tyler slammed down his soda cup. "All the more reason to get it while you're young."

Simon rolled his eyes. "And to perpetuate stereotypes of gay men as sexually promiscuous and amoral—"

"Which doesn't stop you from getting some in the back hall at Sammie's, does it?" Tyler's voice had an edge to it, a spark John could see.

Without stopping to think why, John glanced at Tyler's head. The usually dull pale yellow was bright, vibrating.

Simon leaned forward, arms on the table. "At least I don't make a habit of reducing my sexuality to a futile effort to remain an adolescent in pursuit of endless gratification."

"No, you just get your gratification on the sly so you can pull out this hypocritical bullshit and act like you care more about politics than dick."

Simon's orange Jell-O shrank, the edges shriveling and receding toward his head, though nothing changed on his face. He sat back in his chair and smirked. "Ooo, hit a nerve there, Ty?"

"I'd be surprised if you could hit anything from what I hear about your technique."

The unexpected argument between the two friends was upsetting enough, but seeing it played out in shifting colors

120

between them made John dizzy and nauseous. He ran his hands over the condensation on his plastic cup of soda, hoping it would keep him from rubbing his face against the cold surface of the table.

"Hey, John, you all right?" Tyler put a hand on his back, more heat, so hot he wanted to flinch away.

"Yeah. Just moved my head too fast, I guess."

"You're really pale, man."

Pale? John's face should be redder than Tyler's T-shirt.

"I'll be fine."

Tyler, Drew and Simon had heard John's condensed version of the accident—fall, brain injury, vertigo—the night they met. Tyler had assured him all the dancing he needed to do was what he referred to as a public dry hump, demonstrating the grind on the dance floor, until John was hard enough to wonder if Tyler would rethink his no-seconds policy. But Tyler had laughed and introduced John to a beautiful older guy named Ramon who danced with John until he almost came in his pants. Then with a knowing grin, Ramon had led him to the back hall and finished what the dancing had started with steady strokes of his hand in John's unzipped jeans.

Tyler's urgent voice pulled him back to the present. "Anything help? Want more soda? Some sugar?"

John was about to shake his head and then remembered. "No. I'll be fine as soon as everything stops spinning."

He'd gotten better at filtering out the edges of the world, the hum of color that came with the sounds. He even had a name for it now, thanks to a cute nerd in the library and the internet. Synesthesia. And it was uncommon but not weird. Some people were born with it and sometimes it happened after a brain injury. But none of the articles said anything about colors around people's heads that seemed to show what they were feeling. He didn't usually concentrate on it the way he'd been doing just now. Except when he'd been inside Mason, watching his face, watching those colors because John had wanted to get it right.

"I don't know, John. You don't even look like you could make it back to the dorm." Drew's hand hovered close, but he didn't touch him the way Tyler had.

John didn't know if he'd make it out of the cafeteria without passing out or puking. His muscles felt shredded, like he'd been working out for hours. "I'll just sit for awhile."

"I'm going to wait with you," Tyler said. "But I'm sure Simon has someone to go be holier than thou with someplace else."

Simon flipped him off but got up. Gavin and Garrett left too. It wasn't hard to guess what they were going to do.

Drew stood up but hovered. "I can stay."

"I'm fine. I've been living with it for months. I just have to wait a few minutes."

"Maybe, but you didn't see your face," Drew said.

Tyler put his hand on John's shoulder. "Thought you were going to face-plant on your diet Sprite. Would have been a shame to get a straw stuck in one of those baby blues."

"They're gray," Drew pointed out.

"Oh really." Tyler grinned. "Hey, Johnny. Think someone's sprung on you."

"Fuck you." Drew laughed.

John fought the urge to look at his head, to see what those usually calm, gray crystals were doing as Drew walked off.

"What really happened?" Tyler asked when they were alone.

"I told you. I just moved my head too fast. It gets screwed up."

"That guy, Mason, he didn't screw with your head, did he?"

"No." Mason had nothing to do with John feeling like he'd be better off alone in a dark room for about a week. Hearing about Alex hadn't been a surprise, though the idea that Drew, Simon and Tyler would all agree on something, especially another guy's shining model of perfection, was a shock. Alex must have been something else.

John lifted his head enough to look at Tyler. "Did he screw with yours?"

"Nope. But I've known him for four years, seen him in action. He can be a charming little prick when he wants to be." Tyler's mood shifted. "So, c'mon. Details. Does he have a little prick?"

"Not based on my comparisons." Since Tyler would have to include himself in that list, John hoped that would be enough.

"So what are we talking: Buck Meadows, John Holmes, Aiden Shaw?"

"Huh?"

Tyler gave an elaborate sigh. "Porn stars. God, honey, we need to get you an education. Why else would you have come to this fine institution?"

Chapter Nine

On his way back from breakfast, John ducked into the dorm's central staircase to avoid Keith, who appeared headed for John's room for the fifth time in two weeks. John was running out of excuses and vague "plans", and Keith still didn't seem to get the idea that John wasn't interested. He was wondering if he'd have to come right out and say, "You're a nice guy, but no."

John was up on the second floor girls' dorm when his phone went off with the thumping ringtone and sexual lyrics Tyler had programmed in for himself.

"Hey, meet me out front right now. It's an emergency."

John had gotten used to Tyler's ability to apply emergency to everything from having a paper due in half an hour to having run out of his favorite lube, so John didn't break anything on his way back down the stairs and paused to make sure the hall was free of lurking dive fans.

Tyler had the car running in the fire lane.

"This is Simon's car," John said as he got in.

"Mine wouldn't start. Took the bus uptown," Tyler said.

"So you guys made up?"

"What the fuck does that mean? We were never fighting."

John's cheeks burned and he turned to look out of the window. Simon and Tyler hadn't done anything outward. They acted like their usual selves, it was only the colors around their heads that clashed against each other when they were together.

"Wait. Did Simon say something about me?"

"No." John changed the subject to something that didn't have to do with his burgeoning insanity. "So what's the emergency?"

"Halloween business. You're all set for tonight, yeah? It's like queer New Year's Eve, can't miss Halloween."

"I've got the suit."

They were all going as dead celebrities. With a little hair gel and some side combing, a black suit and an ability to imitate an old training camp roommate's Boston accent, John was going as JFK. Tyler hadn't told John who he was going to be.

But instead of a costume store, Tyler pulled into the parking lot of the Holiday Inn on Wolf Road.

"What the hell are we doing here?"

"Dungeon-style sex party," Tyler said with a grin.

A more fiery blush scorched John's face, accompanied by a flash of hot blood along his dick. A month ago, John wouldn't have had a clue about what Tyler meant. Thanks to Tyler's version of an education, John's brain filled with images of leather and slings and padded whipping crosses. The images explained the blush, but the thick pulse of want in John's dick was from the most vivid image, the one of someone like Mason, someone who whispered "sugar" in John's ear, cuffing him to a hook overhead and warming his ass with a hard hand before fucking him senseless.

"Hell, Johnny. I think you've got a kinky streak there, son. Sorry. Just kidding."

John focused on cold, dick-shrinking thoughts. "Shut up. Why are we really here?"

"C'mon in and find out."

"I'm not getting out of the car until I know what's going on." Which also gave him time to imagine running outside in the snow, jumping into a cold pool, lining up for a physical.

"Scared?" Tyler's taunt was the same John's dad had used to get him off his first three meter. At six. And not to jump, to dive.

Tyler came around and opened the door. "You're sexy as hell when you're pissed off. It's this thing I do every Halloween. It's important to me, and I want you to come, okay?"

"Okay." John levered himself out of the jeep.

The warm fuzzies of being wanted turned to cold pricklies when Tyler opened the door to the Hudson Room and John got a chance to read the sign: *Annual Psychic Faire.*

"I'm not going in there."

"Is this some kind of religious thing?"

Whenever John explained that he hadn't gone to high school, everyone assumed that his parents were fundamentalists. They kind of were, if sports counted as a religion. Since John didn't feel like explaining why, he let everyone believe what they wanted.

"No. It's not like that."

"So. C'mon. I'm paying."

"You're really into this stuff?" Tyler seemed like the last person who'd be reading a horoscope to plan his day.

"It's not all hokey. There's this card reader I see, she's really good."

"No crystal balls?"

"Nope. Don't you remember?" Tyler gave John a gentle shove toward the door.

"It was over too fast to notice."

"Is that an insult to me or a compliment to you?" Tyler's teasing managed to get John through the door, but after two steps he knew he should have given any excuse—the truth included—to wait in the car. It was eye-wateringly bright, a constant clatter of colors forming and breaking in a hundred kaleidoscope patterns. He shut his eyes.

It didn't help. The colors were still there, some of them taking on human outlines, played out on a screen that seemed farther away than his tightly shut eyelids.

Tyler came back for him. "What's the matter?"

Denial was instinctive by now. "Nothing."

"C'mon. I'm just going to talk to this one woman. I want her to do you too."

John couldn't even manage to turn that into something suggestive. Why hadn't he told at least some of the truth? The room made his head spin, triggered an icicle ache behind his eyes. He could have just claimed a headache and been halfway to the car.

Tyler's reader wasn't far along the square of tables advertising different services. Her fee for readings was on a sign without any mystical embellishments.

"Tyler. Happy New Year. Good to see you." She rose and leaned across the table to offer Tyler a hug.

"Happy New Year, Rachel."

"New year?" John asked softly.

"Yeah. Halloween's the end of the old year for Wiccans and some Pagans."

"Samhain," Rachel said with a smile.

"Rachel is a friend of my mom's. Rachel, this is John. I want you to do him next."

Rachel didn't look like the skirted, bangled gypsy John had envisioned. With her short brown hair, black top and jeans, she could have been anybody's mom. Except that most people didn't get quite so wide-eyed when they looked at him, even if they

K.A. Mitchell

knew about his medal and accident. And he'd never met anyone whose colors turned to bright mirrors that burned against John's eyes even after he squeezed them shut against the glare.

"Are you okay?" she asked, even though John had a feeling she knew he wasn't and that she even knew why.

"Yeah. Just a headache."

"Sorry." The word held more genuine regret than a casual expression of sympathy. She turned to Tyler. "Are you sure you want your friend to overhear this?"

"Oh yeah." To John, Tyler said, "Rachel's always telling me how much ass I'm going to get. Even the cards know I'm a stud."

"Hmm." Rachel selected one of three oversized card decks from the silk-covered table as Tyler pulled a couple of twenties from his wallet.

In her hand, the space around the deck was bright, no color, just like the cards gave off some kind of shine. Nausea had been slithering in John's stomach since he read the sign at the door. Now it punched free and leapt into his throat, forcing his breakfast up until his nose and mouth burned with bile. The sensation was almost familiar from the few times he'd been stupid enough to eat before competition.

Except this wasn't vertigo or a headache or even pre-competition nerves. It was terror. Terror rolling icy sweat down his back, turning his joints to water, dragging his balls in close and tight.

The mirrors around Rachel's hair turned white, almost the same pale yellow as Tyler's, as she watched him shuffle the deck. When she took the deck back, the glowing white alternated with the yellow. Two colors. Like Mason.

Shit.

Was that it? Was Mason...what Wiccan? Psychic?

John looked away, eyes searching for anyplace that didn't shine like a freshly shaken glow stick. The booth next door was refreshingly ordinary, though a line of people awaited the service it offered. Kirlian Photography, *See Your Living Aura* the sign promised. As opposed to a dead aura? From his vantage point, John could see the image of whoever was being photographed on the screen, but it just looked like the kind of pictures that came from having the lens open extra long. A blurred edge.

"Yeah. Not exactly what it looks like, is it?"

John turned slowly toward the voice and found a man with a balding head and a grizzled beard alternately blowing and sipping on a mug of coffee. "What isn't?"

"Auras. Reading people. As if some computer can see them." The man's tone was dismissive.

John's heart slowed a little. Just conversation.

"Ever check your own?" the guy said.

"My own what?"

"Aura, or whatever you think of it as."

I try like hell not to think of it at all. John's heart raced again, but he gave the man an all-purpose shrug.

Either the guy read John's aura or his body language because he figured out John didn't want to talk.

"Well, I've got to go find some sugar. This coffee tastes like crap and I need the caffeine to rev up my sight enough to make it through all the readings I've got scheduled."

Rev it up? John almost grabbed the guy so that he could beg to learn how to turn it the fuck off. But his tongue got stuck in his mouth, his legs melted to the floor. *If I say it out loud will it be true?*

It wasn't true. It was Halloween and a psychic fair and the power of suggestion. He had a traumatic brain injury that had altered his perception. He didn't *read* anything.

"Bullshit." From his outburst, Tyler didn't seem to be having any more fun than John was.

"I never said anything about your adherence to a standard of virility, just that you know that you are getting bored and seeking balance, a connection on a higher level."

"No fucking way am I bored or missing out on anything."

Rachel raised her eyebrows as Tyler loomed over the table. "If the reading were completely off base, it wouldn't affect you like this. You don't know anyone who would be a Page of Pentacles?"

"Not unless he's got a hot ass."

"It's not fortune-telling, Tyler. It's just an opportunity to consider your path."

"Oh, I'll consider it. While I get my dick sucked by every hot guy I can find. And I won't be bored or seeking a connection. C'mon, John."

John transferred his cane to his other hand and started after Tyler, but Rachel's voice stopped him short.

"John."

He was afraid of what she'd say, and afraid not to hear it. He wished he could just storm off like Tyler. He turned back and waited.

"I owe Tyler an apology."

John's chest hadn't sighed with relief that hard since he watched Zhao over-rotate his last dive and knew he had the second medal. "He'll be fine."

"I did my best to focus on him during the reading, but I was getting a lot of interference. I guess I could have been more diplomatic."

"Okay." Diplomatic was one way to put it. How weird was it to have a friend of your mother do a reading on your sex life?

"Please sit down for a minute, John."

"Tyler—"

"He'll wait. He's angry and he needs some time to think it through."

John sat in the chair Tyler had vacated. He tried not looking at Rachel, not looking at the cards, not looking at the table, and ended up staring at the tip of his cane.

"The reason I had trouble with Tyler's reading was interference. I don't usually work with a spirit guide, it's usually more intuitive for me with the cards and the subject. Do you understand what I'm saying?"

"No, ma'am." John glanced up and then back down to where his cane scuffed the mottled dead-mouse-colored carpet, leaving a dark furrow against the nap.

"Okay. Let me try it like this. When I made the connection to whatever helps me read cards for people, I got a competing connection, like another radio station trying to come in on the same signal."

John made an X over his line on the carpet then scrubbed it out with his toe and looked back up at Rachel. Her mirrors were back in place, but now they held only a dull shine, like they were antiques, brassy with age.

Rachel went on. "I focused on Tyler as much as I could, but it was very insistent. I know this will sound crazy, but I have three messages for you, John."

John dug his cane deeper into the carpet, biting back a question about Rachel being supernatural voice mail.

"The messages may not make sense to you now, but they might later."

John was pretty sure that he didn't want to hear the messages, so he forestalled her with a question he really wanted answered. "Did you actually hear something, like a voice?"

Because if he could see colors in thin air, maybe people heard things that weren't there either and Rachel knew how to turn it off.

"Not really. I get impressions for the most part, so it's not quite an exact quote though the message was really clear."

"A spirit guide? Is that like a famous dead person?" Was he about to get career advice from Abraham Lincoln?

"No. It could be anyone, anything. The impression I got was that the spirit was your age—strong, friendly enough, but kind of irritated. And male. He made me want to smile."

John looked down and realized he'd drawn an A in the carpet with his cane as Rachel spoke. He swallowed and ground the lines to nothing with his heel. One of his hands was braced on the table for a quick getaway, and Rachel picked it up. He surprised himself by not jerking free.

"Are you ready to hear this now?"

He definitely wasn't. And he wouldn't ever be. But now his tongue was superglued to the roof of his gritty, dry mouth. His body refused to obey his mind's demands that they all get the hell out of Crazytown before they became permanent residents. He met her gaze.

"Okay," she said. "Yes. The colors are what you think. Help him."

John's skin crackled and burned, everywhere except where Rachel's palm pressed cool against his own. He wanted to jerk free but he couldn't. *It's not fair. Not fucking fair,* he wanted to shout. Why was she waiting? Why couldn't she just deliver the whole pile of you-thought-your-life-was-fucked-before bullshit at once?

"The other two messages are for you to give someone else." Her eyes became less focused, like she was looking inward for the right way to say it. "For your first. Tell your first they aren't just dreams. And no three-ways." She delivered the last with a smile.

Your first. Mason. From his dead lover. *Hey, Mason, I don't know if you remember me, but we fucked a few weeks ago. Well, this psychic and I have been playing telephone with Alex and he's got a message for you.*

John must have stood up, left the Hudson room under his own power and found the men's room, but all of that was gone, banished to the same black hole of forget-it-for-your-sanity as his last two trips off the dive platform. Because he didn't remember anything after hearing the message until Tyler found him in that last stall, head on the cool porcelain of the tank lid, mouth bitter with bile, his revisited eggs and sausage disappearing as Tyler pushed the handle.

"Holy shit, John, why didn't you tell me you were sick? Are you hung over?"

"No. It's just vertigo."

"It gets as bad as this? That sucks out loud."

No shit. Tyler left and came back with a wet paper towel. John rubbed it over his face and then left it on the back of his neck. Finally, he was able to make it out to the sinks. Tyler held John's cane under one arm as they washed their hands. John wondered where he'd left it, but he didn't have enough energy to ask. All he wanted to do was stick his head under the thin spitting stream from the faucet.

"You better not be sick. If you fuck up my favorite holiday by giving it to me, I'll kick your ass."

"I swear to God you can't catch this."

Chapter Ten

"Where's Drew?" John could use a little of his friend's calm, quiet presence now. He tugged on his suit jacket. It felt short and tight, picked up at Goodwill because the two suits he had Tyler had declared too modern for JFK.

"He's meeting us at Church with Tyler." Gavin pushed off Simon's bed and turned his ball cap to the side. At least for tonight John could tell him apart from Garrett. Gavin was some famous OD'd dead DJ, and with a microphone and belted shirt, Garrett was a dead gay boy-band singer. They were both music fans. Another thing to coo and fight over, another way to have trouble telling them apart.

They had all covered their faces with white powder and put on a grayish lipstick to make them look dead. John had worn makeup before for photo shoots and studio interviews, but John was glad Tyler hadn't decided to make them celebrity zombies. This stuff itched enough without fake blood on top of it. Would he recognize Drew? He was supposed to be some TV show actor John didn't know. At least he'd figured out Simon's costume right away. He'd put on a beret and fake moustache and army fatigues and made a convincing Che Guevara.

"Who's Tommy coming as?" Garrett asked.

"Probably zombie Jesus," Simon said.

The four of them climbed into Simon's ancient jeep and headed downtown. Church was a converted fire station on

Church St, more nightclub than bar with a cover high enough that John had only been there with them once. Colored strobes and stained glass made John dizzy enough to be glad they couldn't afford it. John was already wishing they'd just gone to Sammies when they walked down from their parking spot and saw the line wrapped around the building.

"Hey."

An arm and a familiar voice beckoned from the upper third of the line.

There were a few grumbles as the four of them squeezed in next to Tyler and Drew.

Tyler made a choking disgusted noise. "For fuck's sake, Simon, you were supposed to come as someone recent, or at least, you know, hot."

"Suck me."

"In your dreams. Especially in that fugly mess."

John stepped between them so at least they couldn't see each other to snipe at. Tyler was wearing a pink-striped shirt, one arm rolled up and a set of handcuffs dangling from his wrist.

"Who are you?"

Tyler pointed at some marks drawn on the inside of his forearm. "Brad Renfro. Heroin addict. But..." he leaned in to glare at Simon over John's shoulder, "...hot. Speaking of which, check this out." He jerked his thumb at Drew.

He wasn't dressed as Tyler Ment—whatever that guy's name was. He was James Dean from his slicked hair, tight white T under the familiar jacket, to the thumbs hooked in his jeans. His lips looked incredibly full and not at all gray. Hot. Yeah. No shit. John had never looked at Drew's lips before.

"Um. Why aren't you wearing makeup?"

"It itched. Besides, it's not like people don't know James

Dean is dead."

"And hot." Tyler slung his non-cuffed wrist around Drew's neck, but it was more like he was shoving him at John.

"That too." Drew's hazel eyes sparkled under the streetlight.

John grinned.

Music throbbed against the brick wall, giving John time to adjust to the color wheel of sound before they hit the door. Next to him, Drew was familiar and new, a friend turned into something else by that costume. With his hair slicked back, he was all cheekbones and full lips. It wasn't only that. It was as if the costume gave him a sexy confidence, something that stirred the blood in John's dick the way just having Drew as a friend never had.

Was it bad to fuck friends? Tyler teased him about their one shot and it wasn't awkward, but John hadn't known Tyler then. And the other guys John had been with, a random dance partner, a guy from sociology class, the cute nerd at the library, they hadn't been memorable enough to be a friend—or awkward. As far as really memorable sex went, well, John couldn't imagine being friends with Mason.

Supposing John believed it and wanted to, exactly how was he supposed to deliver that message? It wasn't like he could pass it through Lizzy, or get Mason's number to say, "Hey, your dead boyfriend called the psychic hotline. No three-ways."

He knew he already half-believed that message. It wasn't enough that John would never dive again, never launch into that controlled flight, muscles working perfectly to slide him safely into the warm water, now he had to run messages for dead people? Read the colors above their heads and what? Help? How? He couldn't even fix his own mess of a life. He'd even made Simon put on the makeup. After what the man at the psychic fair had said, John was too afraid to face himself in the mirror.

The six of them found enough space near a wall to stand together. John leaned toward Drew at the same moment Drew came toward him. Instead of knocking heads, which John thought would probably happen given the way his day was going, Drew moved so that his mouth brushed by John's ear.

John jerked back. "I'm going to get a drink. Want anything?"

"Just water," Drew said.

"Okay." John concentrated on threading his way through bodies, focusing on the shifting spaces between them rather than the colors over their heads. If a stimulant like caffeine boosted this ability for that guy, couldn't a depressant like alcohol turn it down? John remembered Mason's bottle of Jim Beam and ordered a double bourbon on the rocks like they did in movies. After paying the cover, the cost of his drink and Drew's water almost turned John's wallet inside-out. He had just enough for cab fare in case he got stranded.

Even on the rocks the liquor burned, the taste reminding him of Mason's mouth that first night. He downed half the glass before he went back to his friends, and aside from adding to his already shaky balance, the alcohol didn't do anything to stop the colors around people's heads from moving in and out of the rest of the strobe lights in the bar.

Tommy was there when he got back. Older than Simon and Tyler, Tommy had graduated to the real world of jobs, and didn't go out with them very often, but John knew him right away, despite the slicked gray wig of his costume. The long gray hair, a white karate outfit and a length of rope around his neck. Even John knew that was David Carradine.

"You are a sick fuck, Tommy." Tyler clapped him on the back.

"Fuck you very much. Hey, new guy, thanks." Tommy reached for John's drink, and John spun away to down the rest of it.

The alcohol and his screwed-up brain would have sent him to the floor if Drew hadn't caught him, warm and solid.

"Thanks."

"Thanks for my water." Drew took it from under John's arm but kept his other hand on the top of John's ass. John finished off the drink and handed it to Tommy.

Tommy sucked in an ice cube and rolled it on his tongue, the tip poking pink through a hole in the middle. "Nicely done."

The warmth that hit John might have just been from the bourbon but he'd had liquor before. He'd never had friends like this before though.

"Hey, John."

It was Keith. Keith who couldn't take a polite no for an answer, dressed as a convict, but with a sleeveless jumpsuit, fake tattoos covering his solid muscled arms.

"Hi."

"Keith, right?" If there was someone Tyler didn't know, John hadn't seen it yet.

"Yeah. Hi."

Even with the pounding mix from the speakers, the long pause that followed was awkward. John's skin prickled, and he looked up to the second floor with the open balcony. Mason leaned there, no costume, just a black T-shirt. He was watching them.

"I didn't know you guys knew each other," Keith said into the comparative silence. "Do you guys know who this is?"

"Keith." John tried to stop him, but maybe Keith had been knocking back doubles too.

"John Andrews," Keith said, like that made it obvious.

Tyler stuck out his hand. "Hey, John. Glad to meet you." He rolled his eyes.

"No." Even Keith's hoarse voice carried his frustration over the thump of music. "I mean the John Andrews, the diver, the guy who won two gold medals at the Olympics four years ago."

Tyler's hand tightened on John's. "What?"

John tried to free his hand and looked at the floor.

"Yeah." Keith's proud smile suggested he'd had something to do with John's win. "He'd have won another one this time if he hadn't fallen and hit his head."

"What, like Louganis?" Tommy asked.

Tyler and Simon were staring, and John could see the connections clicking in their heads. He didn't want to look at Drew. Glaring at Keith wasn't helping shut his mouth any faster. At least Gavin and Garrett were off dry-humping on the dance floor. Not that someone wouldn't tell them.

"And that's how you got hurt?" Simon asked.

"Not really. I went up again and fell and hit the deck," John confessed.

Tyler punched John's shoulder. Hard. "Asshole. I can't believe you didn't tell us. Do you have any idea how much ass that's worth? How many guys would want to fuck an Olympic medalist?"

"Which sure as hell leaves you out of it," Simon said.

"No way. I get the leavings. Consoling the ones who don't make the team. What a waste of time." Tyler's yellow crystals deepened to gold, solid and strong.

"Every time I think you cannot possibly be more shallow, you just create a whole new standard of disgusting." Simon put a hand on Tyler's shoulder like he'd shove him, but actually it put them between John and Keith.

"I live to astound," Tyler said.

John suddenly realized what Tyler had been doing. He'd pulled all the attention away from John and onto himself. And at least for Tyler, knowing about John wasn't going to make any difference. At that moment, John wanted to hug him.

"So hey, man. Thanks for over-sharing." Tyler gave Keith an unfriendly look. "But we were just going to go dance. Nice costume. You got some kind of new gay hanky code working there?" He flicked at the blue bandana on Keith's head.

Keith glared at Tyler, lips in a thin hard line. "Just because you've never done anything to be proud of—"

"Oh trust us. He's proud of his own breathing." Simon rolled his eyes but moved up to stand next to Tyler and their— hell if John was going to call them auras or start adding extra *e*'s on words like *shoppe* and *faire* and *olde*—Simon and Tyler's *colors* no longer sizzled at the edges but overlapped in a warm shade of red-gold. "So the dark blue bandana is traditionally the color for anal, left pocket top, right pocket bottom. I don't know about wearing it on your head."

Tyler grinned. "I can't believe we stumped Mr. Gay Encyclopedia. It means Keith wants to put his head up his own ass."

Keith hadn't done anything that deserved Tyler and Simon coming at him like a pair of forwards in water polo. What he'd said about John was true, whether John wanted it known or not. He was trying to think of something to say when Drew tugged gently at his arm.

"C'mon. Let's go dance."

Drew didn't say anything for a minute, just moved against John's body, arms draped over his shoulders, and then burst out, "What an asshole."

It was far more emotion than John had ever heard from his friend. "Are you pissed I didn't say something before?"

"No." Drew leaned in to speak right into John's ear. "'Cause I already knew."

"You did?"

Drew pulled his head back and nodded, those surprisingly full lips curved in a sexy smile. "Your picture was on the cover of lots of magazines when I was in high school. That spread in *People*? Damn, you were hot."

John thought of a few of the magazines he'd had as a teenager, innocent enough at a casual glance, but what he imagined from the picture of a sweating sports figure or half-dressed actor. And then he'd—

"Please tell me you didn't."

"I did."

"Oh. Shit."

Drew shrugged. "And you're still hot. Hotter in person."

"Why didn't you say anything?"

"I figured if you wanted people to know, you'd have said something."

"Thanks." He was about to offer a more substantial thanks, but then he remembered his empty wallet. "I'd buy you a drink, but I'm kind of tapped."

"It's all right. I actually owe you one anyway. Bourbon, right?" Drew leaned in again, his breath hot, tickling John's ear.

"Are you trying to get me drunk?"

"Would it do me any good?"

"Um." Drew was safe. Nice. Sexy enough to get John interested, but...

But the look he could feel aimed at his head from the balcony wasn't "sexy enough". It was hot. Just thinking of the man behind that stare turned John's crank in a way no pouting mouth on a good friend ever could. He shot a glance Mason's way. John didn't need one of those aura charts that had been for sale at the fair to know that the way the crystals sparked around Mason's head meant he was jealous.

John gave Drew a shy smile, one that had always worked

when interviewers started on the personal relationship questions. "Can I let you know?"

Drew dropped a kiss that was almost a lick on John's neck. "Been waiting a while. I think I can wait a little longer for the real thing."

Mason didn't know which of the scene queens John was grinding with on the dance floor, any more than Mason knew why he'd dragged his ass to Church tonight. Halloween was an easy night to get laid, but it wasn't just an itch that had him leaning on the rail on the second floor. The pole from the old fire station went right down to the stage, empty now except for a couple of guys dancing, one of them wearing nothing but a gold banana hammock, rubbing against the pole like it was his best fuck buddy.

John was giving the James Dean he was dancing with almost the same treatment. He didn't seem off balance enough to use his cane. Mason knew all about how those hips worked, how that thrust and grind felt, how tight the ass under James Dean's hands felt wrapped around his dick.

Remembered for damn sure since it was the last piece of ass he'd had. He'd gotten busy with the computer—it was almost ready to go, a few more tweaks from Lizzy on the casing—and then he just hadn't been interested. He didn't miss company. He must have scared the shit out of Lizzy with his talk about seeing Alex's ghost because one of the housemates was always home when Mason was. He couldn't get a glass of milk out of the fridge at three a.m. without someone shuffling by on the way to the bathroom, or to have a "snack". Did she really think he'd kill himself?

He lost sight of John in a crush as the DJ tossed in an old Backstreet Boys song and the dance floor got impossibly crowded. When he found John again he was on the second floor, headed into the bathroom. He had to hang on to the balcony rail to keep himself from following him in, backing him into a stall and finding out what John had been learning.

John came out and went into one of the dark alcoves that had probably been where the bedrooms were. There were couches in them. Not much light. They weren't designed for conversation.

No one followed John. James Dean was probably in there waiting for him. Except he wasn't. He was back with the rest of the crew John had come in with. As Mason watched, Tyler grabbed James Dean's arm and pulled him aside for a conference. Maybe James Dean had changed his plans.

Mason couldn't think of a single good excuse for following John into the alcove. There was only one reason to be there. He couldn't even muster up a lame excuse about reminding John about the fish bowls full of condoms left around the upstairs. He'd probably walk in on John bent over one of the couches. Blood pumped sweet and thick in Mason's dick at the thought of yanking the guy away and taking his place. Would that ass still be good and tight? Would Mason still need to stretch him nice and slow before he worked it in?

Fantasies aside, John would probably tell Mason to fuck off, and he'd deserve it, but he headed to the alcove anyway. He'd barely gotten past the curtain when a hand shot out and yanked him onto the couch.

"I knew you were going to follow me."

After just one time, how could Mason possibly remember John's voice? The fresh-cut-grass smell from his hair? Mason had ended up half-sprawled on John's lap. Pushing himself up enough to get a good look at John's face in the dim light, he said, "Maybe I wanted to see who the lucky winner was tonight. See who got a piece of this." He slid his hand under John's hips and squeezed his ass through the thin material of the suit trousers. Damn. A jock again. The guy liked flaunting his ass. Mason had to shift to get his swelling dick out of his inseam.

143

"What do you care? You're done with it."

Mason's dick disagreed. Forcefully. Heat flashed along the length, pooling to drip at the tip.

John shoved Mason off and then straddled his lap. John's eyes looked black in the darkness. Black and almost angry as he stared down. "Or maybe you were looking for a three-way."

Mason shut his eyes as Alex's words echoed in his head. *When did I ever give you the impression that I was into a three-way?*

"What?" John's question was sharp, his body tense.

Mason opened his eyes. "Nothing. Is that what you're after, sugar? Bored with one dick at a time already?"

John rocked on Mason's lap, cock pressing into Mason's belly. "You lied to me."

"Huh?" It wasn't enough Alex was using cute guys to bitch at Mason for cheating, now he was getting called a liar?

"You told me you'd show me everything."

John moved like he'd kiss Mason, but Mason stopped John with a hand on his jaw, slid a thumb over his lips. John started a distracting caress with a hot, slick tongue, pulling a groan out along with Mason's words.

"Let's see. We hit blow jobs, rim jobs, fucking both ways, jerking off and some dick-on-dick action. Uhn." A hard suck followed by another sweep of tongue made it hard to remember what he was defending himself for. "Covered a lot of ground in less than twenty-four hours. What did I miss?"

John grabbed Mason's wrist and moved his hand from John's mouth to his cock. Those trousers were so thin, John's pulse thudded against Mason's palm. Or maybe it was just the music.

"But you promised me two more nights." John rocked into Mason's hand. "There's a lot you didn't tell me about."

"Like what?"

"Circle jerks and daisy chains. Dildos and butt plugs. Slings and spreader bars."

A vision of John's tight round ass bent over a bed with his legs pinned apart hit Mason like a porn-filled freight train. If he wasn't sitting, his knees would have buckled. "Fuck." Mason squeezed the hard shaft under his palm. "Been a busy couple of weeks. What did you like the best?" *Please say bondage.* He'd done a little, Alex had liked to take turns tying their hands so they couldn't get themselves off, but God, John's legs forced wide, tied down, waiting and begging for it? Mason's dick rubbed against the slick spot in his shorts. He was going to come in his fucking jeans in a minute.

John's gaze aimed a laser beam at Mason's crotch, turned it into ground zero, then treated him to a flick of tongue on his lips. "I haven't decided yet. Why?"

Want tore through Mason like a January wind off Lake Erie. He didn't know he could still feel something that strong and sharp. Didn't know anything would make him believe he could fill that hole inside. Shoving the suit coat off John's shoulders, Mason wrapped his fingers around solid muscled arms, holding on against the surge flooding the aching hollow inside him. Yeah, Mason had wanted guys since Alex died. Wanted sex and friction and the oblivion of release. But this. This was more than that. This was firing up the motherboard and for the first time everything came online. With him. John.

"I want..." Mason didn't care how. On the spreader bar in his fantasy or here in this dirty dark corner, Mason just wanted John.

"What?"

"You."

"How?" The one word had a hundred filthy promises in it.

Mason wanted to laugh, but his throat was too dry. He

might have John's arms pinned in his grip and trapped by the sleeves of the jacket, but John knew damned well whose finger was on the power button. "Anything. Whatever you want."

"I want this." John shrugged free and knelt between Mason's legs. In a single breath, Mason's cock was free of his jeans and in John's mouth.

Again John didn't stop for any preliminary licks or kisses, but dove in with a determined pair of lips and a flexible, tireless tongue. Going without and John's skill was a combination guaranteed to put Mason over the edge in about fifteen seconds. After a brief struggle with his fingers digging at the couch like that could stop that sweet climb, he slid into the heat, grabbing John's head, trying to find a grip on hair slick with gel. John must not have minded, or maybe it was exactly what he wanted because he moaned around Mason's dick and gulped him in deeper, past that soft-tight-hot muscle in his throat and right on into a blinding orgasm.

Mason's dick stopped pumping, but his heart kept slamming against his chest, breath burning the back of his throat as he looked down to watch John wipe his mouth with his thumb.

Christ. Where could they get a spreader bar and some cuffs at one a.m. on Halloween? A twenty-four-hour hardware store?

John smiled at him, a smile Mason felt in his gut, and maybe it was because he'd lost more than half his brain cells out his cock a minute ago, but it was probably just an inborn Kincaid determination to be fucking miserable because he opened his mouth. "Wow, Mr. President. I'd say you were a natural, but we all know how hard you trained for that position. Not to mention all the practice you've been getting since."

John wiped his hand on Mason's pants and stood, leaning in so that their faces were close together. "For your information, this..." he flicked a finger against Mason's hyper-sensitive dick, "...is the only cock that's been in me since I got here."

Mason managed to keep his lips sealed against further imbecilic outbursts and watched through pain-watered eyes as John picked up his suit coat and straightened up.

John took a step away and then turned back. "Oh. And another thing I've got to tell you. Your friend who doesn't like three-ways says they aren't just dreams."

Chapter Eleven

Mason was too impatient to be quiet, but it wouldn't have mattered anyway, Lizzy was a light sleeper. Still, a desperate, focused energy lent him enough speed that he was almost out of her bedroom before she snapped on the light.

"What the fuck are you doing?"

He had the box holding the computer clutched against his chest. He didn't think he'd have held his firstborn with more awed affection and fear.

"I need to use it for tonight."

"I'm still putting some of the case on. Why the hell do you need it now? I thought you went out."

"I did. But—I just need it."

He took it down to the kitchen. She followed him, of course.

He ripped away the cardboard around the brass and glass rather than fuck it up by lifting it out of the box, and powered it up.

"Mason. What are you doing?" She sniffed suspiciously. "Did you switch to vodka?"

"No. I'm not drunk." The operating system made a nice background hum, booted up and waiting for Mason's input. With any luck, he could get *someone else* to input the data. "I want to talk to Alex."

"Mase—"

"I know how it sounds. Look. You know how I told you about Alex being angry? Well, I know he's got more to say. And I figure if he's trying, that he could use this."

She sank into a chair. Her lips moved a couple times like she was choosing her words carefully. "Did you have another dream?"

"Not tonight. I kind of wanted to do this alone."

"Tough." She folded her arms.

"I'm not going to smash it. We put too many fucking hours into it for that."

She didn't move.

"I don't know if with you here he'll—"

"What? He'll show? Can you hear yourself?"

"I'm not drunk and I'm not crazy."

"Then you're high. It's Halloween and you're telling me a ghost story." Lizzy's lips thinned into a hard line.

"It's more than that."

"Explain to me how someone who makes fun of Carrie for reading the horoscope in the paper suddenly believes in ghosts. And not only ghosts, but ghosts who can instant message from beyond."

"Because John gave me a message."

"John?" Both Lizzy's brows shot up on that.

Mason looked at the screen where the cursor waited, blinking patiently. "If I can explain it, will you leave?"

"That's almost too easy, but all I can say is maybe."

So he did. He told her exactly what Alex had said in the dream, and then how John had quoted him, how he'd said it was from someone who didn't like three-ways.

Lizzy scrubbed at her face with the heels of her hands. "Don't you think it could all be a coincidence?"

K.A. Mitchell

"Why the hell would he say it like that?"

"Why the hell would Alex talk to John? They never met. And why wouldn't he help you more, then? Explain what Alex meant?"

The screen wasn't big enough to hide behind, and Lizzy wasn't going anywhere. "I kind of pissed him off."

"John?"

"Yeah." But Alex too, for all he knew. Maybe Alex was warning John off Mason. Okay. *That* was crazy. The whole thing was crazy. But he knew that John hadn't wanted to say anything, might not have said anything if Mason hadn't been such a dick. John hadn't come up with that for kicks. The first line about three-ways maybe. But that last thing he'd said. He'd known what it would mean to Mason. Which was why John had disappeared, maybe into that group of friends, and Mason wasn't about to go begging favors from Tyler Granger.

To Lizzy he said, "The computer was Alex's idea from the first. I'm just going to sit here. Not drink. Not do anything but wait. And the worst that can happen is I feel like an even bigger ass in the morning."

"Then I'm sitting with you."

"I thought you said you'd leave me alone."

"If you aren't fucking nuts, I want to be here. And if you are fucking nuts, I have to be here. So deal."

Short of physically carrying her back to her room which would wake up Kai and Carrie and involve bruises from all three of his housemates and possibly the police, Mason couldn't think of a way to get rid of her. He wasn't up for more physical abuse. His dick was still sore from John flicking it with his finger.

They waited together.

Mason didn't fall asleep, but staring at a blinking cursor in silence for a few hours did make him zone out. He blinked and looked over at Lizzy. She was asleep, head pillowed on her folded arms. A piece of hair had slipped out of her braid and plastered itself to her mouth. He pulled it away.

He'd been waiting for it, but the voice still sent his heart skipping hard against his ribs.

"Sometimes I forget how beautiful she is." Alex looked like he wanted to touch Lizzy's hair too, but he stopped, one hand hovering near her cheek.

Alex wasn't see-through or anything, but Mason knew this wasn't like the time on the porch. Alex might be here, but Mason wouldn't be able to touch him.

Mason's breath whistled between his teeth as he sucked in air. "Alex." He clenched his fists to keep from reaching for him. "What do you want? What am I supposed to do?"

Alex nodded at the computer. "It's not that easy. Don't you think I'd have tried it?"

Why couldn't Alex just answer a direct question? It was like the early days of the internet, when conversations didn't happen in real time, and they might be having parallel discussions on separate topics.

"I hate this," Alex snapped.

Sick sweat prickled on Mason's skin. Did Alex mean the computer or the limited conversation? Alex had to be proud of the computer; it had been his idea from the first. Mason and Lizzy had just made it real.

But Alex wasn't looking at the computer anymore. He was glaring at Mason. "And sometimes I hate you for it. Why couldn't you just let go?"

Bigger bubbles of sweat broke across Mason's skin, hot and cold like a fever, his gut heaving in the face of Alex's anger.

"Don't. Alex, please. Baby, don't hate me. I'm sorry."

Alex's eyes were always dark, but now they were a perfect dark sky, enough dark to blot out the brightest high-beam headlight. Like the one that didn't pick up the deer in time.

Mason shivered under his sweat.

"Then fix it. I need you to fix it."

"I can't. I don't know how. Damn it. Why didn't you drive? I should have been the one to hit the tree." But by the time Mason was yelling, Alex was gone, Mason was awake and Lizzy was still drooling on the kitchen table, hair again plastered to her cheek.

"Fuck."

He'd whispered, but Lizzy jerked awake anyway. "What?"

"He was here." Mason looked at the computer, but it was still only a blank screen and a blinking cursor, though the cursor was halfway down the page now.

"You fell asleep."

"No, you fell asleep." He ran a thumb over the thick ridges of red streaking the light brown skin of her cheek. "Nice nap face."

He looked at the cursor again. Maybe he had fallen asleep and leaned on a key. The space bar? He and Alex hadn't been talking out loud. Lizzy would have heard them. It was easy enough to check. He had the computer repeat the most recent keystrokes.

Some useless movement of the tab, the enter, and then in the midst of it three letters: N O J.

John knew it was too much to hope for that Mason wouldn't understand the message he'd flung at him last night, or that Mason wouldn't know exactly where to find John. Simon and Tyler had probably been hanging out in the same lounge on the second floor of the campus center for years. Simon could probably trace the history of gay students staking out this lounge through a few decades. Either way, Mason intercepted John before he turned the corner into the lounge.

"What the fuck was that about?"

John knew what Mason was talking about. But since they'd crossed into the freak zone, John was going to make Mason actually say something. John had already taken the first step. "What the fuck was what?"

"Last night."

"It was a blow job. It can't have been that long since your last one. And by the way, a huge sucking mistake." John looked past Mason to the lounge, to that square of couches where the conversation wouldn't be any more serious than who would bottom if Aiden Shaw and Buck Meadows made a porn video together. They sure as hell wouldn't be asking about messages from dead people.

"I'm talking about what you said."

"I said a lot of stuff."

Mason's arm moved, a sudden flash that started things spinning. For a second John thought he'd pissed Mason off enough to get a swing of his fist and was ready to block it, but Mason just scrubbed at his unshaven jaw before placing his hand flat on the wall next to John's head.

"You gave me a message from Alex."

It sounded a lot crazier out loud. But who was John to judge crazy when the colors around Mason's head shifted faster despite the forced quiet in his voice. Red and white flashing, a nauseating spin like the lights on top of a police car. John didn't want it. Any of it. "I've got to go."

"Where? Got an urgent blow job to give?"

"Fuck you and get out of my way." But John whispered it. He could raise his voice. Even though the open spaces of the campus center echoed with hundreds of voices, his friends would turn at the sound of John yelling. He didn't need them. He could do this himself.

Leveraging his cane between them, he moved around Mason.

"What did he say to you?" Mason grabbed John's arm.

John shook it off, but the crystals, the white ones, slid at him like a dozen icicles flying from the roof, a comic-book freeze ray attacking, firing splinters of cold to stab at his head. And that was not going to be his life. "It was Halloween, you stupid shit. I was screwing with you. Like a ghost story."

"Bullshit. Because you knew. You knew what he'd said to me. How could you know?"

Pain exploded at the back of John's eyes from those bright shards of white. He stumbled and wrenched his gaze away. Drew looked up and then got to his feet before reaching down to smack Tyler's shoulder. Drew. Soft, flat gray. Even Keith with his almost negative light would be perfect after this. John tried to walk away again, but his balance was fucked and he ended up against Mason's chest, those powerful arms around him, keeping him upright.

John pushed again, but Mason didn't release him. "I don't think my boyfriend is going to like this."

"Yeah? And how does he feel about you blowing other guys?" That rumble against his ear. That rich, deep-purple voice blocked the pain and the spinning for a second. Mason's lips moved to brush against John's neck. "Is it Granger? He'd pay to watch it. Hell, I'd pay to watch it."

John got free and latched onto Drew. It should have felt better, but it was almost worse, the cold in his head replaced with a dull hot throb like a full body bruise. "Drew, this is

Mason."

"Hey, Drew." In a blink, Mason was the sexy charmer who'd talked John into giving him a second chance, promise in his voice and a hint of dirty fun in his smile. "Sorry, man. No harm meant. Your boyfriend tripped. Mind if I borrow him for a minute? He's got some notes I need for a class project."

Tyler flanked them on the wall side. "You're taking classes? I'd heard you were back to blowing your scholarship on liquor and dick."

"Nice to see you too, Tyler." Mason turned his dark gaze to John, who was working hard on not puking. Mason's and Tyler's colors were jammed together, like too many pieces in a puzzle, bulging and receding, convex to concave. "It's not for me. It's for Lizzy, right, John?"

"Lizzy? Still got the same hag? Can't she find a straight guy to hit on?"

"Kiss my ass, Granger."

"Keep on dreaming. John, you ready for lunch?"

If John wasn't so nauseous, he'd have smacked Tyler for talking about Lizzy like that, but the only thing John was ready for was some quality time with his head in a toilet. He hadn't puked from his scrambled brains since the first month of rehab. He locked his back teeth.

"I think we're just going to head back to his dorm."

"You two lovebirds do that." Tyler was more than a foot shorter than Mason but just as solidly built. He looked straight at him. "Don't you have to go somewhere else?"

"I'll call you about the notes, John." Mason backed off.

Had he ever given Mason his cell number? Would Lizzy give it to him? Neither of them had been to his room. God, those tiny slits of windows looked more like protection than prison right now. "I'll give them to Lizzy myself."

Drew steered him into another one of the doors that sprang up like secret passages in a Scooby-Doo cartoon. Scooby-Doo, ghosts, his life was a fucking cartoon. Except that he didn't think Velma would unmask this ghost at the end to find old man Warner, the caretaker, who would complain about "meddling kids." And he couldn't change the channel.

In the solid white passageway, John gulped in some air and leaned against the wall.

Drew didn't say anything, didn't try to touch John, didn't ask questions he couldn't answer. Every breath in the quiet monochromatic hall pushed the nausea back until John could unlock his jaw and straighten up. "Thanks."

"It's okay. Vertigo?"

It was an easy escape. Not exactly a lie. "Yeah."

"Does anything help?"

"This." John pointed at the halls where there was nothing but the pale silver whisper of their voices. "You."

"Yeah, well, I am your boyfriend, right?"

John looked at the still calm blue-gray around Drew's head. "You heard that?"

"Yeah." Drew grinned. "Holy crap. I hope your face looks like that because of your vertigo and not from the thought of me as your boyfriend."

"I get a headache with it too." Again, not a complete lie. He did get a headache with the vertigo, with the colors, with anything having to do with his fucked-up head; he just didn't have one at the moment. "I think I'm going to the dorm to crash."

"It's all right. I don't exactly know if I'm looking for a boyfriend either. But I wouldn't mind tucking you in." Drew's leer was funny rather than obnoxious.

Why didn't safe and cute and funny and nice make John's

dick as hard as it got after thirty seconds of arguing with a screwed-up bastard like Mason? John had been sticking to Tyler's no-second-date policy, and it worked just fine. But Mason made John want to shove the policy and his hands down Mason's pants.

"I'm just going to go back and crash. Blow off my afternoon classes."

Tyler would have had something to say about blowing off classes. Mason would probably have thrown John's oral practice in his face. Drew just said, "Okay. But I'm going to walk you back to your dorm. I don't want to have to read about you passing out in the middle of the Podium on Facebook."

Chapter Twelve

Mason knocked on John's door, waited the three seconds of patience he managed to eke out and knocked again. To Mason's surprise, John looked relieved when he discovered Mason as the punch line to "Who's there?" Resignation covered his relief as he stepped aside to let Mason in.

"How did you find me? Lizzy?"

Mason shook his head. "She keeps your secrets well." There were two places to sit, the bed and a desk chair. Mason took the desk chair. Fun as a horizontal derailment might be, Mason wasn't leaving the room until he got an answer out of John.

"So how did you find me?" John avoided the bed too, leaning on the wall, arms crossed in a way that was puzzlingly familiar.

"They have these amazing things called computers nowadays. Anybody with a little determination can find out whatever he needs to know."

"Yay for the information age."

John wasn't making it easy, but what had Mason done to make John want to do anything to help a guy who either acted like a raving lunatic or a heartless asshole? Mason chewed on his lower lip and then he dropped everything at John's feet. Every hope and every fear, every bit of armor he'd managed to use to keep himself safe since he heard Alex's neck snap when they hit that tree.

Looking up, he said, "I need to know."

"I don't," John said, words clipped and somehow shorter than even their one syllables. "I never wanted to know any of this."

"Please."

John shut his eyes, squeezed them to slits. "Since I fell, I've been—they called it a visual perception distortion. All I know is I see things differently."

"You can see him?" Mason looked around and over his shoulder.

"No. And I didn't even get the message." John was watching him again.

"But you knew. You knew what he'd said to me."

"No. I didn't know. Someone gave me three messages and I passed them on to you."

Mason had to hang on to the chair to keep from jumping out of it, shaking John as if that would make the information run out faster. "Who? And three? I only got one."

"You got two. No three ways. And they're not just dreams."

Mason tightened his grip on the chair. "And the third one?"

"It was for me."

"Alex said something to you? What?" Was he jealous? Did Alex know, did he care that John was the first guy Mason wanted as more than something to help him jerk off? He remembered what Lizzy had said. Alex wouldn't want that, would he?

"It was for me," John repeated.

Much as Mason wanted to push, he had another line of questioning. "And who gave you the messages? You said you see things differently. Like ghosts or what?"

"I—I saw a psychic. She gave me the message."

"What?"

Mason would have sworn John wasn't one of those woo-woo types. But then Mason would have sworn he wouldn't ever be having a serious conversation with someone about a message from a ghost, either.

"How'd she know about me? You told her you fucked someone with a dead boyfriend?"

"I didn't go see her. She came to me. And, she said she had to tell me something from someone young, someone full of energy who made her smile."

That could have been anyone. Maybe it was all a crock of bull, and John had just figured on Alex as the only recently dead young guy he knew. "Did she ask you for money?"

"No."

"Did she give you a name?"

"No."

"Then how do you know the message was for me?"

John blushed, pink flooding his creamy skin, and for a second Mason's bigger head almost lost control of the conversation. How could the guy deliver blow jobs like that, hang around with Tyler Granger and still manage to blush like he'd never heard the word fuck in his life?

"She said that the message was for my first."

"Your first what—oh." Mason didn't think he'd ever been able to blush, but other parts of him sure felt an increased flow of blood. He'd never thought about how hot it would be to be someone's first anything. "So then we've got to talk to the psychic."

"I delivered my message. You can talk to the psychic."

"But you were part of the message. What if she won't talk to me without you? How am I even going to find her?" Mason turned on his best charm, his best little-boy-trying-for-an-extra-cookie, get-out-of-detention, please-Alex-baby, don't-be-mad-at-me look and poured it on John.

John's answer was a wicked grin that looked out of place on his smooth, innocent face. "You aren't going to like this."

"What?"

"She's a friend of Tyler's."

There must have been something left of his charm, because John called Tyler and never mentioned Mason as he got the number for Tyler's psychic friend.

"So when do we call her?"

John tried to hand off the number, but Mason grabbed his forearm before he could pull away. "What do you really want, John?" An emotion darted across John's face, something too quick for Mason to read, a ripple in a calm pond. "I mean, if you're like me, you want everything to go back to the way it was before the accident fucked everything up. But since neither of us can have that, what do you want now?"

John pulled away, but he wasn't trying hard and Mason just followed the motion and let it pull him to his feet. John's wrist locked around Mason's forearm too, but he wouldn't meet his gaze.

"You're looking pretty fucking spooked by all this shit," Mason said after they'd stood there in silence for a minute. "I know I am." He put his other hand on the back of John's neck, not trying to move him, just rubbing his thumb against the muscles at the base of his skull, muscles so tight they made Mason's own head ache with the tension. "What do you mean you see things differently? I'm not going to tell anyone else."

John relaxed a little, a tiny softening in the grip on Mason's arm, head turning into Mason's touch. It felt good to offer someone else the kind of comfort he couldn't seem to take. Not even from someone he loved as much as Lizzy.

Mason softened his voice. "Are you seeing ghosts? Is that kind of shit for real, because honest, after last night, I'm ready to believe anything."

"Not ghosts," John whispered.

Mason didn't say anything else.

"But it's still crazy," John finished.

"Last night I tried to get my dead boyfriend to talk to me on a computer. He spelled out your name. I'm not exactly in a position to judge from crazy."

John twisted free and took a few steps back. "Cover your face with your hands and think of something, something that gives you a strong feeling."

Mind reading? Mason could buy it. He covered his face and pictured John face-down, ass opening for Mason's fingers and tongue.

John laughed. "Yeah. You've got a dirty mind. That's not exactly a tough guess. Try something else."

John already knew about Alex, so Mason dug back in his memory for something long gone. That first report card in middle school, the neat perfection of a solid row of A's.

"Happy," John said. "And proud—no. Ashamed."

Because of course he'd shown it to his parents. His mother had started to praise him but his father had ripped it up. *Only sissy boys do that good in school. You a sissy boy?*

He lowered his hands and looked at John. The shame receded, but it left him feeling kind of sick. "You can read my mind?"

"No. I don't know exactly what you were thinking about, just the way it made you feel. It's... After I fell, I saw colors with sounds."

"Like—what do they call it—synthe—synesthesia?"

John's eyes widened.

Mason shrugged. "I've read about it. One of the guys who invented the web, the one that gave everyone the whole www, he has it. Couple other physicists and mathematicians."

"Maybe I've got a new major, then. But yeah. That was it at first, and then—" John swallowed hard, and Mason thought John was going to clam up. "I started seeing colors everywhere, but mostly around people's heads."

"Colors how?"

"They change a lot. Especially when people have strong feelings."

Mason thought about that. Maybe John was reading the temperature changes, like a mood ring. Energy couldn't be created or destroyed, so Alex was energy in a different form that some people could see. Just because Mason couldn't understand it right away didn't mean there wasn't a logic to it all.

"Do you have to concentrate to see it?"

"You really think I can do it?"

"Even without your demonstration. Why, are you going to turn around and say 'just kidding'?"

"No. But it is kind of—"

"Crazy?" Mason smiled.

"Hard to explain."

"What do you see now?"

John looked away. Mason couldn't imagine it was that bad. He was excited, like he'd just figured out how to hack his favorite game to make it do tricks the designers never saw coming. This could be something really amazing.

"It gives me a headache."

"Sorry. Maybe I should—" Stop thinking? "Can't you turn it off somehow?"

"I wish."

"I bet." Mason thought most people were annoying enough when they kept their feelings to themselves. Having the knowledge forced on him all the time would be enough to make him pass out. "Is there any time it's better?"

"Just worse." John tipped his head at him and Mason realized why some of his gestures looked familiar. Lizzy. John had been studying Lizzy, copying her mannerisms. He didn't remember the folded arms or the head tilting before. If John tried a single eyebrow raise, that would confirm it. But why? How could you go through life and not have your own way of talking to people?

The knock at the door was softer than Mason's had been. John rolled his eyes—that gesture seemed pretty universal— and went to answer it. Mason didn't recognize the guy at the door, but John did. And Mason didn't need to have a mood ring built in his brain to know that John wasn't happy with his new guest.

"Hi, Keith."

The other guy's voice was a harsh whisper, like Darth Vader with laryngitis. "I'm really sorry, John. You have to believe me. I thought they knew—or they should know. I mean—it's important and then they acted—"

"Keith." There was almost panic in John's voice. He started to push the guy out of the room. "Shut up. This time, please, shut up."

"Who's with you?" Keith peered around John.

Mason grinned, waved and flopped on the bed like he lived there, boots and all.

"Keith."

Why didn't John just tell the guy to fuck off and shove him the hell out the door? Mason would have added the threat of a beat down, but maybe people did things differently in John's home-schooled, moved-around-a-lot world.

John managed to get Keith out the door and into the hall. The dorm construction wasn't exactly soundproof, as Mason had learned freshman year, but it was enough to keep him from hearing the conversation. Or maybe John was whispering now too. And then John got loud. "What I want is to be left alone, for God's sake."

John came back into the room. His face was unreadable as he took in Mason stretched out on the neatly made bed.

"I'm surprised you didn't introduce me as your boyfriend to get rid of him. I could have taken off my pants and everything."

John managed a light smile. "I hear that doesn't take much of an incentive."

"So what'd he do? He know about your color thing?"

John made a face like someone had poured battery acid in his coffee—or been forced to drink the healthy shit Kai sometimes made and called "tea." "You're the only person I've told." John looked away. "I thought— You said I could trust you."

"You can. I don't exactly want it known that I'm trying to chat with my dead boyfriend either. I'm not interested in another counseling session with psych majors at university health services. So what did he do? Out you as a kinky queer to the Young Republicans or something?"

"No."

"He looks the type. Kind of buttoned down and repressed."

John smiled again. Mason liked it, wanted to keep making it happen. And he didn't have to ask himself when the last time was that he cared if he could make someone else smile. He bit his lip.

"C'mon. What could you possibly say that would freak me out?"

"Since it seems like confession time, I was an Olympic

diver. I hit my head on the platform. Keith saw it on TV, and he told all my other friends. It kind of pissed me off."

"Right. And then you went on to do a brilliant dive, wowed the judges and got a perfect score. Sorry. Saw *The Greg Louganis Story*. Saw the Olympics too. I never miss the swimming stuff. And trust me. I'd have remembered your hot ass."

"You believe that I can see colors around people's heads that tell me what they're feeling and you don't believe I won a gold medal in Olympic diving."

"Oh, and a gold medal too? Now I know you're fucking with me."

John was good. He could almost believe it. It went nicely with the whole moved-around, tutors-instead-of-high-school thing. Except, like Mason said, he watched the Olympics. Besides, the idea of Mason fucking an Olympic gold medalist was insane. That would be so far out of his league it wasn't even funny. Alex had been far enough out of Mason's league, but from the first time they hooked up, it had been too late to keep them from falling for each other. And then you couldn't tell that stubborn shit anything.

John started laughing, proof that he was screwing with Mason. John delivered everything with that quiet deliberate voice that he probably convinced a lot of people whatever he wanted them to believe. But an Olympic medal, not fucking likely.

John agreed to call the psychic, actually seemed kind of relieved about it by the time Mason managed to convince John to pick up his cell. After a second, Mason could tell John was on voice mail. As he delivered the message, he watched Mason's head, making him wish for a second he could see what John saw. He almost rolled an eye from the socket trying to look up at his own forehead.

"I don't know if you remember me, but I'm John, Tyler's friend. You gave me a couple messages from a spirit guide—"

Mason mouthed the words *Spirit guide?* with incredulity. People really talked like that?

John held a finger over his lips as if Mason had spoken aloud and went on with the message. "We—I—was hoping you could explain a couple more things for me. Uh—" He held his hand over the speaker and whispered, "Are we going to pay her?"

"Why don't you cash in your gold medal? Yeah, I can come up with some cash."

"We can pay you." John left a number that Mason instantly committed to memory, and flipped his phone shut.

Mason sprawled back on the bed and propped himself up on his elbows. John hadn't come near him since he'd told him what he could do, and Mason wanted John smiling again, not frowning with that little line popping up between his brows, so as much as Mason wanted to know what John saw over Mason's own head, he didn't ask.

John folded his arms, Lizzy-like, again. "So now what?"

"I thought you could read my mind. But I guess if you could, you'd already have your pants off."

John's hands went to his fly and then he stopped.

"Do you really have a boyfriend?" Mason asked.

"Would you care?"

"No, but you might."

"I don't." John peeled off his jeans.

"Care, or have a boyfriend?" Mason wriggled out of his own, aiming his sweatshirt for the other side of the room.

"Either. Are we going to talk or have sex?"

The hesitancy Mason had found hot that first time was gone, but Mason liked the new confidence. He peeled off his

167

briefs. "Talking's fine with me, sugar."

John just watched, like he was waiting for something in those colors only he could see. Mason bit his lip until he tasted blood to keep from asking if he could see Alex, even though he'd already said he didn't. The idea of Alex watching them filled his throat so full of bitter he couldn't breathe.

Mason sat up. "Wait a sec." He pulled the cord with Alex's ring over his head and tucked it into the pocket of his jeans. "Okay."

John moved closer but not close enough to touch. Mason had to reach out to pull him down onto the bed.

"You said I didn't show you everything. C'mon. Tell me. I owe you now."

"Confession time's over." John kissed him, a kiss that reminded Mason of what John's mouth could do with a cock in it, a kiss that was hot and wet and as slick as good sex itself. Mason slid his hand down and cupped John's ass, forcing their dicks to grind together so he could feel John's as it filled and tightened, jerking against his own.

He squeezed hard, pulling the skin wide around John's hole so he could feel the air on it, make him want a touch, a tongue, a cock to tease it open.

John bucked down against him, dick spilling a little spit of precome against Mason's, pulse of blood and a silky heat pushing him faster into need-it-now. He wet a finger in his mouth and slicked John's crease, coming back for more and more until he got the skin around his hole nice and wet.

"Now, c'mon. Tell me what you want."

"Just do it."

"Not until you tell me every one of those kinky fantasies you're blaming me for not showing you." He dipped his finger in, just the tip, just enough to make John fuck against him harder.

168

Mason gave him a little more and John tried to follow the finger with his ass even while keeping pressure on his dick. "Asshole."

"Yes it is." He felt John grin against his shoulder. "And I'm going to make it feel good if you tell me what I want to hear." He went into the first knuckle and then back out. "Spill."

"Want to be held down. Tied down so I can't even jerk myself off."

"God, yes." Mason slipped his finger in deep until John grunted.

"Let you—him do what he wants, can't close my legs, can't grab him, just let go—and—"

"I will. Swear to God, sugar. I'm gonna give you that." Mason rolled John onto his back and slid down, licking and kissing while working that finger in John's ass. "I'll make you beg to come. Beg to get just the lightest rub on your dick because you're going to need it. Need it so bad." He started with a wet kiss on the head of John's dick, kept his mouth tight and slipped that thick ridge over his lips and tongue.

"Better not. Break your. Promise. This time," John panted out.

Mason raised his head. "No way. You're not getting out of it either."

He could make a spreader bar. And they sold some other shit at Steel under the bar. He screwed his lips back around John's cock and forced that thick ridge over his tongue until it pushed against his throat, a spasm made him gasp and swallow around John's dick. It hurt, made his eyes water and made him feel like he was choking to death, but every time he took John that little bit extra, the moan and the way John's body spasmed was enough to make him forget how much it hurt.

Because John was stroking his head and whispering "please". John, sexy and innocent, wrapped up in that aloof

K.A. Mitchell

"don't care" package, was anything but cool and indifferent as he urged Mason to *never stop, God never stop.*

Mason felt the gland under his finger and pressed up and used his thumb under John's balls to press down, and John sobbed like he'd never come before in his life.

"Oh, fuck, goddammit, why." John's fists hit the bed next to his hips, thudding again and again, and if Mason blacked out first he wasn't stopping. He gave up on trying to swallow, on everything but relaxing his throat enough to let John get deeper and deeper.

John's dick pulsed against Mason's tongue, and he knew John was about to unload. A second of gut-clenching panic as Mason remembered his chewed-on lip, but he was in this too far to stop now. One deep inhale through his nose, and he got down as far as he could, then John's legs shook like he'd buck Mason off before he started pouring come so far back in Mason's throat he couldn't taste the bitter, just the heat, the slippery weight of it stealing breath until he choked again.

He wiped his face on John's thigh, buried the come and tears and spit and sweat in the dark hair. John jerked and made a sound like it hurt as Mason eased his finger out. What had he said, no one had been in him but Mason? But he wasn't running with Tyler Granger and not fucking every shiny new guy he saw. So— "Sore?" he asked aloud.

"A little." John reached down and cupped his cheek. "Could have pulled off, you know."

"That's not what I remember you saying."

"It's okay, though. You can fuck me if you want."

Not if he was sore. Not if he hadn't been doing it a lot. "You got some lube? I'll just go right here." He rubbed the mess he'd made on John's thigh.

John handed back a pump bottle and yeah, that size and brand, it wasn't for light use. Mason lubed his dick and climbed

170

up behind John. "On your side, cross your legs."

John followed directions just as quick as he had that first night, creating a nice tight space between his thighs. Mason worked his cock in until the tip of his dick poked John's balls, while the base hit John's asshole with every stroke. And his thighs, smooth and slick and then the whisper of hair as he got farther, the tug on the skin of his dick. Mason wrapped one arm around John's shoulders and one over his thighs and pressed down. "Tighter, sugar."

John locked his legs like a vise and it hurt damned good. Every time Mason pushed forward under John's balls and against his ass, dragged on the thin skin between, John let out a surprised grunt. And when Mason moved faster, John made a sound like he was coming again. Mason rode John's body, arms keeping every inch of them together, tongue tasting the sweat on the back of John's neck. A couple more strokes and John made another sweet gasp and shuddered when the first shot of come hit his balls. Mason gave into the long hot spasms as release took him hard and fast, then flopped back against the cold wall.

"Next time, s'gonna be in you. Pound you forever."

John rolled face-down on the bed with his arms blocking his face, blocking his view of...what?

"Did you see something?" Mason asked.

"I told you I can't see Alex."

"I remember." It wasn't as if Mason wanted Alex to be here. Especially not when he had someone's dick down his throat. Mason lowered his chest onto John's back, grabbing one of his hands and trying to entwine their fingers. John let Mason take his hand but didn't squeeze back, just left it there.

"You all right?"

"Fine."

"What's it like?" Mason knew John would know what he

171

meant. What was it like to see people as walking mood rings?

"It sucks."

"And not in the way you like it, huh?"

No laughter from the still form underneath Mason, only John rolling to dump Mason onto the mattress before climbing out of bed. Tall frame, lean muscles on display as John crossed the room, picked up Mason's pants and tossed them at him.

"Here's your hat, what's your hurry?" Mason asked as he grabbed the pants in midair. Habit had him pulling the cord holding Alex's ring out of his jeans pocket. The ring didn't make him miss Alex any less, but it felt weird not to have it. "You gonna let me know if your psychic calls back?"

"Sure. What's that worth? I get to fuck your ass?"

"Where the hell did that come from?"

John blinked and then shrugged.

"Yeah, whatever." Mason yanked the cord over his head. "Got a towel or do I get to wear a load home?"

John opened the closet and threw a towel at Mason. After scrubbing at his belly, crotch and thighs, Mason started dressing. "So you'll call me?"

Without putting on a stitch, John picked up his phone and sat on the vacated bed, legs spread wide, like he wanted Mason to get a good, long look at that half-hard cock, the head still shiny wet. "What's your number?"

Mason spat it out, but before John had finished tapping, the phone went off. John turned away before answering with a brief exchange of greetings and identities. There wasn't much for Mason to go on from this side of the conversation. He angled himself to watch John's face.

"No." And then a pause and a big blush before, "Yeah...okay," and then a resigned "Yeah." A longer pause. "Where's that?" He covered the phone and turned to Mason.

"Can you get a car? At about seven tonight?"

"Sure." Lizzy could drive them. Except it was Monday and Lizzy had a class she couldn't miss. Lizzy would lend him the car if he dropped her off, but then he'd have to drive it.

John hung up.

"You don't drive?" Mason clung to a thin thread of hope.

"I can't. I told you." John pointed at his head.

Mason had driven since the accident, driven himself to job sites while working for his uncle this past summer, but not with anyone in the passenger seat. Not since Alex. And he'd sworn he was never doing that again. Never putting someone else's life on the line like that. Maybe they could take a bus. Maybe they could get a cab. Mason stalled a little. "Do you want to get dinner before or something?"

"What, like a date?" John laid disgust as thick as tar on the last word.

"Okay. Enough. What the fuck is your problem?"

"I don't have a problem."

"Of the two of us, which one is acting like an asshole?"

"Yeah, well, I've always been a quick learner."

Maybe Mason deserved that. "Fine." He headed for the door. Or maybe he didn't. "Listen, one of the reasons I don't date girls, I mean aside from them having a pussy instead of a cock, is this kind of head-game shit. I've seen Kai go nuts with it. So stop throwing a fucking tantrum and tell me what the hell is pissing you off."

"And you think I'm pissed because I won't have dinner with you?"

"I get that things kind of suck for you with what you've got going on in your head, but maybe I can help you."

"Well, we both know what that's about."

"You think you know."

173

"Are you going to tell me you don't want to help me, spend time with me because you think Alex is going to show up?"

"I'm not saying I don't want to talk to him. But I like spending time with you too. And not just because you have a great cock."

"Instead of a pussy?" For a microsecond, John's grin flashed, and then it was gone. Maybe Mason had imagined it.

"Right. So where is this place?"

"Off Sand Creek, in Colonie."

"I'll pick you up around quarter of."

Chapter Thirteen

John recognized Lizzy's old magenta Ford Fiesta when Mason pulled it into the fire lane in front of State Quad. John didn't know why he'd assumed Mason would have his own car, other than the fact that all the people John had met who lived off campus had cars—even if, in Tyler's case, the car didn't always work. Maybe it had been Mason's car in the accident, but then wasn't that what people had insurance for?

Mason barely acknowledged John when he slid into the passenger seat, and guilt tickled John's stomach. He had been rude, but no ruder than Mason usually was. Remembering why they were there took care of the guilt. John hadn't asked for any of this.

"You were right this afternoon," he said.

"About you having a great cock?" A tiny smile curved Mason's lips, but he didn't glance over as the car rolled slowly down the asphalt toward the campus perimeter road, and his grip on the steering wheel remained bone-white. They cleared the last row of parked cars, and despite the lack of oncoming traffic, stopped for a long time before swinging left. John was used to Tyler lurching through traffic like he was daring John to grab the panic handle over the passenger door.

"That too," John agreed, eyes tracking the dark blue growl of the slow-moving van in front of them. "But you were right about the things I see being a lot to deal with right now. And I don't want a lot of extra crap in my life. But I want—I like having sex with you. So after we talk to Rachel, can we just do that, the sex?"

"As long as you didn't just call me extra crap in your life, yeah, we can do that."

John had kind of called him that. He twisted his lips. "So what would you call that, then?" And how often would they be doing it? Maybe tonight?

"Benefits, no friends? Fuck buddies, I guess. Does that include the kinky stuff?"

"It could." John leaned back against the seat.

The highway had four lanes and a fifty-five-mile-an-hour speed limit, but every time John looked over, the arrow on the speedometer hovered between forty-five and fifty. "You don't have to worry about me getting sick. It's no worse in a car than walking. Sometimes it's even better."

Mason's voice was thin, strain blanching the rich color from it. "I'm not worried about you getting sick."

They slowed a long way before the red light. "Then—" The realization might as well have been a cartoon light bulb, the answer so glaringly obvious it hit John like a spotlight. He stared hard at Mason's colors, strong even in the dark. Red and white, both dull and flat, but trembling slightly. Fear. "Is this the first time you've driven since the accident?"

"No." The crystals shook even more tightly, matching the grip Mason had on the fur-covered steering wheel.

John was pretty sure Mason was telling the truth, but something was making Mason drive like he kept expecting the road to suddenly drop away from underneath them. When they sat again at a stop sign, Mason looking left and right and left for long moments, John wondered if he would act like this if he had to climb up a dive platform. Except John couldn't. Couldn't even get ten feet up before the world went gray, then black and he slid back to the deck. Mason didn't have a brain injury, he could still drive. If he'd relax, he might even enjoy it.

The shaking crystals slowed, then warmed, red stronger and brighter than the white. Mason's shoulders dropped away from his ears, and his hands shifted on the wheel as he steered them down a side street. He turned his head and caught John looking at him.

"What do you see now? And I don't mean Alex."

"You look like you feel better."

"I don't think it takes whatever you see to tell that, but yeah. I do. Thanks."

"I didn't do anything." But a shock raced through John, muscles on alert, everything braced like his name and dive had just been announced. What if by thinking about Mason relaxing, John had made it happen? The idea that he could change what people felt was crazy, but was it any crazier than seeing the crystals in the first place? He tried to make the kaleidoscope on Mason look happy, and Mason started to smile. John swallowed.

So much for thinking things couldn't get worse. Maybe he should move to an uninhabited island somewhere.

"We're here."

Even though John remembered Rachel looking pretty mom-like and normal, he still expected something far more dramatic from the room she called her office. It was just a small room with a separate entrance. Other than a few plants, it held only normal-looking chairs and a table. No beads dangled, or incense smoking in a bowl or glow-in-the-dark stars gleaming on the ceiling.

At first, caution made John squint when he looked at her, but the bright mirrors he remembered were muted. She greeted Mason like she had John when Tyler introduced them, a friendly smile and a repetition of his name. Nothing dramatic,

177

not even a handshake. Her eyes didn't roll back into her head, her lips didn't begin passing on messages from the dead. John let out the breath he was holding. Until she spoke.

"Mason, would you mind if I ask John to help me carry in some coffees for us?"

The excuse to get John alone was obvious, but Mason was polite, turning on the charm John was beginning to find as familiar as it already was good at distracting him from why he shouldn't be going along with Mason.

"Not at all, ma'am."

John followed her through a door to the kitchen.

She took out a box of cookies and started pouring coffee into mugs.

"None for me, thanks," John said quickly.

"I like some caffeine when I work. Helps me focus," Rachel explained.

The guy at the fair had said the same thing, about caffeine revving up his reading. John couldn't imagine what he'd see revved up. That night with Mason after the Brewed Awakening shake had been more than enough of a warning.

"Does your friend take cream and sugar?" Rachel put the glass carafe back into the coffee maker and opened the fridge.

"Both, I think."

"He's adorable." She handed him a plate to put cookies on.

Adorable? John wondered how Mason would like being called that. He made John blush, made him squirm, but mostly Mason made John wish a lot of things were different, and not just that he saw colors that didn't really exist. He was running out of names for them. He'd need to carry around a big box of crayons to start comparing them.

Rachel stirred a generous amount of sugar and cream into both mugs but didn't say anything else. When she'd returned the creamer to the fridge and just leaned on it, waiting, John spoke. "I thought you wanted to talk to me."

"Actually I thought you would have questions for me."

Questions. More like wishes. *Can you stop it? Can we just make it go away?* "What's happening to me?"

"I don't know."

John blinked hard, lips tight against a sigh of frustration.

"I wish I had a better answer for you. I can *feel* you looking at me, but not why. It's possible that anything we talk about will only give you more questions. But before we get started, I thought there might be something you didn't want me to mention in front of your friend."

John stared at her mirrors that got brighter as he watched. "When I look at people, I see—I guess they're like auras? Only to me everyone ever has just one color, and it shows me how they feel. But with him, there are two colors, and I don't know if I want him to know it."

"I don't think we have a choice. If an X-ray showed you had a broken bone, you'd need to be told, right?"

John thought of the incomprehensible shadows and colors on the brain pictures he'd been shown in the hospital. "Yeah, but this doesn't show up on a CAT scan." He had no idea exactly what all of those pictures had meant, but he'd have remembered if one of those doctors had said *And here's the part that means you'll become a psychic freak for the rest of your life.*

"It doesn't show up like that, no. But this is about him more than it's about you. That's something to keep in mind."

"I guess."

"Why don't we pool information and see if we can't figure out what's going on. If you want, I can get you someone else's number, someone who does work with auras."

"No." John liked Rachel. And the thought of having to

explain this again to another stranger was more nauseating than all the vertigo he'd had in the past month. "Have you heard from him again, Alex—the spirit, I mean?"

"No. Not at all. And I've done readings since. With you two here, things might go differently, but don't expect easy answers."

Why should anything about this new life be easy? And he'd thought training twelve hours a day was hard.

Mason was sitting at the table, drawing something on the tablecloth with his fingernail, but when they came in, he jumped up and took John's water and the plate of cookies from Rachel.

When they were all sitting down, Mason took a long sip of coffee. "Hot and sweet, the way I like it. Did John tell you that?" Mason's smile flirted with both of them.

"Are you always like this?" Rachel smiled back.

"Pretty much, ma'am."

"You can't give me that bad-boy charm and call me, ma'am. You make me feel—"

"Cougarish?"

This time Mason's smile made John's hand clench into a fist in his lap. It was either that or use it to push his dick down.

"You're worse than Tyler." The coffee mug didn't hide Rachel's grin.

"I take that as a great compliment, Rachel."

"You know him then?" Rachel gave a little laugh.

"Too well." Mason spoke with distinct regret.

There was nothing little about Rachel's laugh that time. "He's always been hell on wheels."

"If you've known him that long, you have to promise to give me some inside information. Something that'll set him back a little next time we face off."

"We'll see."

John knew Mason would get his inside information. Rachel was hooked. Everyone liked Mason. John included. Though he'd meant it when he said he didn't need extra crap in his life. Particularly not spending a lot of time with someone who wished he was with someone else.

Rachel turned to a shelf behind her and took out a blue silk-wrapped bundle. "Why don't you tell me something about Alex while you shuffle these." She took the oversized card deck out of the silk and passed it to Mason.

After seeing the deck dwarf Rachel's hands, Mason's fingers were long and confident as he shuffled the cards. "Alex was the best thing that ever happened to me."

It wasn't as if John didn't already know that. Know how perfect Alex had been. He just wished he could make himself understand that being jealous of a dead person was stupid, but it was harder when he heard it this time, in Mason's rich dark purple voice that rubbed John's skin like soft, warm fur. The cards had their own sounds, sparks of silver and whispers of gold as they shifted in Mason's hands. Maybe if John could just concentrate on that, on the perfectly normal nameable, documentable synesthesia, he could ignore everything else.

"Alex came out when he was twelve," Mason went on. "He said his parents were a little freaked but came around fast. He was already so popular in school, it just became another thing that made him cool. Alex could make gay cool in high school." Mason shook his head. "He led a charmed life until I drove him into that tree."

The red and white exploded, a laser burst of light in John's watering eyes. He blinked and looked away. A long round of silence followed. John expected Rachel to ask some Oprah kind of questions, but one of the things he was learning was that in real life, in addition to not thinking that the Olympics were the most important thing ever, real people didn't act at all like they

181

did on TV or in movies.

"I don't think he's mad about that, though," Mason said into that silence.

John saw what Rachel was doing. By not asking questions, she was getting more of Mason's thoughts. All she did was tell Mason to fan the cards out face-down on the table and select one at a time.

The first one was kind of pretty, a woman draped with flowers petting a tame lion. Rachel nodded and asked Mason to pull another card. He turned it over to show a family dancing under a rainbow made out of cups. John didn't need to read the Tarot to see how perfect things had been for Alex and Mason. And a five-year-old could figure out the next one, which was labeled "The Lovers" and had naked people on it.

"We were really close. Not just sex." Mason tapped the naked people card. "It was awesome, but it wasn't how we stayed close. We—he talked a lot. About everything."

The next card had a little boy and girl in a garden made up of cups full of flowers. John wondered if the next one would have puppies on it. He hadn't touched the cookies, but he felt as sick as if he'd eaten the entire plate by himself.

"There was some weird stuff once. We had tickets to something, a concert down at the arena. When we were about to go in, we could only find one ticket, but we'd had them both in the car. So I went out to get the ticket and Alex went in."

John really couldn't see a point to this story, but it turned the colors sharp and angry.

Mason went on. "I was halfway to the car when I got a text from Alex saying he'd found the ticket in his coat, but they wouldn't let him back out to give it to me or even let him hand it over the turnstile. I had been backstage enough with Alex at a couple of places and I knew my way around. I found a stage door, picked up a case and blended in with the stagehands, then walked right by security and found the way to our seats.

"The thing is, when we talked about it later, Alex swore he was the one who snuck through to meet me. He remembers the shape of the case, the red straps on it. I swear I can remember backstage. Sometimes I can remember sending the text from the inside, but that could be me getting it. I remember all that, but not the concert. Weird, right?"

The hard lines of red and white blurred to a flow of pink.

Rachel smiled. "Believe me. I've heard stranger things."

"I guess so."

Rachel swept the deck into a pile but left the cards Mason had pulled face up on the table, her eyes straying to them from time to time. "John, why don't you tell Mason what you're seeing."

"It feels like we're seeing a marriage counselor," Mason muttered.

John thought it was more like Dr. Phil. "How would you know?"

Mason leaned close. His face was serious but his voice was teasing. "Tell you later, huh?"

"Okay." John looked down and then realized Rachel and Mason were waiting for him to speak. He took a deep breath. He wanted to say okay again, anything to not tell Mason this, but Rachel was right. Mason needed to know, wanted it badly enough to drive here. You couldn't be a coward and do a handstand dive off a thirty-five-foot-tall platform. John could do this.

"You know how I told you I see these colors around people that tell me what they're feeling? Even if they're hiding it? It's just one color. Lizzy's is a golden yellow. Carrie's is green. Kai's pink."

"Oh man, I cannot wait to tell him that."

"Please don't."

"It's okay, I won't. So what's mine?"

"I think yours is red. But you're the only one who has two colors. Red and a white."

Mason might get by a lot on charm, but John already knew he wasn't stupid. "You mean Alex?" He looked at Rachel. "Alex is haunting me?" He glared back at John, making him want to flinch away from the sharp pressure of crystals shattering and reforming. "Why the hell didn't you tell me? That's why you wouldn't look at me today? He's here, all the time?"

"I don't know. Sometimes, like when we—" John felt the blush hit his cheeks but he couldn't do anything to stop it. No one needed to read auras to read him. God, why did they have to do this in front of someone else? Someone his mom's age. "—you know. It goes away. The white. It gets hard to see. But when you touch that..." he pointed to Alex's ring, "...it gets brighter."

"I did this?" Mason turned to Rachel again who might as well have donned a black and white shirt to officiate the meet. "Did I trap him here?" He shut his eyes. "Baby, I'm so sorry."

The white exploded, splintered into John's eyes, his head. He put his hands up to protect himself, but flesh did nothing to keep it out. The shards kept digging into the soft places inside, hammering away until they drove him down, hunched in his chair with his head under his hands.

He could hear them, see their voices. The sharp dark anxiety in Mason's repetition of John's name, the cool wet green flow of Rachel trying to find him, and then her telling Mason to leave the room and his slow, grudging acceptance.

The shower of crystal needles stopped, though whether it was because Mason had taken Alex with him or because somehow Rachel's mirrors were all around him he had no idea, but she had her hands on top of his and was calling his name.

He lifted his head to her reassuring smile.

"I guess we're on the right track then," Rachel said.

Mason paced in the kitchen. *Alex, baby, please. Don't hurt him. I didn't mean to trap you. I swear, I'll fix it. But you're not like this. I know you. You would never hurt someone like that.* He repeated his pleas aloud and slammed his lips shut, straining to hear what might be going on in the other room. He thought he'd fucked up before. Now he'd done worse than kill Alex, he'd damned him to this...nothing. And then he'd gotten John hurt. Or worse. What was going on in there?

His chest ached, a ten-month-and-three-and-a-half-week-old ache, where the steering wheel had slammed into him, a crushing paralysis of fear. He had to do something. But anything he did could make it worse. He yanked the cord over his neck and squeezed it in his hand. "Please don't hurt him, and I can fix it." After carefully placing the ring on the counter farthest away, he knocked on the door.

"He's all right," Rachel called. "Just give us another minute."

A minute to what? Pour John's brains back into his head? Mason's fist was clenched to pound on the door. What good would that do? His chest tightened again and he rubbed the spot where two ribs had cracked, close to the sternum, but not on the side of his heart. Nothing that didn't heal. Nothing like Alex's snapped neck.

It felt a hell of a lot longer than a minute before Rachel called him in.

"You okay, John?" Mason was afraid John wouldn't look at him, but John turned to face him, gaze steady and unafraid.

"Yeah, it's better now. Rachel thinks maybe Alex got excited and tried to connect." John might not have been scared, but he looked beat to hell.

"So I guess we should head out. Um, what do we owe you, Rachel?"

"This is on the house, so to speak." Her eyes made a skyward arc. "I helped put things in motion. And I want you to call me and let me know how you're doing. Especially if anything like that happens again."

"We will, be damned sure about that." Mason was man enough to admit when he was in over his head, and he hadn't been able to touch solid ground since John gave him that message—maybe for longer.

"Thank you, Rachel."

"Are you sure you won't take some cookies, John? Any kind of work depletes your energy."

"No thanks." John wrinkled his nose. "I'm still feeling kind of sick."

"Okay. You boys be careful. And keep an eye on Tyler for me. He's headed for a rude awakening."

"I'll be looking forward to that." Mason ducked back into the kitchen for Alex's ring and tucked it in his pocket before they left.

John didn't say anything as Mason backed them slowly out of Rachel's driveway. Couldn't blame him. It had been a serious mindfuck of an evening. And it sure as hell wasn't going to finish up with the kind of fuck Mason had been hoping for.

One thing he had to do right away, though, and he hoped John didn't know enough local geography to figure it out until they got there. Barely resisting the urge to pat the ring he could feel weighting his left front pocket, Mason drove them farther out into the suburbs, heading for Holy Redeemer Cemetery.

Even when they got on the Northway, John didn't say anything and the silence was starting to make Mason even more jumpy. "So what did she say?"

"She thinks I can help you." John's voice was soft but flat. He was always in control, but right then he sounded like every emotion he'd ever felt had been sucked away.

"How?"

"That because I can see it, I can somehow untangle you. Your auras, she called them."

"But it hurt you." *Alex hurt you*, but Mason couldn't quite get himself to say that out loud.

"Yeah, it did. Still does, a little."

Mason wasn't letting much take his eyes from the road as he scanned for deer coming out of the dark, but his peripheral vision still picked up John rubbing his eyes.

An exit took them to a state road. Worse and worse in the dark. Mason might be babbling, but it was better than the silence. "You remind me of Lizzy like that. She gets migraines."

"I got them too, after I fell."

"Off the diving platform, right?" Mason teased.

"Whatever."

"Maybe you should have had some caffeine, she says that helps."

John made a disgusted sound.

"Worst one she got was after a Chinese food binge. She blamed the MSG."

"What?"

"Monosodium glutamate. It's a sodium, like salt, a naturally occurring amino-acid in crystalline form used as a—"

"I know what it is. What does it have to do with headaches?"

"Lizzy says it's a migraine trigger. Something about latching onto neurotransmitters. She did a paper on it for statistics."

"And caffeine helps her, makes the headache better."

"Yeah."

An intersection brought them to a little patch of strip malls. John leaned forward. "Pull in there." He pointed at a Stewarts convenience store. "Please," he added, but Mason was already signaling.

"You need aspirin or something?"

"No." John hopped out of the car before Mason had put it in park. "I'll be right back."

Through the plate-glass windows, Mason could see him cruise the aisles, examining packages and filling his arms. Maybe he had the munchies. It's not like Mason was in a hurry to get where they were going. It had to be done. Tonight.

And it was going to be final.

He'd lived through the sound of that ritual clod of dirt hitting Alex's coffin, even though he'd had to go to the funeral in a wheelchair. He could make it through this.

Just as Mason was getting an itch for a pint of Heavenly Hash ice cream, John came out with a bag stuffed full of crap. Just from a glance, Mason could see Ho Hos, mesquite barbeque chips, and Cool Ranch Doritos.

"If you were hungry, we could have stopped somewhere and got a burger."

"This is fine." John tore into a bag of Cheetos and stuffed a few fat curls into his mouth. He didn't offer to share, and Mason backed out of the lot.

By the time they were on the road to the cemetery, John had finished off the bag of Cheetos and washed them down with a caffeine-free Diet Coke, which seemed oddly health conscious for a guy who had just cleaned out Stewart's snack rack. He cleaned the orange dust from his fingers with strokes of his tongue, then sucked the last bits off with loud smacks that shouldn't have made Mason's dick come alive, not here, not now. But Mason's dick had always had a conscience-free head.

John's smile was oddly reminiscent of someone stoned out of his mind, and Mason wondered exactly what John had been up to with Rachel in the kitchen. Maybe she had to get high to work her psychic mojo. He ripped open the bag of Doritos and crunched away, apparently oblivious to the fact that Mason had stopped the car next to the fence with the elegantly lettered sign naming the neat shadowed rows beyond as the Most Holy Redeemer Cemetery.

Mason turned off the engine and pocketed the keys. "I'm going to try something."

"Bury his ring?" John said around his crunching.

"Did you read my mind?" Again, Mason found himself trying to see the top of his own head.

"No. Just guessed." John waved at the sign with the bag.

Mason had expected an argument or a complaint about wasting John's time, anything but him munching away as complacently as a cow in a pasture. "All right. So I'll be back in a little bit."

"Okay."

It was almost nine, and the cemetery gates had long since been closed, but even the gothic spikes on the fence weren't a deterrent to a kid who'd grown up in a Dunkirk trailer park. Mason tossed his jacket over the spikes and swung himself over the four-and-a-half-foot-tall fence. He wished he could say he had a hard time finding Alex's grave because that would give him a few more minutes to stall, but he'd seen it awake and in dreams way too many times for that. Go two rows behind the mausoleum guarded by St. Michael wielding a sword, turn left under the thick hemlock branches. There were fresh flowers in front of the small stone, and a bird feeder had been erected beside it. Alex would have liked that. His older sister probably thought of it. The flowers would be from his grandmother, and that little toy car from his baby brother.

"Hey, baby." Mason crouched down, then knelt. "Look who's on his knees now." Through a throat tight as a fist, he squeezed out, "Miss you." He'd never felt better here, just worse. Better was in the dreams when he could be with Alex, except maybe that was the problem. "I'm so sorry if I did something and kept you here. I know how much you wanted to talk to God. You had all those questions for him."

He started scraping a spot in the sod, tearing through first with his finger, then with the keys. "The computer's coming out great. Lizzy did an amazing job. You'd love it. And I know she'd want me to say hi for her." He was really stalling now. He wiped away a little snot with his sleeve. Not crying really, just not completely dry-eyed. And it was damp out. "So why I came was this." He dug out Alex's ring and untied it from the cord. "I gave it to you, and I guess it was pretty dickish to take it back. If that started this, I'm really sorry." He carefully put the silver band in the hole he had made and covered it back up. "So you keep yours, and I'll keep mine. I'll always wear it, babe. Never gonna forget you. But—" He twisted and pulled and finally yanked the ring off his left hand and jammed it onto the ring finger of his right. It burned there, awkward and out of place. "I know I can't keep you here. Just being a selfish jerk as usual."

He patted the chunk of sod back into place. "I know you're not jealous, we talked about it, about how we'd never want the other to stop living if—we just thought it would happen a whole lot later, but—please. Don't hurt John anymore, okay? Even if this doesn't fix it, he's not the one who screwed up somehow, I did." He wiped his eye. "So please. Don't do that again. Fucking scared the piss out of me." Mason's fingers twisted in the grass. "God, I suck at this. In the car, you know, I just wanted to say goodbye. Just say I love you, but you were already gone and that pissed me off so much." He made himself let go of the grass over Alex's grave and carefully brushed his hands clean. He didn't want to take anything with him this time. "So if you can hear me, goodbye. I love you. And I'm so fucking sorry."

He got up and forced himself to walk away without looking back.

He made it as far as the other side of the mausoleum before he had to stop and lean on Michael's robe to catch his breath. His face was wet, but he wasn't crying. He looked up and blinked as rain spit at him, light at first, then soaking. It felt good until he remembered he'd have to try to drive home in it. Drive John home in it. His foot slipped the first time he tried to swing over the fence, hung him up, sleeve twisted around a spike. Then there were hands on him, lifting him, easing the pressure of the spikes on his ribs and chest.

John eased Mason down to the ground then freed his jacket and handed it to him.

"Thanks."

John didn't say anything, just wiped the rain off his face and got back into the car.

Mason turned the key and flipped on the interior lights. "So?"

John looked closely at him and smiled, a blissed-out, giddy smile. He couldn't have looked happier if he was getting his dick sucked. "Nope. Don't see it." John sighed.

Mason turned his head. "Are you sure?"

John moved his head more slowly. "Yes. I don't see anything."

Could it be that easy? John looked too relaxed and happy to be making shit up. Alex was gone. He'd always been gone, but Mason hadn't been ready to accept it. The realization should have cut fresh and sharp, but unlike the last two times he'd stared at the cemetery gates in a rearview mirror, all Mason felt was relief. He'd fixed it. Alex was at peace; John was safe.

John's food-to-mouth speed had slowed, but he reached back into his Stewarts bag for a Ho Ho. After he'd peeled back the plastic, he offered one of the chocolate cake rolls to Mason by pressing it against his lips until they parted for a mouthful of cake and creamy filling.

"Thanks," he said through the gooey mass stuck to the roof of his mouth. He couldn't resist sneaking a glance over to watch John put the rest of that chocolate tube in his mouth. A sweet rush that had nothing to do with processed snack food pumped through Mason's bloodstream. *No, thank you,* Mason's dick seemed to say.

Was it wrong to want this now with Alex's grave dirt under his nails? Was it any different than any time he'd wanted to fuck since he'd lost Alex? Yes, because it wasn't just wanting to fuck. It was wanting John. Wanting to give John what he kept asking for, tie him down and make him shake and fall apart begging for Mason's cock in him. Take everything John was offering, be there at the beginning, watch him learn everything you could do with two bodies working together to get to the perfect moment of release.

Mason had never cared about how many lovers Alex had had before they got together. There wasn't anything new about the act itself with Alex. Alex had taught him what the feelings were that went with it. What it was like when you actually gave a shit about who was looking up at you with his mouth around your dick.

Wrong or not, he couldn't seem to get his head—either head—to think of anything else as he drove back to the city.

"So where are we going now?" John's voice sounded thick, but maybe that was because of his mouthful of chocolate and icing.

"Did you have any plans?"

"Nope."

Mason uncurled a hand from the steering wheel and placed it on John's thigh. A light touch was all he would risk, but it was enough to feel the jump of muscles, the electric connection between them. "What about now?" He put his hand back on the wheel.

"Maybe."

Chapter Fourteen

John recognized Mason's neighborhood as they got closer. He'd been hoping Mason would want to have sex, but now with the contents of a whole bag of snacks distending John's stomach, he wasn't so sure he wanted to. He glanced over and then remembered that he couldn't see what Mason was feeling. The shimmer of color had begun to dim somewhere near the bottom of the bag of Cheetos. They should come with a special offer emblazoned on the package. *Now With Special Anti-Aura Glasses, Free Inside.*

The MSG on his neurotransmitters—if that's what had done it instead of one of the other chemical additives—couldn't block the vertigo being stirred up with sudden motion or the synesthesia of sounds and colors, but that didn't matter. Mason's red and white crystals had faded into a shadow, the faintest hint of something above the edge of his hair. John couldn't wait to see if everyone else's colors had turned off. This was the best thing that had happened since he fell off the platform. Even if he couldn't find MSG in a pill form, he'd eat Cheetos until they needed a forklift to get him out of a chair if it meant he didn't have to see what everyone was feeling all the time.

Mason pulled Lizzy's car onto the parallel strip of sidewalk that passed for a driveway and turned it off. He twisted in his seat to face him and pointed at his hair. "Still no...?"

"Nothing." John wasn't lying. Exactly. Mason wouldn't have been able to tell. John only blushed when he talked about sex, and he had plenty of practice telling interviewers that he didn't have time for a relationship because he wanted to focus on diving.

Still, it wasn't totally a lie. There was no white around Mason's head. Or red. Mason just hadn't figured out why John was suddenly a snack-food junkie, and John had no plans to tell him either.

Mason shifted back around and looked through the windshield. Everything was wet, light bouncing in that way that gave everyone a chance to have double vision, but it wasn't raining anymore.

Mason pocketed the keys. "I feel like getting some coffee. You mind taking a walk?"

"No." John was so relieved to get a piece of reality back, he wouldn't have minded a ten-mile hike. Besides, he wanted to see some other people, confirm that their colors were gone too. And it would give him a chance to settle his stomach, though he stuffed a bag of flavored chips in his jacket pocket just in case before popping open the door.

The world tipped in that familiar way as his brain dealt with the air-pressure change, but this he could live with. The cane, the not-diving again, he'd put up with that if he didn't have to take the colors. Mason waited patiently by the back of the car and then they walked out to the shiny street.

After a few blocks, Mason turned south on Ontario to find a darkened Brewed Awakening. "I forgot they closed early on Mondays," Mason said.

"It's all right."

"Maybe for people who already pigged out, but for people still hungry and thirsty, Dunkin' Donuts is a poor substitute—if they're even open."

K.A. Mitchell

The wind blew against them as they walked back up Madison, and John wondered why this had seemed like a good idea. There wasn't anyone else walking around the Pine Hills neighborhood at ten thirty on a cold rainy night, so he hadn't even gotten to test his theory about the MSG.

"You said you'd tell me about the marriage-counseling thing you mentioned back at Rachel's. Did you and Alex go to one?"

"No. That was with my folks. When I was in middle school, there was this time when we had to go to court-ordered family counseling."

"Why?"

"I got into some trouble. At school." Mason shrugged and looked away.

If it weren't for the MSG, John would have figured out what Mason wasn't saying, at least what he wouldn't let John read on his face. The fact that John was actually looking for it surprised him, and then it pissed him off.

"I thought maybe there was stuff you weren't saying about Alex."

"No." Mason shook his head. "We didn't fight like that. Not like my folks."

John didn't want to be disappointed, but he was. This was why he'd said he just wanted to have sex. So that he didn't have to keep remembering that he was competing with Mr. Perfect, who was dead and unlikely to do anything to lose that title in the future. Mr. Perfect certainly wasn't going to fall into the pool or fail economics because the acronyms and numbers kept jumping around, or say something incredibly stupid because he'd never been around real people all that much.

The rain hit again when they were still blocks away. Just a few drops, then a flood, coming at them sideways, soaking through jacket and jeans in minutes. The rain was so cold John couldn't believe there wasn't ice in it, and he looked at Mason's head, wondering if it was Alex again. But the rain was striking everything, including the few other people making a run for the glow of the twenty-four-hour grocery store up ahead.

"Can you run?" Mason asked.

"I can try."

John took off next to Mason, outdistancing him for the first hundred feet, but then a car broke the reflected light in one of the huge puddles in the parking lot. The ground heaved under him. John tried to put his cane down for balance, but it was tucked up under his arm and he was falling, the sickening lurch in his stomach telling him there was no catching himself this time, and then Mason caught him, yanked him back to his feet.

"All right?"

"Yeah."

Mason kept a hand under his arm as they jogged through the parking lot and made it into the store. They might as well have gone swimming in their clothes—in November. Even the comparative warmth inside the store couldn't chase the chill out of John's bones as he stood blinking in the light.

"C'mon." Mason pulled him along to an aisle that appeared to be a catchall, bath stuff like soap dispensers, beer pong sets, children's toys, light sets, clock radios and best of all: a couple of sweatshirts bearing names of the local colleges and towels. He dug out his wallet. "I've got forty on me."

John took out his bank card. His parents topped his balance off at a thousand each month. "I can get whatever we need."

Mason looked at the card and then back at John. There was probably another remark coming about John's imaginary gold medal, but when Mason only shrugged, John again found himself trying to read what was only a shadow.

K.A. Mitchell

"Fine. Get some stuff to get dry. I'll take a large. I'll meet you back at the checkout."

When Mason had disappeared from the end of the aisle, a group of dripping guys came down for a beer pong set. John stared as hard as he could, but they had nothing, not even the faint shadow he could see around Mason's head. He grabbed two bath towels and a couple of U Albany sweatshirts and started back to the front of the store.

The woman lingering in front of the ice cream freezer was a blank. So was the space above the bleached and teased hair of the older woman who checked them out. Though when she pulled the pen out of her mouth to ask if they had an Advantage card in a raspy voice, it wasn't hard to guess she was counting the minutes to her cigarette break. John handed over his bank card when she gave them the total and hoped he wouldn't have to use her pen to sign, but the machine had one of those automatic screens.

Mason stuffed a twenty in his hand as they left the checkout lane. "For the sweatshirt."

"Okay." John did his best to wedge his wallet back into his soaked jeans. He didn't argue. Some people were weird about money. He'd always had it, first his parents', and now his own, a chunk he'd earned from endorsements, and then from disability and insurance. Which he'd earned in a different way. "It's still pouring."

People hovered at the door, trying to time their break for their car. John and Mason seemed to be the only other people on foot.

"I know," Mason said. "But I've got an idea. C'mon."

They moved in and out of shelter in front of the grocery store, and the rest of the plaza storefronts, all closed, past the liquor store, the locksmith, the Chinese food buffet, until they got to the corner.

"We're not going to get any wetter. Tie up your bag."

John twisted the plastic handles into a knot. Mason pointed out a lighted storefront partway down the side street. "That laundromat is open until midnight. Ready?"

John felt more like he was swimming than walking and wished one of the towels was that super absorbent chamois he used between dives because one baby blue bath towel wasn't going to be enough for this.

They climbed the steps and Mason pushed open the door. It smelled wonderful. Fluffy, warm and clean, the scent strong enough to trigger the synesthesia to fill John's head with creamy yellow clouds. Best of all, the little laundromat was empty.

Mason got some change from the machine and peeled off his soaked army jacket and shirt and threw them into a dryer before digging out one of the towels and sweatshirts. John looked out onto the dark street and tried to hunch down behind the industrial-sized washers in the front.

Mason laughed. "It's eleven o'clock, it's pouring and it's Monday. No one's going to see your chest." But he tossed John a towel and a sweatshirt.

John came back with his wet clothes to find Mason stripping off his jeans.

"What?" Mason said when John just stared. "I'm putting on the towel and I've got briefs on. And I'm fucking freezing." He tossed his jeans into the dryer. "C'mon."

John looked again at the window to the street.

"Are you running around in nothing but a jock again?" Mason grabbed one of John's belt loops and tugged him close.

"No, but..." He'd been on magazine covers in a Speedo, but that wasn't the same.

"I'll hold up the towel."

John backed away.

Mason sighed and looked around. The sudden grin on his face made John's stomach turn over in a good way. A perfect on-target-rotation way.

After crossing to the corner under the vending machine for detergent and dryer sheets, Mason bent down and fished a thin strip of plastic out of the clumps of lint and dust. "C'mere."

He crossed to the door at the back which was clearly labeled Employees Only, and worked the plastic between the door and the frame. A click, a tug and Mason opened the door.

"How did you know how to do that?"

"I told you I got into some trouble at school? That was how."

The laundromat smell was older in here, tinged with a dampness that made the edges of the creamy cloud curl up like old paper. Even with just the light from behind him, John could see why there wasn't a big lock on this door. A mop and a couple of broken machines weren't worth the trouble of keeping safe.

They might not have broken into a bank vault, but John still jumped when Mason sneezed.

"Fucking dust allergy."

Given what John had seen of the usual disorder in Mason's bedroom, he thought that was unlikely.

"Go on in and take your pants off. You can wait in here until they dry with your masculine modesty intact. Though really, sugar..." Mason's hand grazed John's hip, "...you've got nothing to be ashamed of."

John shivered and hurried through the door to peel off his soaking jeans, resting his wallet on top of one of the skeletal machines. Mason waited, outlined in the doorway. "Socks and sneakers too."

He picked up John's jeans and stood over him as he bent down and worked on the wet laces.

"Any excuse to look at my ass?" John asked.

"Don't need an excuse, right, fuck buddy?"

Mason's tone was so cocky, John wanted to fling the sneakers at him, but the second lace was knotted. Finally it came free and he shoved them at Mason.

"Be right back."

The dryer started thumping and then there was an odd crackling noise. John heard Mason's puzzled "What the fuck?" and then the dryer opened, shut and started again. Mason came back to the storage room with the flattened bag of chips John had stuffed in his jean jacket pocket.

"Still hungry?" Mason asked dryly.

Now would be a great time to explain that John had no idea whether Alex was really gone because he couldn't see anything, or that the neurotransmitters wired to his third eye or aura detector or whatever were clogged up with a flavor-enhancing food additive. He really should come clean. But all he did was bite back a giggle at the pun.

"Rachel got you stoned, didn't she? Something in the cookies?"

"No. Just a sugar high, I guess."

Mason turned and dug into his bag from the grocery store. He had two self-heating coffees, activated by a pull tab. "It's not up to Brewed Awakening standards, but you want one?"

Caffeine was the last thing John wanted. He gave a tiny shake of his head. Not only didn't he want to lose the effect of the MSG, he was already jumpy enough with being almost naked in a public place and breaking and entering on top of that. From the way Mason was looking at him, John thought public sex might be next on the list. If it kept him from thinking about the other things, that would be fine.

Mason finished his coffee in a few big gulps and then tossed the bag of chips at John. "Want to lick out the crumbs?"

John squared his shoulders to face him. "I could lick your cock instead."

"If it seemed like you were into it."

"I—what makes you think I'm not?"

"Experience." Mason's voice was tired, the dark purple sluggish and rippled. He spread his towel over the top of a washing machine and hopped up to sit on it. "It's okay to not want to. After everything that happened tonight, I'd say that seems pretty normal."

John peeked out of the door and then shut it until only a thin crack of light came through. Picking his way carefully across the room to protect his bare feet from metal scraps, he stood next to Mason. "I kind of thought you wouldn't want to." Mason's ring was on his other hand now, silver gleaming in that narrow band of light. John tapped it lightly.

"I kind of thought I wouldn't want to either." Mason's feet swung, heels softly tapping the empty aluminum. "But I did."

He reached into his grocery bag and held up a bottle of lube and a box of condoms.

"I didn't see you get that."

Tyler never left home without basic supplies, as he called them. Was Mason the same way?

"That's because you were staring at Gloria's hair, doing your head thing. Pick up any good gossip? From the way she winked at me, I'd say she thinks you're my sugar daddy."

John felt the heat start in his cheeks and turned farther into the dark. "No. Nothing."

"I want to thank you for helping me with Alex and everything."

"A thank-you fuck?" John thought of conversations around Tyler's lunch table. "Is that worse than a pity fuck?"

"No, that's not what I meant." Mason slid off the machine. "I want you, John." He leaned in, coffee-flavored lips barely brushing John's before he took John's hand and put it on a thickening cock. "That's not pity or gratitude. And trust me, springing wood is not something that normally happens after I visit Alex's cemetery. That's you."

Mason's words curled inside, bringing warmth back to everything that had shut down in the cold. John slid his hand up and down, the heat of the flesh underneath the thin cotton briefs bleeding through to his palm. With one arm pinning John close, Mason breathed warmth along the side of John's neck until soft lips reached his ear.

I don't know if he's really gone John was going to say, but the truth got stuck in his throat. It wasn't that he knew for sure Alex was still here. And if half the truth made things easier for them both, why say anything? Why didn't John get to have this? He wasn't forcing anything on Mason. He'd made every move.

But guilt left a burn like acid on the back of John's tongue and he turned away from Mason's kiss.

For a second he thought the harsh buzz was another freakish thing his brain was doing, letting him hear Mason's anger and disappointment, but it was only the dryer going off. Mason stepped away, swinging the door wide and letting in a flood of light and the smell of hot rubber.

"The sneakers are still wet, but the clothes are mostly dry and the rain stopped. It's about ten minutes fast walk to the house, want to try for it?" Mason called back.

If nothing else, the clothes would be warm. "Yeah. Let's try."

They made it back to North Pine without getting soaked

again. Mason stopped halfway between the porch and the car. "You can take your chances and have me drive you back uptown, or you can come in for the night. I'm sure Lizzy will take you back up in time for classes."

"I'd rather go back now," John said.

"Kind of figured you would. C'mon."

Mason didn't seem as tense on the drive back to the campus, but he didn't say anything either. When he stopped in the fire lane, he shifted in his seat. "Do you want me to walk you inside? You look like you're really crashing from that carb load. And it's been a hell of a night."

That might have been part of the sick feeling in John's stomach, but not all of it. He couldn't blame it on vertigo either. "I can make it." He took a grip on his cane.

Mason nodded. "I meant what I said about helping you with your head stuff."

But he wouldn't if he knew that all the help John wanted was to turn it off. "Okay."

Mason turned back to face the dash. "If you decide you want to give that fuck-buddy thing a shot, let me know."

Chapter Fifteen

John really was dragging ass by the time he hit his hallway. He was nauseous, from a gut full of guilt and Cheetos, trying to walk in damp pants that felt like he'd come in them but without the fun memory. Worse, the first guy he saw had a smear of purple over the top of his head, and he knew the MSG was saying good-bye-been-fun to his neurotransmitters. His door looked like the gate to heaven, and all he wanted to do was face-plant on his bed and never move again.

"Where the fuck have you been?"

The harsh whisper startled him and he had to hang on to the wall to keep from landing on his ass. It had to be Keith. But when John had slowly moved his head to see who had a hold of his forearm, he found a really pissed-off Drew, his gray dark and sharp as pencil scrapings against the white dorm wall.

"Huh?"

"You were a wreck when I left you here today so I came back to check on you. Where did you go?"

That had only been today? It felt like a week ago. The real answer: sex with Mason, trip to a psychic, a cemetery, and almost public sex in a laundromat was out of the question so John just said, "Out."

"Who with? I called Tyler. I called everybody I could think of. I even asked that creepy Keith guy if he'd seen you."

John pulled his arm back. Drew was acting like a jealous boyfriend. A lot of crap had happened today, but John was pretty sure he'd remember if he'd actually agreed to something like that.

"I went out with Mason."

"Kincaid? What the hell for? I thought you guys just had a one-time thing."

The fact that Drew was keeping track of who John had slept with was creepier than anything Keith had done so far. John sagged against the wall. Drew touched him again, the same kind of friendly supportive grip he'd offered dozens of times, and it felt like a handful of spiders under John's skin.

"We didn't have sex." Another not-quite-a-lie. They didn't while they were out, and John was too sick and tired to blush at the memory of the sex they'd had. "Like Mason said, he needed help with a friend's project. We were working on it."

"The next thing you'll tell me is you were at the library."

"Drew—"

"It's not going to happen, is it?"

John knew what he meant, and he wished it could. That a nice guy who cared enough to make sure John got home safe was the same kind of guy who made John want to get on his knees and beg to be fucked, but John had been using a vault's worth of coins in the wishing well this past year, and none of them had come true.

What he really needed now was a friend. One he could just talk to about all of this crazy stuff that was going on in his head, but the only person he could talk to about it was the one person he couldn't. Because he was too busy lying to him. Why couldn't that have been Drew instead?

"No. It's not." At least he could be that honest with Drew. "I wish things were different."

"Bullshit, John. If you want things different, you make them that way."

The gray over Drew's head leveled a thousand points at John. He wanted to reach out and smooth them flat, but he was so tired he couldn't remember how he'd done it before.

"Are we still friends?"

"At least I'm good for something. I don't know." Drew walked away and left John hanging onto the wall.

He didn't undress, didn't give a crap about the nasty fuzzy feeling on his teeth, he just fell onto his bed and dreamed.

First it was the laundromat, except they weren't in the back in the dark anymore, they were downstairs in the one in the dorm and Mason was fucking him over a machine that shook through the spin cycle, vibrations shuddering through John's cock, and he was going to come without even touching his dick. But then he was on a couch in a room he'd never seen before. An ugly orange couch that sagged in the middle, in a finished basement in some house he'd never been in.

Mason was next to him and good thing too, because John's balls ached like they were in a vise and he had to get off. He reached for him and a loud cough stopped him.

A sexy guy stood in front of them, black curly hair, green-striped button-down shirt open to his waist and pale blue jeans fraying around his bare feet.

"Yeah. I'm not too sorry about the interruption." The guy nodded at John's crotch. John looked down. He was dressed now, but Mason was in a pair of boxers.

"Alex?"

"Duh," the guy said with an elaborate roll of his eyes.

"John, what are you doing in my dream? In Alex's basement?" Mason asked.

John wanted to ask Alex the same thing, but this was

clearly Alex's show.

"We need to talk," Alex said.

"I hate it when you say that. It means you need to talk, I need to listen," Mason said.

"Well, you do." Alex's voice had a smile in it. He was hot. And he probably was a really nice guy, but talking to a dead guy in his dream left John a little too freaked out to come to any sensible conclusion.

"Despite your noble self-sacrifice..." Alex waved his left hand with the silver band on it in Mason's face, "...I'm still fucking here, thank *you* very much." He turned that last on John. "And before you go turning this into a big pity party for yourself, I'm not jealous. Okay. A little."

Alex smiled at Mason again and reached a hand toward his face. No skin touched, just an arc of white, like the one that had given John such a headache.

"He's probably an all-right guy since you like him so much," Alex said. "I want you to have a life, babe, I do. I just didn't figure on a whole after-life's subscription to fucking box seats for it, okay? Now fix it, John. You already know how. You've been doing it all along. Fuck, if I had that kind of talent, I'd have been a lock for a Tony every year."

An actor who could make people feel what he wanted? John guessed that would come in handy. But John didn't want to use people like that.

"Trust me, John," Alex said. "You don't want to have to see me again."

Coming from a ghost, that was a pretty effective threat.

"Now it's my turn." He leaned down and kissed Mason, a warm spark that shot from their kiss and shocked John like he'd touched a live wire. "Goodbye, love."

Mason jerked awake, the touch of Alex's lips still buzzing across his mouth. He put his fingers over it and flipped open his phone to call John, the lying son of a bitch. It was only six thirty in the morning but he was going to call him anyway until he remembered he still didn't have his fucking number.

Fine. He climbed out of bed. This would be better in person. He could look John right in the eye and have him explain how he could lie with Alex's fucking soul on the line.

Damn, he was a hell of a liar, him and his gold medal. Was any of it real? The colors he said he saw? Last night at that psychic's house—no way had John been faking that. And when Mason came back from Alex's grave, John had been so different, so happy, he had to have been telling the truth.

Mason went to ask if he could borrow Lizzy's car again, but her bedroom door was open and she wasn't there. She was in the kitchen, cradling a bowl of cereal like someone was going to take it away from her.

"I need the car again."

"Where's John? I thought you guys had a date."

"He'd better fucking be in his dorm where I left him."

"And you'd better be planning on taking the bus with an attitude like that. What happened?"

"How well do you know him? Have you ever caught him in a lie?"

Lizzy thought for a second. "No. He doesn't talk about himself much. It's kind of a relief."

"Is that at me? I thought you wanted me to express my feelings about Alex."

Lizzy cocked her head. "Ooooo. I think that was the bus. Should be another one in twenty minutes. Then there's the fifty million stops on the way uptown. You should make it there by eight if you walk a couple stops ahead."

"Fuck you. Will you give me a ride?"

"Calm down and eat some cereal while I shower, and I'll think about it."

"I want a waffle."

"I bought the cereal especially for you."

Mason looked at the counter. "Wheaties? Thanks. I fucking hate Wheaties."

"Have some anyway or no ride."

Mason was going to bring up PMS, even if he got called a sexist pig, but this fell into a bizarro category way beyond a hormonal explanation. Lizzy didn't do bizarre. She did annoying, and nagging, and maternal, but not insane.

He picked up the box. Some jock was on it, two gold medals around his neck over a red-white-and-blue pullover. Like he told John, he'd watched the Olympics this past summer, especially the men's diving and swimming. He looked at the guy's face.

At John's face. Familiar smile, tilted gray eyes. His hair was a little longer now, face a little older. You could get something like this made, hell, you could do it yourself with Photoshop. He looked at the spot where John's neck met the jock's torso. Smooth. Nothing to suggest it had been airbrushed in. So it was a good fake.

He looked at the top of the box. It wasn't even opened. Good thing, the cereal had expired three years ago. Not this Olympics. John would have been—the seventeen-year-old who won the first double medal in men's diving for the U.S. in years?

Mason stomped up the stairs and pounded on the bathroom door. "Where the fuck did you get that?"

Lizzy yelled back, "Ebay. Expensive too, damn it."

"So you guys had it set up, made? What for?"

"Jesus Christ." Kai flung open his door. "I've got a fucking test in two hours. Do you guys mind?"

Lizzy opened the bathroom door, hair and body in towels, water still running. "Sorry, Kai." She took the box from under Mason's arm and hit him over the head with it. Twice. Hard. She handed the box to Kai. "You want in?"

Kai aimed it at the back of Mason's skull, thumped him once, gave the box to Lizzy and went back into his room.

"Shit. It's for real." Mason rubbed his throbbing head.

"Yes, dickhead. It's for real. John fell onto the deck while he was training for last year. That's why he needs the cane. I can't believe he didn't tell you. No wait. Maybe I can."

"He told me."

"And?"

"I thought he was screwing around."

She aimed with the box but Mason ducked, and she had to grab at her towel before it swung free. Mason got the box out of her hands and stared at it.

"Why did you do it?"

"So you could see you're not the only one life screwed over. Shit happens. Big, ugly, bad shit, for no good reason. And there are other people out there who get that."

"So he wasn't lying about it."

"Are you sure they didn't screw up your IQ test? You know, he can't ever dive again. He did that—nothing but that—for most of his life, and now it's just gone."

John talking about tutors, saying he moved around a lot, flashing his bank card at the store like he was loaded. He hadn't lied. Probably hadn't lied last night, but he sure as shit knew how to make lies by omission work for him.

Mason sat on the hallway floor with the cereal box in his lap. "Will you give me a ride now?"

Lizzy went back into the bathroom for a minute and then

came out and sat next to him in a T-shirt and underwear. "This is more than just the diving thing. This is that Alex-talking-to-John stuff too. What's going on? What did you guys do last night?"

She'd probably beat the shit out of him if he told her he took John to Alex's grave. "I can't tell you. That's his stuff to talk about, but you can ask him. Just give me some time to talk to him first. We'll meet you later."

After that dream, John was expecting Mason to come hammering on his door as soon as he could get uptown. Going to the food court would just put the confrontation off, so he waited in his room. By the time his wait had stretched into an hour, he wondered if it really had been nothing more than a dream. He'd managed to convince himself he'd imagined it all, so he didn't have any of his practiced excuses ready when Mason tapped on his door at 7:45.

John didn't even look at his face but at his head, to the white pulsing there, the red reeled in tight and close. Angry, but controlling it.

"Can I come in?"

John moved to let him by and shut the door. Mason leaned against John's desk. "That was a hell of a three-way, huh?"

John almost laughed. "Yeah. Alex's basement?"

"His parents' house. Up in Saratoga."

"Oh. Crappy couch."

"Try fucking on it."

John had to fight to not look away, because if he did, he'd admit to them both how much that stung. Not that Mason and Alex had had sex, but knowing now that John had seen Alex, how crazy it would be to think John could mean anything to

Mason.

Mason rubbed his palms down the thighs of his jeans. "I'm having a hard time knowing what to believe in right now, and you bullshitting me is not helping."

"I didn't lie. There was nothing there after the cemetery." John sat on his bed.

"But there is now."

"Yes. Two colors, like before."

"Has that ever happened before? Has it ever stopped?"

"No."

"Was it just me or—?"

"It was everyone. I didn't know it would work." That was the first excuse. He'd had that one five minutes after the dream where he'd been caught in a lie by a ghost. Something he hadn't believed in since he was eight.

"That what would work? What did you do?"

"You know how you told me about Lizzy's headaches? You said MSG makes them bad, caffeine makes them better? I figured out that caffeine makes the colors...stronger. So a lot of Cheetos would have the opposite effect."

Mason bit his lip like he was trying not to laugh. "You've never taken a course in logic syllogisms, have you?" It didn't matter, the crystals sparkled with his humor.

John would rather Mason yell at him than make him feel stupid. "What's that supposed to mean?"

"It means it was a lucky guess."

"But I was right." He'd take instinct over logic as long as it worked.

"Yeah, you were. But why did you do it?"

"Why?" John pushed off the bed and paced across the room. "Why wouldn't I try anything to get rid of it?"

"I don't know. It seems like it would be kind of neat sometimes. Like playing poker."

"I'll sign up for the World Tour tomorrow."

"Seriously."

"Seriously? It's everywhere. It's all over. I can see when people are fighting or people want to fuck or know when a professor is full of crap. I don't want to. I don't want any of it. I just want my goddamned life back."

"The one where you were an Olympic diver?" Mason didn't sound like he was teasing that time.

John put his head against the door to his room. Where was he going to go? He didn't fit anywhere. He'd thought he might start to fit in here, and then Tyler had to drag John to that stupid psychic fair, and it all spun out of control.

Mason had brought a backpack with him, and John heard him rustling around in it, the cool silver-green whisper of nylon, the dark blue rumble of the zipper. "Like in this picture?"

John turned around. Mason had that damned Wheaties box.

"Where did you find that?"

"In my kitchen."

"Must not clean very often. They haven't made that box for years."

"Still, you lied again."

"I did not." If there was one thing in his life John was proud of, it was those two medals. He'd worked hard enough for them.

"You didn't say you won two gold medals."

"Platform and springboard." John touched them on the box.

"And that's really how you fell?"

"Not in competition. Nothing so dramatic. I clipped my head

doing a reverse in practice six weeks before the Olympics. Didn't even break the skin though it hurt like hell. Must have done something to it, though, because I went right back up and walked off the platform sideways. At least that's what they tell me."

Mason sucked in his breath. The red was soft, glowing like something you could warm yourself in.

John shrugged. "Could have been worse. Could have died."

Mason looked straight at him. "Do you ever wish you had?"

John didn't want to answer that. He'd asked himself that once or twice, when they told him not only wasn't he going to make the Olympics, but that he'd never be able to dive again. Never take on gravity with nothing but strength and skill to make falling look like grace. And he'd never been sure of his answer.

"I did," Mason went on. "Over and over. I wished it was me. Would have been glad to trade places with Alex. So that's why— I know you don't want to, but that's why you have to help me. Help him. After that, you can stoke up on all the MSG you want. Hell, I'll buy you a pallet of Cheetos. Just don't leave him stuck like this."

If Mason had come in here breathing fire like John had expected, it would have been easier to fight him, easier to demand to be left in peace, but when Mason just asked, it was hard to say no. "I'll try."

"Thank you. Now it's my turn to make a confession."

John looked up. Mason's red stayed clear and honest as he said, "Lizzy wants to know what's going on. I didn't tell her, I figured it was your story to tell."

John thought of Lizzy looking at him like he was crazy and hung back when Mason would have gone through the door. "I can't."

"She's waiting."

"You're going to have to do it."

"You still have to come with me."

They stepped out of the dorm and walked to the Podium at the center of the campus. The sun was bright, warm for November, like the weather was trying to make up for being so shitty yesterday.

"What's it like?"

"I told you. It sucks."

"Not the color thing, the being-an-Olympic-diver thing."

"Oh. A lot more work than you'd think. A lot of time on trampolines doing the same moves over and over and over. That might have saved my life."

"What do you mean?"

"I don't remember, but I guess I blacked out. If I hadn't practiced so much, I wouldn't have been able to curl into a ball when I fell."

"But you still hit your head."

"Yeah."

"Bet you wish someone could turn off gravity."

"No. Gravity's what makes it fun. You've only got a second or two and you have to make it count. Every single muscle you move has to count. That's—" John looked out at the thousands of people soaking up the unexpected warmth. Sometimes he could forget what he'd had, forget that he was stuck down here now with everyone else. He swallowed. "It's what I miss the most." Proud as he was of his medals, he'd trade them, trade all the attention and approval he'd gotten, to be able to live in the air again just two seconds at a time.

Lizzy was sitting on a square planter on the science side of the big rectangle above the lecture halls. The warm gold above her head was the same as he always saw it, clear and steady. Big too. John thought of what he'd learned so far. The bigger the spread of the color, the more sure the person was they were in the right and wanted to convince others too. And clear and steady meant no deception, practical thinking.

"I don't think she's going to believe you," John said.

"Us, you mean. You're going to help."

"Everything okay, guys?" she said as they came up. No change to the color, but she did start swinging her feet where they dangled against the cement.

"Yeah." Mason nudged him.

"Fine."

"So is someone going to tell me what's going on?"

John just watched as Mason started the explanation, the same way John had. Fall, vertigo, perception.

Lizzy's feet stopped drumming. "What do you mean perceive things differently?"

"Cover your face with your hands, Liz. And think about something. Something you have strong feelings about. It could even be a memory."

She raised her palms to her face. "If you guys are taking a weird picture of me to put on line..." Her threat trailed off.

A shimmer at first, desire so strong John felt it in his gut, then the shine huffed out in a mist, fogged and reformed to the usual way he saw Lizzy.

"Arou—desire and then sad. Not really sad, but something you want but can't have."

Lizzy lowered her hands. And that was the look he'd been dreading. Fear. Her crystals drew in tight. "Did you read my mind?"

"No. I don't know what made you feel that way. Just what you felt. And I don't mean to, it's just there."

"Body language," Lizzy said firmly, her assurance pouring out again like honey over a biscuit. "You're just really good at

217

reading body language."

"I wish."

Mason tried to get back to the story. "So John was at a psychic fair—"

"How can you believe this?" Lizzy interrupted, staring at Mason.

"Well, I haven't had time to form a hypothesis and set up a control group, but it's been pretty fucking reproducible so far."

"No," Lizzy said.

"Look, brain activity, including thought and emotion, can be read on a thermal scan, yes?"

"But there are layers of tissue in the way."

"Temperature change is a frequency change. John can see that frequency. His brain reads it back to him in a way he can process."

"John?"

"I know it's not really there. I just see it."

She was wavering, the edges pushing out and then receding as she fought her way through her disbelief. When Mason explained about Alex, about dreams and messages and something about a computer, the crystals went solid as a shield. Like Rachel's mirrors, nothing was getting past that.

"Mase, I know how much you miss him."

"Don't." Mason snapped the word with so much force people walking by turned to watch. "Don't try to take the easy way out," he said more softly. "Fuck, I wish it was that easy. I'd be happy to just have an occasional dream visit and move on, but he's stuck. It's what he's been trying to tell me, and I'm not going to leave him like that."

"How can you do this to him? I thought you would be good for him." Lizzy, John's first friend here, for awhile his only friend, turned that anger on him.

"I'm not. I don't want—" Something inside him wanted to reach out, press down on that gold shield and calm her fears. It wouldn't be like making her understand, only speed things up a little. He forced it back, hands fisting at his sides. "—any of this. I don't want to be doing it."

"Ghosts, Mason?"

"Energy can't be created or destroyed. You're the one who sat up with me the other night."

The crystals turned clear again, but stayed in a protective wall. Lizzy hopped off the cement box. "Well, it's better than art history. But, John, if you're fucking with him, I'll kill you, okay?" She gave him a bright smile.

Chapter Sixteen

John had never felt particularly comfortable sitting around the kitchen table in Mason's house, even when Lizzy was on his side. Now with her aiming narrow-eyed stares like her threatened homicide was seconds from reality, he really wanted to be somewhere else. After five minutes of splitting her glares between the two of them, she folded her arms and said, "Now what?"

Mason looked at John. The white and the red were as tangled as he'd ever seen them, overlapping and snapping along with Mason's frustration with Lizzy's stubbornness.

"I think I'm supposed to find a way to separate their auras." John hated using that word, but he couldn't think of a way to put it that Lizzy would understand.

"Auras? What happened to frequencies?"

"That's my word," Mason put in. "You're not helping."

"Really? Good," Lizzy said.

"John, tell Lizzy what Alex looked like in that dream this morning."

"Oh no, you've had time to talk, probably even showed him a picture. That doesn't prove anything."

"Then ask him something." Another red crystal, thin and brittle, snapped and reformed.

Lizzy sighed. "What was he wearing?"

"A green-striped shirt and jeans. Really faded jeans."

"What about his feet?"

"His feet?" Did anyone look at feet in a dream? Did Alex have an extra toe or something he was supposed to have noticed?

"They were just feet."

"In ratty sneakers, right?" Lizzy prompted.

"No. Bare."

"Ha," Mason said. To John he added, "Alex took off his shoes anytime he could."

"Shut up. You could have told him that anytime."

John was tired and his head was already starting to hurt. "You know what, Lizzy? I don't care if you believe me or not. I don't even care if you hate me. I just want to do this and never have to see any of you again."

Lizzy's shield stuttered. Mason's angry popping slowed. Then he laughed. "Damn, sugar. You're sexy when you're pissed off."

John looked down. He'd stood up and was pushing down on the table to loom over them. He jerked his hands away like the surface was on fire. "Can we just do this?"

"Sure," Mason said.

"Go right ahead." Lizzy shrugged but didn't move her arms from their tight fold over her chest.

John clenched and relaxed his jaw. If he were going to have to deal with this psychic crap, now would be a good time for telepathy so that he didn't have to say this out loud. "Mason. Don't you remember what I told Rachel about when you're most—um—apart?"

Mason's brow furrowed for a second and then he smiled. "Yeah, sex. Guess that lets you out, Lizzy-love."

"Really? All this bullshit and you're just going to fuck each

221

other's brains out?"

"Born lucky, what can I say?" Mason's tone was light, but the red still sizzled and shattered, the white popping in the spaces between. From what John could tell, even Alex was still pissed at Lizzy.

Mason shut the bedroom door behind them. "Sorry about that."

"She's right. I do sound insane."

"*We*. And we know otherwise because we've lived it." Mason perched on the edge of his mattress. "You ready?"

"I guess." Was there something else to be done? Candles? He thought of the ghost traps from *Ghostbusters*. "Don't cross the photon beams."

Mason grinned. "You're a funny guy. You hide it well under Mr. All-American Olympian."

"Shut up. You didn't even believe that until this morning." The compliment had John fighting a blush that for once didn't have to do with sex. "How should we start?"

Mason leered, but then his face got serious. "Kissing, I guess."

John sat on the bed next to him.

"Wait just a second." Mason closed his eyes. The colors had settled but were still kind of equal—and tangled. He opened his eyes. "Okay."

There was the familiar tingle when Mason's lips brushed John's, but even as their mouths slid open, John knew in a second he was going to be sneaking a look at Mason's head. He tried to concentrate on the feel of Mason's tongue, but Mason broke first, laughing.

"That's not working so much, is it?"

John glanced at the overlapping flash of color. "No."

Mason dropped back on the bed. "You could blow me."

"Easy for you to say." John couldn't imagine trying to focus on doing that right now. "Do you think it would work?"

Mason's laugh was short and full of regret. "No."

John flopped next to him.

"Let's try this." Mason sat up. "Take off your shirt."

Mason ripped his T-shirt over his head and tossed it on the floor. John copied him. Mason eased back down and pulled John with him so that they were pressed chest-to-chest. Mason's heart thumped fast and hard against John's ribs, but he was pretty sure it was fear and nerves rather than any other kind of excitement.

Flipping John onto his back, Mason started stroking his hands over John's pecs and ribs, just hard enough not to tickle. The touch was warm, but nothing like when Mason brought his mouth to John's nipple and flicked it with a pointed tongue.

John opened his eyes and saw the space between the red and the white, and though his hands never left where they rubbed Mason's back, he reached out and moved the white, pulled it away. Mason's eyes were closed, tongue tracing a pattern on John's chest. John kept tugging, shifting the white away from Mason's head.

John couldn't say which happened first, but he lost his grip and there was an explosion of sparks behind his eyes, and then a deep stab of pain.

Mason rolled off, hands squeezing his skull like he had to keep his brains from leaking out. "Ow."

"Yeah," John agreed.

"Did it work?"

John didn't really have to check, but he did anyway. "No."

"Fuck." Mason rubbed at his forehead. "Is that what happened to you at Rachel's?"

"No. That was a million times worse than this one."

"Shit." Mason shook his head hard, like pain was something he could scatter away like rain in his hair. "Okay. I'm in if you are."

"If Alex is trapped, why isn't he, I don't know, making this easy?"

"Do you think we should call Rachel?"

"Let's try again."

Mason grinned and climbed back on top of John, pressing their hips together. "I was actually starting to get hard."

John didn't answer, didn't wait this time. He just pulled, pictured what it should be, two separate bursts of color, the red here and the white...

Exploding in a shower of sparks that shook the room, made the bed heave under them and gave John a stabbing hot migraine in every nerve of his body.

And the white nestled back against the red over Mason's head, covered it, because the red wasn't moving, it was flat and close and dim. Mason wasn't moving.

"Mason." John shoved at him, managed to flip him onto his back. God. What happened? He remembered his first-aid courses and checked Mason's vitals. Breathing and pulse okay. But why didn't he wake up? John called him, shoved him, slapped him, shook him.

"Hey! What the hell was that? What are you guys doing?" Lizzy kicked at the door.

John jumped up and flipped off the lock. "I don't know. I was separating them and it just— You felt that?"

"Yes. And the fucking power is out." She went to the window and stared across the backyard. "I thought a transformer blew but everyone else has power." She kicked Mason's foot. "Mason Jackson Kincaid, don't you even pretend to be out of it so you can't talk to me."

"Lizzy, he won't wake up."

She dropped onto the bed and went through the same motions John had. "What did you do to him?"

"Like I said—"

"Yeah, that aura-separating bullshit. Whatever freaky stuff you guys are playing with stops now. And, Alex, if you are here, let go of him. I don't for a minute believe this was his fault. You're the one who was always afraid of losing him." She put her hands on Mason's shoulders like she'd shake him, and something flung her back, dumping her on her ass on a pile of clothes halfway across the room.

Mason sat up. "What the fuck was that?" He blinked and clutched his skull again. "Jesus."

Lizzy hadn't moved. Just sat there where she'd fallen, mouth open, shrunken yellow crystals sizzling.

Alex still hugged Mason's head. As John watched, the white flowed back into the spaces between the red.

"Still here," John said before Mason could ask.

"Alex?" Lizzy said. But she wasn't talking to them. She was talking to the room.

"What happened?" Mason asked.

John filled him in.

"Yeah, he had a bit of a temper."

"What?" But what John really wanted to say was *I thought he was perfect?*

"A break-things temper," Lizzy added. "And more stubborn than you, even."

Mason shrugged.

"And you tell me this now?"

"Well, I didn't think it mattered before. He was dead and I

couldn't say stuff like that about him."

John rolled his eyes. "Stubborn and a temper. What the hell am I supposed to do now?"

They adjourned to the kitchen for a discussion. "Maybe Alex hates that you turned the bedroom into a sty," Lizzy suggested.

"That's really helpful, thanks." Mason slugged back some cold coffee from the carafe.

"Ugh, wash that please."

"I do it all the time and you never know."

"And I backwash in the orange juice."

"Really?" Mason sounded interested.

"No. That's disgusting."

John watched their—he hated the stupid word but it fit now—auras come back to normal as they bickered. His own heart was still racing and pain spread out like a full-body toothache. "It felt like I was doing it right. Like it was almost finished."

Mason and Lizzy turned back to him.

"I think you should call Rachel," Mason said.

"She doesn't really do auras."

"Yeah, but she knows a lot more about this stuff than we do."

"It's too bad we can't amp him up to get a better reading." Lizzy cocked her head at John. "Feed more juice through the meter."

Mason looked at the carafe in his hand. "We can."

"No," John said. "No way."

"You said the colors are stronger on caffeine."

"You were unconscious," John reminded him.

"Because you lost control of him. With the caffeine..." Mason did that thing where he looked through his lashes.

"I thought this didn't fit the logical syllogisms or whatever."

"You already proved the hypothesis once," Mason said.

"And I'll be here to keep an eye on him," Lizzy said.

"No."

"One Brewed Awakening shake," Mason coaxed. "And then we'll try something else."

"I'll go get it." Lizzy grabbed her keys off the table and was gone before John could argue anymore.

"I'm not drinking it."

Mason dumped the rest of the coffee in the sink and started washing the carafe. "What do you want, John?"

"I told you. I want my old life back."

"The one where you sucked off some asshole who was so closeted he wouldn't even touch your dick? The one where you trained all day and lived two seconds at a time?"

"It wasn't just like that."

"You never talk about friends or family so yeah. I think it was just like that." Mason put the carafe into the machine, then turned and leaned on the counter.

"Don't you want it back? If you could just go back and fix it all, make the accident never happen, wouldn't you?"

"I can't do that."

"But wouldn't you?"

"I don't want Alex to be dead. I told you. I'd give my life up for his in a heartbeat. But there's a lot that's happened since I don't want to erase."

John didn't want to look at him. Didn't want to read the colors over his head to find out if this was all bullshit to manipulate John into doing exactly what Mason wanted. One corner of the tile near the back porch door was gone, the shadow making it look like a big empty hole instead of just a missing piece of vinyl.

"Like you," Mason went on. "I probably wouldn't have met you and I don't want to take that back."

"Yeah, because how many psychic freaks are you likely to trip over in life?"

"Well, probably not many who give head like you and have such a gorgeous ass. I may only have gotten in it once, but that's not something I forget."

John looked up. The white was calm now, the red strong and clear. He could just brush the white away—but he was afraid. So Mason wasn't lying about liking sex with him, big surprise. "Well, I'm sure sex isn't something you have a hard time getting."

"It's not. But unlike you, I don't mind having some feelings with it. And I like knowing about all the crap you have going on in your life."

Mason was still telling the truth.

"But why does it have to be all this crap?" John didn't know he was going to say that until it slipped out of his mouth. He probably looked pretty stupid feeling shocked by himself.

"I don't know. That's what life is. But if you really want to turn this off, eat your Cheetos and ignore it, then drink the fucking shake, help Alex and then go back to whatever the hell you were doing."

Hanging out with Tyler and talking about guys they did or wanted to with the occasional socio-political lecture thrown in by Simon might not live up to Olympic diving, but it was easier than dealing with this. Almost anything was easier than dealing with the way Mason was looking at him, like there was something wrong with wanting to be normal.

John hadn't made up his mind when Lizzy came in through

the back porch. She had a box of those greasy breakfast rolls with her too. As good as they smelled, John's stomach was too queasy to think about eating.

She put the shake on the counter next to John and held up the box. "I could only get four. Last ones from the morning batch." She put them on the table. "You should probably eat something to go with all that caffeine and sugar, John."

"I'm not hungry."

Mason came over and leaned close to John's ear. "Drink the fucking shake, John, and then you can get out of here." It was déjà vu from that party where they'd met, minus the smile. *Wanna get out of here?*

Mason walked out of the kitchen.

"What did you say to him?" Lizzy followed him. "Do you think this is easy for him?"

Their voices died away. John picked up the shake.

He didn't even taste it, just gulped it down, let it join that cold knot of anger in his stomach. Mason. Tyler had said he was manipulative. That didn't even begin to cover it. And here John was again, one more time in his life doing what he was told, doing what someone else wanted because that was the easy way.

Diving wasn't easy. He'd been doing it so long he couldn't remember deciding to do it, but it wasn't easy. He made it easy by smiling and telling everyone how much he loved it.

As he sucked down more shake, the cold spread out from his stomach, tingling in his fingers and toes, like he was taking those steps to the edge of the platform. But that excitement was gone for good. All he had left was this cold hard rage inside.

Mason had made it easy for him. So he'd make it easy for Mason.

The shake was gone, and Lizzy's voice got louder, almost a

high silver shriek. "I don't care. I'm not letting you guys do this without me keeping an eye on you. What if something happens again?"

John went to find them. "It won't."

It was bright. Not just the sound-colors, but their auras. John felt like he could flick those shimmers into any shape he wanted. He wrapped that power around his hands and held on tight. He could see everything now, see where Mason was holding onto Alex, the tangle of too much need on both sides.

"What won't?" Kai came in through the front door. "Jesus, I heard you guys screaming on the street. What's going on?"

Lizzy's gold dipped a bit, that wistful feeling he'd caught before. Kai's pink leaped toward her like it would drag her back to him itself. They both wanted it and whatever was keeping them from having it was stupid. At least they should get to have what they wanted. *Just kiss her* was all John meant to think, but the pink went hard and clear and strong. Kai took two steps and yanked Lizzy in tight before slamming his mouth down on hers like he'd been dying to do it for years. For all John knew, he had.

Mason stared at his friends and then at John. The red spiked into a fence of fear.

"I didn't mean to," John whispered.

Mason dragged John upstairs. It only took one look at John's face to see he was just as shook up as Mason was. Kai had been talking about doing that since they were sophomores, but Mason knew his friend would never have the balls—if he hadn't been pushed.

John was still apologizing when Mason shut and locked the bedroom door.

"Okay. I get it. Depending on how things go, and they seem to be going pretty good since they didn't seem to be coming up

230

for air, I don't think it's a problem. But you probably shouldn't tell them." Mason stared at John. "Just don't ever do that to me. Um, exactly what did you do?"

"I don't really know. Sometimes if I think about a feeling, the colors match."

"Even when you're not on caffeine?"

"Yeah."

"Holy shit." Mason wanted to put his back against a wall, but that wouldn't protect him. "Have you done it to me?"

"Not on purpose. When we were driving to Rachel's and you were so tense..."

It was probably a good thing but it still freaked him the fuck out. "Just don't, okay?"

"I didn't know I was doing it before. Now that I figured it out, I can stop it before I do it. Usually."

Mason sat on the bed. "Anything else you think you should mention?"

John looked like he had to think about it. "Not that I know of."

"Damn." Mason felt like he'd run a lot farther than up the stairs.

The hesitancy in John's smile made Mason want to reach out and make it bigger with a kiss. Maybe they weren't so different.

"Still think my crap is interesting?"

Mason didn't have to think twice. "Hell yeah."

John didn't answer his smile. "Are you ready?"

Mason took a deep breath. "Yeah."

"You're going to have to help. I can see the problem now. And I have to kind of move things. I don't know what you'll feel."

"I trust you." He did. He might not be able to see colors or anything above people's heads, but he knew John wouldn't abuse what Mason was giving him.

"Try to relax." John's lips twisted in an almost smile. "Like getting fucked."

"I think I can manage it. Should I lie down?"

"If you want to."

He was stalling again. Now that he knew that hearing Alex's neck snap hadn't really been the end, it was harder. Because this time he had a choice. He could see goodbye coming and try to keep it from happening. All those times Alex had whispered *I need you, babe.* Now this was what he really needed.

Mason told himself it was his imagination, but he *felt* it. Felt the pull inside, like someone was trying to drag his toenails out through his hair. He kept reminding himself that this was what Alex needed, but it didn't feel any better. And then Mason knew it was what *he* needed and the pull went faster, tearing past his chest, into his throat, the back of his skull. He dug his fingers into his jeans to keep from reaching out to stop it and then it was gone. Alex was gone. For the first time since they'd kissed, Mason knew Alex was really gone.

He opened his eyes. Things were a little blurry, but he thought maybe John was rubbing a tear off his face too.

The bed felt huge. Empty. Like his insides.

"Could you stay awhile? Maybe just talk?"

"I can't." John rubbed his face again and left.

Chapter Seventeen

If Lizzy or Kai left his bedroom during the next week, Mason didn't see it. When he stumbled over them feeding each other EBC rolls in the kitchen the next Saturday, he promised he would refrain from heaving at such a blatant display of heterosexuality if Lizzy would give him John's number.

She handed off her phone and went back to licking grease off Kai's lips.

Mason was nauseous, but it was born of pure envy. What if by hanging on to what he'd lost, he'd screwed any chance he had for something real? John didn't need him, something he'd made perfectly clear. Didn't need Mason's help with his aura-reading, or fitting in to a life without diving, or getting laid.

If Mason had gotten his head out of his ass sooner, maybe he would have been there when John did need something.

"You guys got plans next weekend?"

Kai smiled. Mason couldn't remember the last time his friend had smiled without a trace of sarcasm in it.

"You need to catch up on your studying." Lizzy got up. God, had she actually been sitting on his lap? What had happened to her rants on the infantilization of women in patriarchal culture?

"What's up?" Kai asked.

"I want to do something for John."

"Give us a time and a place and we'll be there," Lizzy said.

Mason didn't know how much Lizzy had told Kai about Alex and John, or whether there had been any time to get to it between all that cooing and fucking.

Carrie wandered in, followed by a guy built like a door, tall and solid. Based on Carrie's grin, door guy was definitely proportional.

"You're invited too," Mason said to the ear that didn't have a headphone in it. "Be sure to grab a roll before they're gone," he told door guy before going into the backyard in shorts and a T-shirt. Damn if everyone at 10 North Pine was going to be getting laid but him.

John picked up right away.

Once the *heys* were out of the way, John said, "How's Lizzy?"

"I'll ask her when she and Kai come out of his room."

John sighed. "I'm glad that worked out. I felt really bad about it."

"Have you ever been skydiving?"

John didn't say anything right away and Mason wanted to shake the phone. At last there was a bit of a laugh and John said, "I think with my vertigo I missed my window of opportunity for jumping out of planes."

"Have you ever seen those vertical wind-tunnel things? Where people can look like they're skydiving but they're only a few feet off the ground?"

"I knew some guys who used them to practice rotations." There was a trace of excitement in John's voice.

"They've got an indoor one out by the Schenectady airport. And I thought maybe you might want to go. I know it's not diving, but I owe you. I booked a block of time for this Friday."

When John didn't answer, Mason added, "It wouldn't have to be like a you-and-me thing. A date. Lizzy and Kai are going to go."

"Do you mind if I arrange my own ride?"

Mason pumped his fist in the air but just said, "No problem. But I've got to let them know how many people are actually going to do the flying."

"Okay. But I'll pay for my own ticket."

"Sure." As long as John was in, Mason didn't care about the details.

Even with anticipation making him stare down every traffic light, John wished the trip to the Schenectady Flight Deck took longer than twenty-five minutes. When Tyler heard who was organizing the venture he'd been willing to supply backup, and Simon had supplied reliable transportation. Tyler had even passed on riding shotgun because he knew John got sick in the backseat of a car. As they drove, they listened to some of Simon's comedy collection on his iPod. Tyler and Simon could hold a day's worth of conversation in nothing but punch lines, and John was glad to be able to catch up a little.

The bubbly feeling from laughing the whole way there evaporated as soon as he got inside the building. On a video overhead, someone was in a tunnel doing pirouettes and layout back flips, so sloppy and careless of form it made John's jaw ache. But he wanted in. Wanted it so bad he wanted to run for the tunnel, and fuck all the rules. It would be worth the fifty bucks a minute to live in the air again.

Lizzy came up behind him and gave him a quick hug. Kai shook his hand and thumped his back, and then John was face-to-face with Mason. It was way more awkward to just say hi after having been inside his head than it was making small talk after John had been inside someone's body.

A bearded guy in a blue flight suit came out to greet them.

K.A. Mitchell

After introducing himself as Bob, he said, "I understand we've got three flyers here today. Any special occasion?"

Lizzy smiled. "Just a reunion."

John gave her a look, and she just grinned back.

Bob heartily declared that to be great and then they went over rules and rates and regulations. John hadn't signed this much paperwork since he'd left the hospital, and every bit of it was a lie since he declared he had no preexisting condition of motion sickness or head, shoulder, back or neck injury.

When they were all standing back at the entrance to the Plexiglas tunnel, Bob asked about experience. No psychic powers were necessary to know that everyone was looking at John.

"I've done a lot of platform and springboard diving from the three meter boards."

"A lot, he says," put in Tyler. "He won two gold medals in the Olympics."

Bob was mildly impressed. "No kidding? My son's wrestling coach won a gold medal back in 1988." He looked at John like he should know the guy, like they were all in a gold-medal club and hung out together. There was a buzz and someone they couldn't see or understand talked in Bob's earpiece. He pressed a button. "Copy that."

"So, John. If you get comfortable in there and want to show some stuff, mind if we video it for our website? If we get something we can use, we'll cut your rate in half—for all of you."

"Sure." There'd be more papers to sign, but as long as no one Googled him before he got in the tunnel it would be fine. What was the worst that could happen? He'd bounce five feet into a wall? He had a helmet on.

Tyler was going first. He said it was to check it out and had admitted to John it was so John didn't show him up. They all

236

crowded the Plexiglas to watch. Bob stood on a ring where the wind wouldn't get him and his lips moved with the repeated instructions. The whooshing started, and Tyler was slowly lifted until he was parallel with the ground in the classic skydiving pose. He was right about the level of their heads as he flew, a huge grin splitting his face the whole time he was airborne.

John's throat was dry and his hands tingled. A minute. Maybe thirty seconds. He had to stop himself from counting down the seconds left in Tyler's time.

As John stepped into the tunnel, Bob cautioned him, suggesting John get a feel for the air before trying anything, and John let it all roll out of his head like he always did when he was on the ladder, at the end, muscles coiled and tensed to launch him into flight.

The spongy trampoline safety net almost threw him into the wall, but Bob pulled him back upright.

"Forgot about that," John said, and Bob stepped back.

He didn't guide John up like he had Tyler. It had seemed like it took a while for Tyler to get airborne, but to John his feet lifted the second he heard the wind streaking silver white past his ears. Then he was level. He was careful and discovered the slightest shift of his torso gave a good roll, and it only took an arch of his shoulders to get him moving vertically.

The wind shifted color as the pitch changed, and by straightening up he floated ten feet from the floor. Ignoring the waves of vertigo and the lurch in his stomach, he gently piked into a somersault and over rotated. A rush of adrenaline—spurred by the conviction that he was about to slam awkwardly into the water—cleared his head, but when he looked down, there was nothing but a safety net. He drifted on the air.

It was nice. John could see why it would be useful for people working on correcting their rotations. Easier than a trampoline, less of a price when you screwed up. But it wasn't diving. There was nothing to fight against. No speeding toward an unforgiving surface. No launch into the air with nothing but your skill to keep you from crashing. Diving didn't have a safety net. Disappointment churned his stomach worse than the vertigo.

He snuck a look down again. His friends were watching, and Bob was hoping for good video footage, so he did a lazy back layout. The guy on the video hadn't been so much sloppy as compensating for the way the air cradled you. Keeping the kind of form you needed when you were fighting your body weight and gravity sent you spinning out of control.

A slight drop of his shoulder put him into a slow spiral, and he hung one more forward pike on the way down before getting back into the level position he needed to exit.

"How was it?" Lizzy asked as they traded places.

"Great," he said.

"You looked amazing."

"Thanks."

Sure that Mason would want to watch Lizzy, John headed for the locker room to strip off his flight suit.

But Mason was right behind him. "So?"

Maybe if Mason had given John a minute he could have worked up a decent lie to spin. But the look on Mason's face, coupled with the disconcertingly empty red over his head, had John snapping, "It sucked."

"But you could be in the air and do those spins."

"Yeah. I could. And I might even do it again. But it's not the same."

"Why not?"

"How would you like to know you can have all the sex you wanted but you could never come again?"

The shatter of red and the wince on Mason's face told John

how effective a comparison that was.

"Is it the competition?" Mason asked.

"No. God, no." John yanked off the helmet. "I know you did this for me, and it was nice, but not everything can be fixed." He started walking again, fast, but he'd left his cane in the car, and his head hadn't forgiven him for multiple revolutions. The gleaming metal floor tipped, spilling him down a slope, and John would have fallen if Mason hadn't grabbed him.

"It can be if you want it to be."

John wanted to jerk free, but he wasn't going to add to his humiliation by sprawling across the gleaming metal floor. "That's really deep. You should put that on a motivational poster."

Mason looked at the shining floor and bit his lip. When he looked back at John, his aura wasn't angry, just soft, waiting. "I know I've fucked up every time we've been together. And I know you said you didn't need a lot of crap in your life right now, but it's different now. I'm different now, and I know you can see that."

"Why? Because you're lonely? Because you need someone to need you like Alex did?"

Mason released John's arm, leaving him to fight for his balance on his own.

"I was there, Mason. I saw what it cost you to let him go. You're looking for a substitute. But I just tried that..." he pushed the helmet into Mason's chest, "...and I know it doesn't work."

"You all right, John?" Tyler's question was soft, like he didn't want to startle him.

"Yeah. Just..." John pointed at the floor, "...you know."

Tyler angled himself so John could use him as a cane if he needed him. "Bob needs you to sign a release for the video. That was some fancy shit in there."

Mason handed Tyler the helmet, leaning close enough to whisper in John's ear, "You're wrong."

Being right wasn't much company. Mason sat outside on the back porch steps. John as substitute for Alex? No way. They were so different they might as well have been different species, but that didn't stop John from being the first person since Alex had died that Mason had wanted to be around, sex or no sex. He didn't know if they were going to have the kind of epic love, cue-the-strings-and-montages thing like he'd had with Alex, but he knew feeling like this wasn't something to just quit on, especially not when Mason was right.

If John didn't want Mason back, he wouldn't be fighting so hard.

Mason looked out at the back fence and then the shape in front of the back fence and his heart stopped.

"Alex?" He didn't look the way he had before. Mason could see right through him to the rusted-out grill they'd found at a garage sale. "I thought you were free."

"I am." It was hard to hear him. Like Alex had to whisper or something. "Doesn't mean I won't try to check up on you. Nice job on the computer."

Before Mason could even get his name out again, Alex was gone. If Mason hadn't just lived through the last two weeks, he'd have said he fell asleep sitting out there. But he knew he hadn't.

He ran inside to dig the computer out of its packing. He and Lizzy still had until the Monday after Thanksgiving to turn it in, but they'd already installed a few pieces of software and it did run beautifully. Mason accessed the basic operating system and did another keystroke recapture.

It was a mess, considering Alex hadn't had great

keyboarding skills when he was alive, but Mason managed to convert the message of missing or too many letters and spaces and tabs into something he could read. He supposed he should be glad ghost Alex hadn't crashed the whole fucking system.

Don't freak. I'm not still trapped. Whatever I am now, it makes some things easier and some harder. Like I can't get to your dreams so I tried this. It wasn't all your fault I was stuck to you. I never told you how amazing you were because I was scared I'd lose you if you knew. You couldn't have held me if I didn't hold on too.

John. I think I made it hard on John because I wanted to know if he was strong enough for you and he was. You just have to prove you're strong enough for him. Be happy. Or I'll scare the shit out of you.

Mason blinked hard. Alex always was dramatic.

Strong enough, huh? Mason could work with that.

Chapter Eighteen

Tyler and Simon and Garrett and Gavin showed up at John's door Sunday night.

"Tight jeans and dancing shoes, Johnny, c'mon." Tyler went to John's dresser and threw a pair of jeans at him that hugged his ass enough to make it impossible to get even a credit card in his back pocket.

"I'm tired."

"No. You're pissy. You need to get laid. Do I have a consensus on this, boys?"

"He's right, John. For once," Simon agreed.

"See. Simon says."

"You're never getting tired of that joke, are you?"

"Nope." Tyler grinned.

Just being around them felt better. Completely ignoring John's protests that he didn't give a shit about Mason Kincaid, Tyler and Simon had told him horror stories about freshman-year Mason on the way back from the wind tunnel—well, Tyler mostly—including a few things John was pretty sure were urban legends he'd read online. Going out was better than sitting here not studying for his economics test, even if he did have to watch Garrett and Gavin snuggle. And he could see from their auras it was definitely a snuggling night. Or it would be until one of them got jealous.

"Where are we going?"

"Sammies," Garrett and Gavin said in chorus.

Even though it was Sunday, Simon didn't even try for a spot close to the bar, grabbing something three blocks away.

"Why are we walking?" John asked. He hadn't brought a jacket, and he was shivering.

"It'll make your cheeks all nice and pink." Tyler reached for his arm as they waited for the light to change crossing Central Ave.

"Says the man who doesn't need a cane."

"You can always lean on me."

"Sing and I'm getting a cab," John said, knowing that look in Tyler's eye.

"And I'll split it with you," Simon added.

"Great. Gimme your keys." Tyler reached for Simon's pocket.

"Anything to get your hand on my dick." Simon thrust his hips up.

Tyler jerked his hand back. "You wish."

"John."

John jerked his head around too fast and almost fell. Tyler caught him by the elbow.

Mason had pulled up alongside them, driving Lizzy's car. He leaned over and pushed open the passenger door. "Get in."

"See," John said to Simon. "There were lots of parking spaces."

"Get in," Mason said again.

"I think the man wants you to get in the car, John," Tyler said.

One of the Gs giggled.

"What happened to, 'He's a manipulative asshole who uses

people all the time and you're lucky you figured that out'?"

"I might have said that, yeah," Tyler agreed.

"You set me up." John glared at his friend.

"All this and brains too." Tyler cupped John's ass and gave him a nudge toward the car.

It wasn't like Mason was going to kidnap him. And John really didn't feel like hanging out with Tyler anymore tonight.

"Thanks a lot," John muttered at Tyler.

"Thank me in the morning." To Mason, Tyler added, "Remember what I promised."

"Got it."

John sat down and shut the door. "What was that?"

"Seat belt." After John followed orders, Mason went on, "He said if I fucked this up he'd cut off my balls with a rusty spoon."

As Mason pulled away from the curb, John whistled. "Wow. Lizzy only threatened to kill me."

"It's good to have friends."

"According to you I wouldn't know." John slumped in the seat as they headed toward Mason's neighborhood.

"Did you?"

John thought about training camps, dorms, the Olympic village. Everyone knew each other, people got drunk together and fucked around, but if you were in the same sport, you were never friends. Not like he had now. "Not really. Why did you kidnap me?"

"We never did give that fuck-buddy thing a shot."

John laughed. "You set this up, actually called Tyler who you hate, just because you wanted to have sex?"

"Calling Tyler wasn't that hard. Half of the gay guys in Albany have him on speed dial."

"And one of them wouldn't be your fuck buddy?"

"Didn't want one of them. Wanted you."

"Lucky me."

"Yup."

Mason put the car in the driveway, but instead of going into the kitchen, he led John down a set of stairs into the cellar. It was as full of disused junk as the storage room at the laundromat, and it didn't smell as nice.

There was a weird-looking workout bench in the middle of the cleared space under the single naked light bulb.

John rubbed his arms through his sleeves. "I thought we were going to have sex."

Mason stood in front of him. "I've asked you what you want, but you don't know. Now I'm going to show you what you want. And I'm going to make it easy for you. You said you wished it was easy, right?"

"Yes."

"So here it is. I'm going to help you figure out what you want, and all you have to do is answer yes or no. Do you want to have sex with me?"

Even here in this cold, dirty basement with Mason acting like he really had kidnapped John, he wanted him, wanted that dark voice to keep telling him what to do. "Yes."

"See. Easy."

Pinning John's head between two big hands, Mason kissed him. Slow at first, but still hard, as John opened his mouth and let Mason's tongue sweep inside. The groan spilled out of John without warning, had him yanking Mason closer with an arm around his waist, trying to tell him how much he wanted this with tongue and lips and a press of teeth.

Mason lifted his head and stepped away. "Do you want to see what I made for you?"

"Yes." John walked over to the exercise bench. There wasn't

a bar on the rack, but there were four leather straps dangling from it. The opposite end of the bench had been raised to waist height and padded with a towel. Flat against the floor was what looked like a garden fence post, green steel with holes every inch. The pole was anchored at each end by a fifty-pound weight from the set.

"Do you remember telling me how you wanted to be tied down?"

John wasn't cold anymore. "Yes."

"Do you still want that?"

"Yes."

"Take off your clothes."

It was weird, stripping while Mason just watched, but John's dick apparently didn't have a problem with weird, or the cold, since it filled with blood and throbbed between his legs.

Mason picked up the leather straps. "Do you want me to put these on you?"

"Yes."

They fit snug on his wrists and ankles, not uncomfortable but they didn't slide at all. John's heart started slamming against his ribs. He wanted to make a joke when Mason bent to fasten the cuffs on his ankles, but his mouth was dry. He watched the shimmer over Mason's head instead, warm and thick, like syrup.

Mason pointed at the garden post. "You said I didn't teach you about spreader bars. I'm going to clip those cuffs to that and you won't be able to close your legs." Mason ran a hand over John's ass, and John jumped. "I'll be able to do anything I want to your ass and you won't be able to move away. Or maybe I'll clip them so your legs are together and make your ass even tighter."

His fingers slid down the crease, brushed the hole, circled, tapped. John waited, feeling hypnotized by that voice, like he was already tied down and couldn't do anything except take what Mason wanted to give him.

"Do you want me to clip you to the bar?"

"Yes."

"Lean over the bench." Mason pushed him down with a hand.

It was cold, but that didn't do anything to slow down John's pulse or the rush of blood it was sending to his dick.

The chain Mason used was cold too, and it gave John just enough room so that he could keep his feet off the bar and still bend his knees. If he really wanted to, he could move the weights off. A hundred pounds wasn't a lot, even with his legs apart. Then he felt Mason stand on the bar.

"Lift up." Mason pulled John backward off the bench and stroked his dick. "Yeah." Mason licked the word into John's ear. "You do like this. So hard for me."

It wasn't a question, but he still gasped, "Yes."

A few hard pulls had John trembling, and Mason pushed John face first back down over the bench, holding his dick so that it stayed pointing down under the bench so he couldn't grind against it.

How long had Mason been planning this?

"Can I tie your hands?"

"Yes."

One clip held his wrists together, and then a chain fastened them to the rack. He had a little play, his shoulders didn't ache, but he couldn't touch anything but his own hands.

Mason moved behind him. He hadn't put a blindfold on him, but he might as well have because all John could see were his cuffed hands, the brown leather wrapped around each wrist and the silver chain between them. *What did they say at the hardware store?* he wanted to ask, but he didn't, just rubbed his cheek on his shoulder and waited.

His ass was totally open, balls and cock exposed. It made every little breath of air feel like fingers on him, had him almost vibrating while he waited for a touch on his skin. His eyes were useless so he shut them.

A wet kiss hit the base of his spine, and John arched into it until his shoulders strained.

"Relax." As the word shuddered into him, John tried to obey it.

"Do you want me to rim you?"

That was a stupid question. "Yes."

Mason laid a long lick from John's balls to the top of his ass and back down. John tried to spread his legs farther and then remembered he couldn't. Couldn't reach back and spread his ass open. Couldn't do anything but wait as a lazy wet tongue circled his hole.

John felt the rush of air before Mason's hand smacked across his ass, spreading the sting out. And again, a hard spank that skimmed over his other cheek.

"Do you like that too?"

"Yes." Because it wasn't about pain but sensation, all the nerves in his ass waiting for a lick or a kiss or the slap of skin.

Mason hit John on both cheeks, then grabbed the skin and licked hard over his hole.

"Yes." It didn't matter if there were any more questions because that was John's only answer.

Mason pulled the skin tighter and tongued deeper. It was wet, and hot, and his stubble scratched skin still stinging from the smacks, and if John could have moved he would have shoved his ass back for more. Heat spilled at the tip of his cock, and he grunted, tugging on his wrists. Mason stepped back and spanked John again, leaving a hand against his ass to slide into the crease. One finger tapping against the hole, Mason's other hand milked John's cock with slow strokes.

When the next question came, John had trouble focusing on it.

"Were you lying when you told me I was the last guy to have been in you?"

"No."

Mason slid just the tip of his finger inside. "Have you been fucked since then?"

"No." John rubbed the sweat off his face on his shoulder.

Mason circled with his finger, just that tip around and around while he jacked John's dick, and then he stopped.

John's ass had felt sensitive before, now his skin everywhere felt Mason move around him. He came around to unhook John's hands, and John slid them under his chest so that he could lift his head. Mason was naked, cock jutting in front of John's face. He licked his lips.

Mason gave him a smile John felt in his gut. "In a minute." His expression turned serious. "John, do you think I set this all up for just anybody?"

"No."

"Did I do it for you?"

This was a stupid game. John's chest burned, but he answered anyway. "Yes."

Mason stepped closer, the tip of his cock almost close enough to lick. How full of himself would Mason be when John got that dick down his throat?

Mason brushed the head across John's lips and he licked, tried to suck it in, but Mason would only give him the tip. John's thighs strained as he tried to push his body forward enough to slide down Mason's cock and even the game. With a hand on John's head, Mason pushed in farther, until it wasn't about John sucking, but about Mason fucking across his tongue, against the roof of his mouth and into his throat. He couldn't get his hands up to hold on, couldn't do anything but take it.

Even Roald had never done this to him, but John didn't feel used. This was something Mason was giving him, something he'd made just for him, this space where he told John what he wanted, and John didn't have to decide anything.

Mason was panting when he pulled back, but he re-hooked the chain holding John's wrists to the bar.

"Do you want me to fuck you?"

It came out of him on a sigh. "Yes."

Mason moved behind him. Lube gurgled bright pink before John felt the brush of Mason's slick finger, still lightly teasing. "I'll take it slow, sugar."

"No."

"Then relax."

John let out the breath he was holding, and Mason slammed his finger in deep. The bar kept John spread so wide it didn't hurt, not until Mason went to two, but then he twisted them, pressing down, making it all feel good again. There wasn't anything else to do, so John just let himself float on the sensation of Mason's fingers stretching him, a quick fuck in and out and then that swirling inside, the rub that made John want to melt into the floor.

When he stopped and moved away, John had too much time to think. It had been hard enough to let Mason fuck his mouth, and John was used to that. How was he going to be able to relax enough to let him in his ass when he couldn't move? Mason came back, his cock sliding in the crease of John's ass, just at the base of his spine.

"Can you feel the condom, John?"

He could, now that he concentrated on it. Cooler than skin and way too slick. "Yes."

He hadn't thought of that. He figured trusting Mason not to hurt him was enough, but yeah, it was good to know Mason was thinking for both of them.

Mason slid up and down, and then pressed the tip to John's hole. He wanted to relax, but he could feel himself locking Mason out. Mason stroked a soothing hand down John's back, then raised it for a hard slap against his ass. John's muscles clenched even harder, then relaxed as warmth spread out from the sting and Mason pushed the head of his cock inside.

"You want this?"

John ground his teeth together. "Yes."

Mason backed away, and John whimpered. He wanted it. Hell, now he needed it. If Mason was going to unhook him—but he didn't. Another gurgle and the thick insistent pressure was back, Mason pushed in, a harder sting than all those slaps combined. John grunted and tried to talk his muscles into relaxing.

"I'm going to fuck you, John, and you're just going to have to take it. You won't be able to jerk yourself off, you won't get to come until I'm done. I want you here, spread open under me. I want you so desperate to move you'll shake under me and I'll still keep fucking you." Mason pushed forward another inch, and John's muscles tightened again. Suddenly, Mason was on top of him, holding him down everywhere, voice deep and dark and harsh in John's ear. "Want to fuck you, sugar. Let me in."

There was no conscious control in it, but somehow John's body figured it out and Mason slid in all the way.

"Yeah." Mason kissed the back of John's neck and arched over him. Every movement licked fresh fire on his nerves but John didn't care. A few thrusts and everything felt good. Mason

K.A. Mitchell

started a hard, fast rhythm. John flushed all over with heat, with a rush of adrenaline that made him think of flying, of fighting gravity for that last perfect rotation before he hit the water.

This was like diving in a way that stupid wind tunnel could never be, because something stronger was pulling on him, dragging him down, and all he could control was his reaction to it. He couldn't get himself off, couldn't do anything but ride the feeling and trust his body to turn the shock of Mason pounding inside him to pleasure.

There was no falling, just climbing. Mason's strokes got longer and harder, his breath coming faster against John's neck. John's stomach lurched over and over, every one like he was lifting off the board, but spinning higher. His body started to ache and he needed to come more than he needed to breathe, his balls hard and tight against his body, dick straining for any touch that would take him over, let him land somewhere.

Mason's hips stuttered, and he started saying John's name like it was the only word he knew, which was fine because the only answer John could give was yes. Yes, he knew. Yes, Mason wanted him. Yes, John wanted him back.

Mason slid back, reached around and fisted John's cock, grip almost too tight after fucking air for so long. For a second John was terrified he wouldn't be able to come, that somehow he was just going to have to keep hanging high and alone with all this feeling inside, and then it started to rush out of him and he was afraid it wouldn't ever stop.

John didn't know how long they took to catch their breaths, only that his muscles were still shaking when Mason started unclipping his ankles, dropping kisses down his legs as John flexed his knees.

He freed his wrists and took off the cuffs, kissing the hot spaces underneath.

"Can you walk?"

"In theory," John said, but it was really more of a fantasy since he couldn't even raise his head. But there was something he needed to know. "Have you ever done that before?"

"What do you think?"

John smiled against the plastic bench. "Good."

Mason had been sure it would be a week before he could get it up again, but John had a really nice habit of waking Mason up with a blow job and he planned to reinforce that as much as possible. Though it was kind of disappointing to miss the beginning.

As Mason shifted his shoulders against his mattress, John looked up and Mason's chest got tight. Full. And the feelings needed out. He pushed at John's head. "Fuck me."

John raised his head. "What, now?"

Mason scooted back and grabbed lube and a condom. "Well, maybe later too."

Mason's knees were up around his ears when it occurred to him that John had gotten in some serious practice on this. That swivel thing that hit Mason's prostate with every stroke couldn't be an accident. John was smiling down at him like he knew exactly what Mason had just been thinking. Knowing John, he probably did.

Mason tightened his muscles enough to drag a gasp out of John, and John responded with a harder thrust. When Mason reached for his dick, John nodded and fucked faster so that by the time Mason had shot all over his chest, John was jerking and groaning at the ceiling.

It could have been the blood rushing in his ears, but when John turned, Mason knew he wasn't hearing things. There was applause coming from the hall.

"I hate your housemates."

"We love you too, John," Lizzy called.

"Did I mention this place has really thin walls?" Mason said.

John got up off the bed. Mason's heart started pounding again, but John just dropped the condom in the garbage and came back to fling an arm around Mason's waist.

Mason felt the look and opened his eyes to see John studying him.

"If I said I wanted sex and the other crap too, what would that make us?"

"How do you feel about boyfriends?" Mason held his breath.

"Do boyfriends still sometimes do kinky stuff?"

"Anytime they want to."

John stared hard enough that Mason wondered what he was seeing in those colors. Whatever it was made John smile like Mason had handed him another gold medal. "Then I guess I have a boyfriend."

About the Author

K.A. Mitchell discovered the magic of writing at an early age when she learned that a carefully crayoned note of apology sent to the kitchen in a toy truck would earn her a reprieve from banishment to her room. Her career as a spin control artist was cut short when her family moved to a two-story house, and her trucks would not roll safely down the stairs. Around the same time, she decided that Chip and Ken made a much cuter couple than Ken and Barbie and was perplexed when invitations to play Barbie dropped off. An unnamed number of years later, she's happy to find other readers and writers who like to play in her world.

To learn more about K.A. Mitchell, please visit www.kamitchell.com. Send an email to K.A. Mitchell at authorKAMitchell@gmail.com.

CPSIA i
Printed i
BVOW070956170512

290464BV00001B/35/P

9 781609 281762